DRAGONBORN

THE FLAXFIELD
QUARTET:
VOLUME ONE

Dragonborn

TOBY FORWARD

WALKER
BOOKS

First published in Great Britain 2011 by Walker Books Ltd
87 Vauxhall Walk, London SE11 5HJ

This edition published 2012

2 4 6 8 10 9 7 5 3 1

Text © 2011 Toby Forward
Illustrations © 2011 Jim Kay

The right of Toby Forward to be identified as author of this work has been asserted by him in accordance with the Copyright, Designs and Patents Act 1988

This book has been typeset in Historical

Printed and bound in Great Britain by Clays Ltd, St Ives plc

British Library Cataloguing in Publication Data:
a catalogue record for this book is available from the British Library

ISBN 978-1-4063-3998-7

www.walker.co.uk

And be ye kind one to another. *Ephesians* 4:32

It's no use trying to be clever — we are all
clever here; just try to be kind — a little kind.
*Dr F. J. Foakes Jackson of Jesus College,
Cambridge, to a newly elected don.*

Kindness is a much underrated and undervalued virtue.
Many people have been kind to me over the years,
especially at times when it was greatly needed.
This book is dedicated to them.

It was a house, a group of houses, and
an inn with a sign, with trees framing
the scene. By the inn a dragon,
a Blue and Green.

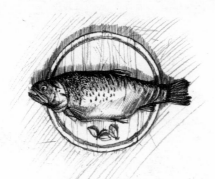

Part One

WIZARD WORK

Flaxfield died on a Friday

which was a shame, because he always ate a trout for dinner on Friday, and it was his favourite.

Sam said goodbye to him at three o'clock and went off to catch the fish, and when he returned just before five, Flaxfield was dead.

Sam was annoyed because the old man hadn't told him he was going to die, and Sam missed him. He waited till seven o'clock, then put the frying pan on the range, dug his fingers into the butter and took a piece as big as a walnut, let it bubble in the pan, and fried the trout, dusted with flour, salted, and, just before the cooking was finished, sweetened with flakes of almond.

Starback got under his feet more than usual. Sam reached down absently and scratched him, but that only made him more of a nuisance.

It tasted good with fresh bread and more butter, but not as good as Flaxfield must have thought, because Sam didn't think he'd want one every Friday. He didn't finish the fish and put his plate on the floor for Starback.

He knew what to do with the body because it was one of the first things Flaxfield had taught him when he started as the old man's apprentice, six years ago. He didn't much like doing the bodies, but he didn't mind, usually. But he *really* didn't like doing it this time. He kept thinking Flaxfield would sit up and tell him he was doing it wrong.

Anyway, he did it right, of course, and then, when he had finished, he sat down on the floor and cried so long that he hurt his throat.

He was twelve years old.

Darkness always came suddenly that time of year, when the days were hot and the roads hard. Sam stepped outside the house and looked up at the sky, as Flaxfield had taught him to. There were many messages there. There always were, but though he sought for something about his old master there was nothing plain to him. Starback scratched his way up the almond tree by the gate and looked up as well, as though he could understand the heavens, which perhaps he could.

Sam slept well, and, though bad dreams were no stranger to him, he had none that night. He was still sleeping when the door opened, and only half awake when a hand shook his shoulder and said, "Breakfast, boy, and be quick."

Sam was dizzy with sleep and stumbled to his feet. Starback cowered behind him.

"Here, catch!"

It wasn't fair. Sam's eyes were less than half open, he was

staggering to stand and the throw was too fast. He still managed to get one hand to it, slapped it into the air, grabbed with the other, it slipped, and he ducked to slap it up again; tossing it from hand to hand he finally secured it, and found it was a folded bag of greasy paper, that squelched in his hands and had a fine tang of faintly scented urine.

"Enough for two there; you can share it," said the stranger.

Sam was used to strangers and used to being ordered about, so he did as he was told. He laid the parcel on the oak table, turned and felt for the tinder box.

"By the clouds, you're slow," said the stranger. "What are you? Kitchen boy? 'Prentice?" He looked at the parcel and gave a grin that showed long teeth. "No, I know. You're Flaxfield's juggler."

Sam scowled, put a little paper and kindling on the ashes of last night's fire and struck the tinder box, raising a spark but no flame. He rearranged the tinder.

"Well? Which is it?"

"Apprentice," he mumbled. Again the spark raised no flame.

"How long?"

"Six years."

Starback was huddled against his legs, with a comforting scratchy feeling. But Sam needed more than that to stop him fumbling nervously.

"Flaxfield must have been getting desperate in his last years."

Sam ground his teeth together.

"Put that rubbish down and light it yourself."

Sam pretended not to understand, and stood dumbly staring at him.

"Well, at least you know not to give everything away all at once," said the stranger. And for the first time a suggestion of respect crossed his face. But not for long. "Light it yourself. I know you can."

"Flaxfield said I shouldn't. He said it wasn't for that."

"You shouldn't. It isn't. But Flaxfield's dead and I tell you to do it. So do it. I was his apprentice once, too."

Sam looked the man in the eye, taking him in properly for the first time. He was awake now and his wits were returning. Long hair, with ringlets at the side, made the stranger's face look longer than it really was. His nose was long, too, and not quite straight. Long teeth and a long tongue in a wide mouth. A friend would have said he looked like a wolf. An enemy would have said a fox. Sam decided fox, a judgement supported by the russet cloak and brown shoes. A wolf would be grey. And a wolf would fight you face to face. Sam decided that this one would fight behind your back. This one was sly, not brave. And all the more dangerous for that.

"Do it!" he snapped. "Or I *will* think that Flaxfield took on idiots at the end."

"You were his apprentice, you do it," said the boy. Starback coughed and whined and clung tighter to his legs.

The stranger lifted his hand and Sam raised his arm in defence. But no blow fell. Instead, a shaft of fire leaped from the man's open palm, streamed across the room and flashed into the range. The dead ashes flared up, licked the kindling, crackled and settled into a cheerful blaze.

Sam lifted his eyes. The old face was grim and set. He looked at Sam with new interest. "You're not as stupid as you look," he said. "You'll need watching."

Not by you, swore Sam silently.

"What's your name?"

"Sam."

"And your real name?"

Sam looked down at the floor then put his knuckle in his mouth and sucked it.

"What's yours?" he asked.

"You can call me Axestone. All right. Now cook the breakfast."

The kidneys were fresh and sweet, with butter, salt and fresh pepper, bread and tea.

"I see I'm the first," said Axestone.

"Will there be others, then?"

"Stars help us. And just when I thought you weren't quite the idiot you look. Of course there will be others. Before the day is out. Now, go and clear this lot up, then gather the willow and keep your eyes open for the others. Let me know as soon as you see someone."

"I can't leave you alone in the house," said Sam.

The door flew open. Sam stumbled, felt the floor tilt steeply, and he tottered through the door, tumbled to the floor, with Starback sprawled on top of him, legs everywhere and claws scratching. The door slammed shut.

"Keep your eyes open for the others," Axestone called.

Sam made a sign with his fingers at the door. It was the one that Flaxfield once beat him for when he caught him doing it, but he was safe now that the old man was dead and he was hidden from the stranger's sight by the heavy door.

"Do that to me again and you'll regret it," said Axestone.

Sam put his hand down quickly. Starback found his feet and raised an embarrassed face to Sam.

"All right," said the boy. "It's not your fault. He made us both look stupid." And he swore quietly that he would repay Axestone double for the insult. ‖

Pages from an apprentice's notebook

EVERYONE KNOWS THAT DRAGONS
BRING LUCK.

The trouble is, you never know whether it
is going to be bad luck or good luck. And,
the worst thing is, dragons have a way of
bringing people the luck they deserve.

That makes it difficult when you meet a
dragon. If you suspect that you are a bad
person, then you deserve a bit of bad luck
from the dragon. On the other hand, a good
person should get good luck. You get the luck
you deserve.

So, whatever sort of person you are, you
behave as though you are glad to see a

dragon, because you want people to think you are good and deserve good luck.

This, of course, is good for dragons, because it means they are made welcome everywhere. But it's also bad luck for dragons, because it means that there are lots of secret enemies, who pretend to like them, but hate them really, and plot behind their backs to get rid of them and do them harm. In this way, dragons are like most people, who can never tell who their real friends are, and who never know who is smiling to their face and all the time getting ready to hurt them as soon as their backs are turned. For the world is full of deceit and danger, and it's as well to know that early on.

As everyone knows, Green and Blues bring the most luck, good and bad. There are seventeen varieties of dragon, all told, but only nine of them have ever been seen by people. The Green and Blue is not the smallest variety, the Snake-

Tail and the Boulder Dragon are smaller, but the Green and Blue grows to the size of a memmont, and so is popular around the house. Also, unlike many other dragons, it can be taught to be clean and it does not smell. On the other hand, you can't decide to have a dragon, like buying a puppy. If you leave a bay tree in a square pot by the kitchen door it's a sign that you would welcome a dragon, and, if one sees it and decides to stay, then it will. Otherwise you have to do without one. Or at least that was what people said. Not that many people had dragons anyway.

Except for wizards, of course, who can let it be known that they would like one to come and stay. Green and Blues like to live with wizards. It gives them a bit of status with the other dragons.

*

The willows were not quite at the bank

of the river, and their shade was welcome, even this early in the morning. Flaxfield said that summers were getting hotter. Sam hadn't seen enough of them to be any judge of whether that was right. Flaxfield was always saying that sort of thing.

Sam selected slender branches, young new shoots that had grown since the last winter, straight and smooth, with fine foliage, the tender leaves a lighter green than the older growth. They had the pliant quality of youth, easily curved and guided. Sweet sap wet his hands as he stripped them. He piled them under an oak.

When he had twenty he sat down under a great oak and stripped them of their greenery, leaving long, slim, smooth wands. It was hot in the sun, cutting them from the tree, and cool in the shade of the oak, stripping them. He looked up often, scanning the hills for approaching figures. There were none.

At first Starback made a nuisance of himself, running up

and down the willows as Sam selected the best branches. But he soon tired of this and dived into the river to cool off.

It was hard work, but Sam made it simpler by not setting himself a time to complete it. He knew he had more than enough time, so he didn't rush. Twenty at a time, he decided to get five lots and then take a rest. That would be a hundred. After eighty, he was hot and his arms ached from the constant flicking of the knife against the greenery, so he changed his plan.

Leaving the piles of willow, he ran to the river and dived in, his body entering the water like a needle piercing silk, leaving scarcely a ripple. Starback squealed with pleasure, grabbed his leg and pulled him deep into the water. Sam was ready for this and he had taken a deep breath before diving. He wrestled playfully with Starback for a while, then tapped him on the nose to tell him it was time to let him go. Starback could breathe under water, so he easily forgot how important it was to let others gasp for air.

Sam lay back in the water, his legs dangling, and kicking just enough to keep him afloat. The sun scattered figures on the surface of the river; green and gold and silver, reflected and filtered from the trees overhead and the eddies and ripples of the water. It brought to the boy's mind the expensive brocades that rich merchants brought to Flaxfield. The old man had spells for cloth which made it easier to work into garments, and which gave protection to those who wore them, or power over others. This simple surface of water was what those weavers and merchants were trying to achieve. But it was free, and better by far, and Sam wore it just by diving in.

He spread his arms and dressed himself in it. Imagining himself a king, or a judge, or, he thought, the most famous and powerful wizard in the world. He turned and dipped his face in the water to cool it. And a sharp pain cut across his back. And another. He dived deep, just as the same pain sliced into the back of his thighs.

Axestone stood on the riverbank, a willow wand in his hand.

"I told you to look out for strangers," he shouted.

Sam paddled, out of range of the switch. Starback snarled and spat.

"I did look out. There's no one for miles."

"And work. I told you to get the willow ready."

"He's done quite a lot, Axestone. He needed a rest." A woman stepped forward from the shelter of the trees and stood next to Axestone.

"He won't get much rest now that Flaxfield's gone. The old man was too soft on the boy. He'll learn what work is when he goes down the mines." Yet another, a man, joined them. Sam had only seen one black man before, black with skin like midnight. Not like this one. This one was the colour of ale, dark winter ale. He stood as high as Axestone, and as slim. They might have been twins, save for the colour of their skin. The same arrogant pose marked them both. But, where Axestone's bedraggled beard was growing grey, this man's was black, and straight and carefully cut.

"Enough of that for now. There are still decisions to make," said a fourth, very old man, older than Flaxfield by the look of him.

Sam felt his stomach churn with fear. How many were there? How had he missed them? And who were they? And why were they here?

"Get out," said Axestone. The switch dangled by his side.

"Not if you're going to whip me again."

"Get out!"

"He's right," said the old man. "He's taken his whipping. And he's made a good start on the willow. Let him be."

Axestone growled at them, more wolf than fox, after all, but he dropped the switch and turned away.

By the time Sam had climbed the bank they were all under the oak, looking at his pile of willow.

"He has chosen well," said the old man. "The very best saplings."

"And the right sizes," said the woman, who was sorting them into smaller piles according to length and thickness.

Axestone nodded. "But not enough," he snapped.

"Then let us make that good," said the dark one.

He unsheathed a long, curved sword, pointed to a willow, and, in an instant, a pile of branches bigger than the one Sam had gathered appeared at the base of its trunk. Each one was trimmed smooth and all were perfectly straight and true.

"Khazib!" Axestone snapped. "Have you forgotten yourself?"

The woman clutched herself in distress. Sam flung himself

in fury at the man, but, before he could reach him, Khazib slapped him away like a fly, and he fell, dazed, on the grass. Starback growled and his nostrils flared.

Axestone waved a hand, and the branches shrivelled and bent, all sap dried up and they were as brittle as old bones, useless.

Khazib walked away without looking back. The woman helped Sam to his feet, then sat him against the rough trunk of the oak in the shade, while the three of them set themselves to cutting and piling more branches of willow.

The old man, before he joined them, fetched cool water from the river for Sam to drink. The boy looked away as it was handed to him. No one had ever waited on him before, and with such courtesy.

He watched them at work, the sweat dampening their brows, as it had his. He remembered the trout he had caught for Flaxfield. The fish were biting well yesterday, so Sam had played with Starback at the river to pass the time. Once, he had fished all afternoon and none had risen. His fingers were sore from baiting the hooks and his hands were wet and scratched from foraging for flies to lure the fish. He was hot, tired, smelly, impatient and bad-tempered. So he conjured a trout. It was a little spell, one he had taught himself, really, like learning how to do a handstand. He had always been able to get most animals to come to him, so conjuring a trout out of the water was nothing.

As soon as he walked into the house he knew he had made a big mistake.

Flaxfield was at the desk. He was always at the desk. It was the only desk Sam had ever seen. More or less everything in Flaxfield's house was the only one he had ever seen. Flaxfield had taken him in when Sam was only three years old, so he didn't really remember much before that. There had been a woman, called Flaxfold, who looked after things. She looked after Sam as well, and taught him to cook and clean, to make useful things for the house — bookshelves and doorstops and bolts. She showed him how to sew and mend clothes, how to grow herbs and vegetables. By the time he was six years old Sam was as good a housekeeper and handyman as anyone in the country.

At the same time, Flaxfield had taught him to read and write. Later, he taught him how to tell his numbers, which plants in the forest and fields were poisonous, where to find the best berries and mushrooms, how to catch a trout with a rod and line, not to touch fire, but how to light one — and four hundred and seventy-two other things.

Then, on Sam's sixth birthday, Flaxfold said, "I'm off now," and gave him the only hug he ever remembered having from anyone.

"Wait," said Flaxfield. Sam didn't remember the old man ever saying more than two sentences to her before. It was as though she was a piece of furniture. He went to the old oak dresser that took up nearly one whole wall of the kitchen. Opening a door, he took out a loaf of bread, some figs, a small bottle of cordial and a bag of silver coins. They had been put there recently, because the bread was fresh, and there was nothing else in the small cupboard.

He handed them to Flaxfold. "You have done all things well," he said. "Go where you must."

To the boy's astonishment, the old man kissed her cheek and smiled.

She said nothing more, but closed the door quietly after her.

"Go and get me a trout," said Flaxfield.

That was the first day that Sam cooked their food on his own. He had done it every day since then for six years. When he came back with the trout Flaxfield said, "Now, wash your hands and look at this. Read it carefully."

Sam read it.

"Do you understand it?"

"No."

"It says that if you sign it at the bottom of the page," he pointed with an inky finger, "then you will be my apprentice for twelve years. I will teach you everything I know and then you will be able to go and work for yourself. It will make you rich if you want to be."

Sam hadn't seen many places and he didn't know very much, but he had read books with Flaxfield and, lately, on his own, and he didn't think Flaxfield's house was like the houses of rich people he had read about, or that Flaxfield was like rich people.

"Are you rich?" he asked.

"I said," Flaxfield repeated carefully, "if you want to be."

"Oh."

"Do you want to be my apprentice?"

"I don't know. What if I say no?"

"You can stay here as my servant, or you can go away and do whatever you want. I'll pay you thruppence a week as my servant, or I'll give you thirty shillings to take with you if you go away."

"I'll be your apprentice," said Sam.

"That's right. Now, sign your name here — *Sam* — and then after it, on the next line —*Cloud*."

"Why?"

"Because Sam is your everyday name, but Cloud is going to be your secret name. That's your first lesson as my apprentice, never tell anyone your special name."

Sam nodded.

Flaxfield frowned at the paper. He tapped his fingers against the table, put his hand into his pocket, hesitated, took it out again and smiled at Sam.

"Is that it?" asked Sam.

"Usually," said Flaxfield.

He put his hand back into his pocket in a rush, pulled out a stubby piece of metal and put it on the table.

"Perhaps we should seal it," he said. "Make it special."

He found a lump of hard red wax and lit a candle. Sam watched as he held the corner of the wax over the flame and it melted, dripping onto the paper below the two signatures. When there was a small pool of soft wax Flaxfield took the metal and pressed it in. When he took it away it had left a mark and the wax was dry again and hard.

"There. That's sealed," said Flaxfield. "Do you like it?"

Sam peered at the wax. The metal had left an indentation, like a coin, with the picture of a bird in the centre.

"Can I see?"

Flaxfield handed him the metal.

"You like it?" he asked.

"Yes."

"You should have it, then."

He found a leather thong, threaded it through a loop in the metal and tied it around Sam's neck.

"Is it mine?" asked Sam.

"You look after it for me."

Sam liked the weight of it against his neck.

"But can I keep it?"

"Will you?" said Flaxfield. "Will you look after it?"

"Yes."

"Good. Now, go and cook that trout."

And that was how it had all started.

From time to time he looked secretly into the cupboard, to see if it was where the bread was kept, but it was always empty. Once, when Flaxfield was there, he opened the door to put a loaf of bread in, but the old man said, "That's not where it goes. Leave that door alone."

When he was ten he learned a hard lesson. He conjured the fish because he couldn't be bothered to dangle a hook any longer. He knew he was doing a bad thing. Which was why he shouldn't have been surprised when Flaxfield was angry with him for doing it.

"Put it here," said Flaxfield.

He put the fish on the desk.

Flaxfield looked into its mouth.

"Where did the hook go in?" he asked.

Sam kicked his toe against the leg of the desk and mumbled.

"Eh?" Flaxfield put his hand to his ear and leaned forward. Although he was old, he could see like a hawk and hear like a dog.

Sam owned up.

Flaxfield nodded and walked out, waiting at the door for Sam to follow him. When they reached the riverbank, he handed the fish to Sam.

"Make it swim."

He dropped it into the water where it floated, belly up and dead.

"Go on."

"I don't know how to."

"Why not?"

Tears ran down his face, making patterns in the dirt.

"You never showed me."

Flaxfield nodded.

"Remember that," he said. "If you can't undo by magic what you have done with magic, then don't do it. And stop crying. That won't make it any better."

Sam wiped his nose with his bare arm.

Flaxfield scooped the fish out of the water. He closed his eyes and began to hum. After a while he leaned forward, dipped his head in the river, his long hair spreading out like a cobweb, and filled his mouth with water. He put his face close to the mouth of the trout and sprayed the water straight between its jaws. The trout flickered. Flaxfield shook it. It twitched. He lowered it gently into the running current. It hung for a second, motionless, then darted to life and swam off.

Sam felt sick. There was something in the air around them that frightened him. Flaxfield's face was grey and his hands shook.

"Go away," he said.

That night, even though it was a Friday, Flaxfield ate cheese.

Sam thought the old man would be angry with him, and he hid. But Flaxfield called him gently and they ate together, more companionably than usual.

"I'm sorry," said Sam.

Flaxfield smiled at him.

"Everyone does it, sooner or later," he said. "You did it sooner than I expected."

"I knew it was wrong. But not very wrong."

"It was as wrong as you could make it," said Flaxfield. "You used the magic you have inside you without thinking and you did something you couldn't undo, and you did it to save yourself trouble. Three things," he ticked them off on his fingers, "and every one of them serious."

Sam lowered his head.

"No more tears. Have an apple with that cheese."

The next day, the dragon arrived and Flaxfield gave him Starback to look after.

"He isn't yours, mind," the old man warned him. "He belongs to himself — everything does. But he's your responsibility. You must feed him and take care of him."

There was more about the right use of magic. Looking back, now that it was all over, Sam realized that he had learned more about how not to use magic than he had about how to use it. He didn't know much about that at all. And now Flaxfield was dead. And he would never know any more.

He was twelve. His apprenticeship was only half over and he didn't know what would happen to him.

Did he know enough about magic to live by it? He didn't think so. He really didn't think he knew enough to make himself rich. And he thought he would be very lonely on his own in Flaxfield's house.

He didn't know much really, he reflected as he looked up into the intricate branches of the oak spreading about his head, the breeze lifting the leaves and the sunlight scattering them with green stars. But he knew that Khazib had done a very bad thing by using magic to save himself the effort of cutting the willow wands.

The shivering of the wands as they fell from the willow disturbed the air, disturbed the spaces between the air, disturbed the steady stillness. A grey-robed figure pacing on a smooth floor, stopped, turned her face to a window and held her breath. She felt the shivering of the falling willow branches, felt the magic that had stripped and piled them, felt the sorrow and felt the loss of the figures on the riverbank. She crouched, sniffed, paused, smiled.

"Flaxfield's dead," she said.

The reply was little more than a clatter of claws, words without breath.

"That's very good."

She drew her robe to her head and wrapped it round her like a shawl, half hiding her face.

"Now it starts," she said. "Now it starts."

She dropped to her knees and licked the floor, a snail trail of saliva glistening against the stone.

"I can taste it," she said. "I can taste the magic rising up."

She lay flat and licked, pressed her cheek against the cold stone. A black beetle clawed its way up between the slabs. It tilted, tottered, settled, walked towards her. She darted her head forward, snapped her teeth together, splitting the beetle. She flicked her head to one side, tossing the beetle into her mouth. Crunched it once, swallowed, licked her lips, sticky with the beetle's soft insides. More black beetles clambered up, crawled over her.

"They know," she whispered. "They know the time's starting."

"What else can you see, Ash?"

She screamed at the clattering shape and it shrank back into a corner.

"Give me time. Let me enjoy this."

She slithered towards it, her grey robe rippling like smoke.

Bakkmann stepped away.

"Can we leave the castle now?" it clattered.

Ash rose up, stood close.

"I'll snap your legs off," she said. "One by one. *Snap. Snap.* You hear me?"

Bakkmann clattered yes.

"With Flaxfield dead," said Ash, "we can do anything. We can leave this place."

She hugged herself.

"At last. At last."

She ran from the room, round and down the spiral stair. The robe billowed behind her, like smoke. Through stinking corridors, pushing aside anything that got in her way, she found the great door. It stood open. It was always open. She paused, moved slowly, stepped up to the threshold and walked through.

As her foot passed through the doorway she stopped and screamed out.

She fell back, away from the door. Her foot snapped off at the ankle and hung in the air outside.

Ash snarled, lunged forward into the doorway, hands outstretched. Again, she froze as soon as she crossed the line. Her arms had gone through, as far as the elbows, then stopped. Her weight sagged. She fell to her knees and her forearms snapped off.

Bakkmann found her, bleeding and slumped on the floor.

"I should have killed him," she moaned. "If he had lived longer I would have been able to."

Bakkmann clattered.

"What's gone wrong?" she asked. "Why am I still a prisoner here?"

"Can you see anything?" Bakkmann clattered.

Ash closed her eyes and sank down again, crouched. Her foot was beginning to grow back. The stumps of her arms had stopped bleeding.

"Nothing. They're at Flaxfield's house. That's protected against us. All I felt was a stupid slip of wasted magic. It opened a door just enough for me to feel what was happening."

She doubled over, put her face to the floor. One hand was restored. The other was back, except for the fingers.

"I can get in," she said. "Just for a moment."

She pulled the robe so that her face was hidden.

"Figures on a riverbank," she said. "A dragon. And a boy."

She hugged herself, moaning.

"What is it?"

She ignored the clattered question.

Bent double with pain, she dipped her head below the window, pulled her robe away and looked round. Her eyes were bleeding. Her mouth was twisted into a snarl. She said something. Almost.

"What's that?"

"It's a boy," she said. "Flaxfield's boy."

Bakkmann clattered louder.

"We have to get him," said Ash. "We have to. The seal. Flaxfield's magic. The boy."

She stared at the slabs of black that made up Bakkmann's face.

"It's not over," she snarled. "Not over after all. It's just beginning. After all these years. He's found a boy and given him the seal." ‖

Pages from an apprentice's notebook

THE THING ABOUT ROFFLES is that there are all sorts of them, but they all look pretty much the same. Some are good and trustworthy, while others can be very sly and unpleasant, and there's absolutely no way of knowing which is which until you have been with them for a long time. They all seem to be very helpful, though a little short-tempered. They only ever come above ground for one reason, to look for stray memmonts.

The memmonts are curious creatures and they often find gaps in the ground that they can wriggle through to get Up Top. They like the sun, but they have no sense of

---

direction, so once they are here, they find it difficult to get back home. The roffles love the memmonts and, although there are many of them and one missing wouldn't matter, they always try to rescue strays.

Memmonts, of course, don't belong to anyone, so the roffles are not recovering their property, just doing a kind thing for a memmont.

They carry almost everything they own on their backs in hard leather cases shaped like barrels that have been sat on sideways and flattened out. Some people say that this is because they were put in barrels as a punishment hundreds of years ago and tipped down the disused shafts of the mines, and then they found the Deep World. Other people say they were miners once, and that they stayed down there and made the Deep World themselves and came to like it better than Up Top. Other people still say that once everyone was a roffle in the Deep World but the people Up Top came through the gaps and liked it here and stayed. No one knows.

Roffles have pointy shoes and they are just over half as tall as a grown man or woman. Roffle babies can walk when they are seven months old and talk like grown ups on their first birthday. Every roffle name begins with the letters Meg. It is a very rare thing to see a fat roffle, but there was a famous one called Megantople, who sometimes came Up Top to go to fairs and make money from charging people tuppence to see him. He spent the money on gold and jewels and took them back to the Deep World, where he became the richest roffle ever. Even now, roffles who are descended from Megantople are very rich and powerful.

Everyone knows how delicious the food is that the roffles grow in the Deep World, but they will not bring it Up Top and sell

it, so very few people have ever tasted it.
Sometimes a memmont, carrying a basket of
roffle apples or plums on its back, will break
through to Up Top, and then the people who
find the memmont can taste them, but this
hardly ever happens.

Roffles love to give advice and help people,
which is a good thing, if it is a good roffle,
but a bad roffle will give bad advice
and false help, just for
the fun of it.

*

Starback

was a Green and Blue. No one ever knows how old dragons are, so Starback could have been a youngster of only a few years, or a very old and wise dragon indeed. It was impossible to tell. They never looked any different, or behaved any differently, rolling about and scampering like puppies however old they were.

Starback watched the wizards working very carefully.

They had worked hard, and cut the willow. The woman, Eloise, had started the weaving and they had all taken turns until the basket was complete. Then they had carried it to the house and gently lifted Flaxfield into it.

The old man's name was Sandage. He supervised it, and he was the one who arranged the herbs around the body, in a very particular order, different from the one that Sam knew. The boy corrected him almost straight away, but Axestone put his hand on his shoulder.

"This is a wizard, boy. No ordinary death. Watch and learn."

Starback kept close to his friend while the rites were performed. Sam didn't look at him. He kept his gaze on the face of the man who had raised him for nine years and given him the only home he had ever known, and who now lay dead.

"Now," said Eloise. "It is the boy's turn."

Sam looked at her and, for the first time, his eyes took in the rest of the room. It had filled. Silently, slowly, one after another, more and more people had entered. Over thirty stood there now. All turned to look at him. There were women there, but most of them were men, and, Sam knew, all wizards. He had no idea there were so many in the whole world.

"What?" he said.

"Sandage was his first apprentice and has performed the preparation. You were his last apprentice," said Eloise. "You must give me the elements to finish this." She seemed changed by the ritual she had performed, but Sam was used to that. He had seen it many times with Flaxfield. It wasn't that anything actually changed, but they looked different. The first thing Sam had noticed about Eloise was that she was beautiful. He had seen very many strangers since coming to live with Flaxfield, but not many of them were women, and he had no idea what beauty was in a woman, yet the first sight of Eloise was enough to tell him that she was. It reminded Sam of a day when he had been sitting with Starback, looking over the steep hill and the tumbling river that ran down east through the forest before changing its mind and doubling back to run past the bottom of the meadow behind the house. The light of the angled sun on the slopes and water seemed to the boy to be the most beautiful thing in the world. And then, without warning, a high, huge cloud slipped over the sun and, in a breath, everything was changed. The greens were darker, the grass rippled, the trees woke and stirred and looked around them, like a crowd at an execution, turning to see the arrival of the prisoner; the river deepened and the meadow breathed out the scent of flowers whose beauty had been hidden by the high grass, but who new-revealed themselves in fragrance. The shadow changed the beauty, made it more, disclosed depths and mysteries. It was like that after magic. There was always more. Flaxfield had seemed more wise, more stern, more old. Eloise, the words completed, was more beautiful, and, suddenly, frightening.

"I don't know what to do," said Sam. "You do it."

"I do not know how to," she said. "Only the last apprentice knows how. He has taught you."

"He didn't. Truly he didn't."

"Then you are no apprentice," said Axestone coldly. "You have lied to us."

There was a tension in the room as thick as smoke and as hard to breathe. He could feel everyone waiting to see if it was true.

Sam wanted to cry. He *knew*, he just *knew* that Flaxfield had never taught him this. How could he forget? He hated Axestone for humiliating him, and he hated Flaxfield, for not teaching him.

Starback nudged his legs. Sam was so upset that even this was not welcome, though he knew the creature was trying to be kind. He put his hand down to push him away, but Starback grabbed it in his mouth and pulled him towards the dresser. He nosed against a small door. Sam opened it. He took out a loaf of bread, some figs, a small bottle of cordial and a bag of silver coins. They had been put there recently because the bread was fresh and there was nothing else in the small cupboard. His hands were not steady. He carried the items carefully to Flaxfield and placed them inside the wicker basket, as close to Flaxfield's hands as he could. Then, he stopped and looked at the still face. "You have done all things well," he said. "Go where you must." He leaned forward and kissed the cold, dry cheek.

The room made a small, comfortable sound, of breaths that had been held being released.

Sam looked around to see if it was right. Axestone nodded and almost smiled.

"That's no good!"

"Ah, Caleb," said Axestone, looking at the one who had spoken. "You have arrived at last. That leaves only Waterburn still missing."

"In plenty of time," said the newcomer. He looked like a sapphire in a bread-shop window. All the others were in travelling drab, or at least in sturdy clothes that drew no attention. He wore a brocade jacket with the cleanest lace at the neck and cuffs, the collar fastened with a jet brooch in the shape of a beetle, with a silver mount, and silk breeches with buckled shoes. His hat, discourteously still on his head, was tilted ironically, as though mocking the solemnity of the rites. "I didn't miss anything. Especially that nonsense this idiot boy just showed us."

"It was Flaxfield's choice," said Eloise. Her radiance had faded now.

"We don't know that," the man scoffed. "There was no magic in it. Flaxfield was a great wizard. He deserves magic at his Finishing. I was his last apprentice." He raised aloft a staff that Sam had not noticed before. It was dark, with a deep shine to the wood and more silver round the neck. Khazib dashed it from his hands and it clattered to the ground, the fine silver-work denting on the red tiles.

"Magic enough has been done today," he said. "It is for the last apprentice to provide the goods to finish the ceremony, and he has. That has been done. We leave now."

Caleb stretched out his arm, palm down. The staff rose and he grasped it. His hand clenched tight with fury.

Axestone nodded to the crowd. Four stepped forward and hoisted the basket to their shoulders. Together, led by Axestone, in twos, they made their way to the river. Sam and Starback nearest the front, as Eloise had made sure they should be.

They reached the river and Eloise completed the Finishing. When she had done, she turned away and walked off by herself as Sam had often seen Flaxfield do. Her steps were unsteady, and she stopped soon and stood and waited for the effort of the Finishing to leave her.

"They don't know about the boy," said Ash.

Even though she was used to its noise now, the clattering laugh made her feel ill. She drew her sleeve across her eyes, smearing the blood but letting her see again. Her arms and foot were completely restored.

"The gap's closed now. They've kept their magic hidden. But I've put a confusing spell there. They won't know that the boy's the one. They won't trust him."

"Will they kill him?"

She tried to stand, staggered, and sank back to the floor.

"They don't kill like that."

The clattering grew fast and loud.

"I would kill him. I would stab. I would jab. I would stab."

As the creature spoke it jabbed out a claw-like leg and clattered more claws on the smooth floor.

"I know you would. Perhaps, one day, you will. Not now, it is enough that I've made some mischief for them. Now get out."

The clacking died down. It slouched away, leaving a faint stink of cat mess. ‖

Pages from an apprentice's notebook

MAGIC IS DIFFERENT IN THE MINES, but nobody really knows why.

Some people say it is because the miners are all descended from one couple, a person from Up Top and a roffle, so they are neither one thing nor the other. The miners do all look alike, so it may be true. Everyone knows that everything, including magic, is different in the Deep World, so it makes sense that people who are half roffle would interfere with magic.

Some people say it is the tunnels, that the magic gets lost in them and can't find its way and can't work properly, but this doesn't seem to be right because magic can find its way through a dark forest, across rivers, and even to the other side of mountains. On the other hand, the tunnels in the mines are like a spiderweb, they criss-cross each other and join up where you think they won't, so the magic may lose direction.

It is very dangerous when magic loses its way. If magic forgets who worked it, then it can't find its way back to its source. So, magic worked for greed may go hunting for someone to return to and go to the wrong person.

Other people say that magic is different in the mines because it is always dark, but magic sees through the darkness, and anyway it is light in the Deep World and magic is hardly magic at all down there.

Because the magic does not work properly in the mines they are very dangerous places for wizards. Even a great wizard will find that

the magic doesn't behave properly in the mines,
and he may hurt himself, or even die from a
spell which is completely harmless Up Top.

Wizards should stay away from
the mines. There's no
more to say.

*

"That boy is a fraud,"

said Khazib. "I think Caleb is right. We have made a mistake."

The others listened and then joined in, as they felt inclined.

"He can't do any magic at all," said Axestone.

"None that we have seen," said Eloise.

"He made a good farewell to Flaxfield," said Sandage.

"It was a disgrace!" Caleb was angry, and, hidden above them, listening in, Sam felt shame scratch down his back.

The other wizards had all gone, not even returning to the house after Flaxfield's Finishing at the river. Only these five remained. They sat around Flaxfield's kitchen table, the evening light making their faces clearer, the highlights and shading accentuated by the gloom. Sam had been sent off to occupy himself.

"We need mushrooms from the wood," Caleb had told him. "Only the puffballs, mind. It's for a special spell. And choose only the best."

Sam nodded like an idiot, took the mushroom basket and set off. Puffballs! Puffballs were good on toast, fried in butter. They made a spell for curing the trots in dogs and you could grind dried ones and put the powder in a lotion to make you look younger [but only for a few hours "and hope that's long enough" Flaxfield had said] and that was about all. So he knew he was just being sent out of the way.

They watched him till he was past the coppice then, as soon as he was under cover, he doubled back, climbed up the ivy at the side of the house, slid into an upper window and crawled down the side of the wall to the smoking-loft over the kitchen fire, which was now cold and dead. Invisible in its cover, he could see most things and hear everything.

"When was the last time you saw Flaxfield?" asked Axestone.

It was Eloise who had seen him most recently.

"At the Tawdry Fair in Cawthwaite. He was buying spices. Four years ago."

"Was the boy with him?"

She shook her head.

Caleb looked around at them. His fingers played over the silver and jet pin that fastened his collar. "Did he ever go to a fair without you when you were his apprentice? No? No."

They all shook their heads.

Before that, Axestone had been the last to see him. Over twelve years ago.

"It was here," he said. "He looked very old and tired." He hesitated.

"Go on," said Khazib, sensing something important. "You have to tell us."

Axestone lowered his head. "He said he had come to the end of his magic, that there was little left."

They waited for more.

"I asked him where his apprentice was. He said he had no more to teach. That he would never have another."

Caleb smacked the table.

"So! I was his last. I should have given him the farewell. I knew it."

"He changed his mind," said Eloise.

"The boy did it well," agreed Sandage.

"That's not the point. He's not an apprentice."

Sam bared his teeth at Caleb.

"Look at him. Have you ever seen an apprentice like him?"

"He is scruffy," admitted Sandage.

"Scruffy?" The deep, mocking voice of Khazib interrupted. "He's filthy. He smells. A castle kitchen boy is cleaner and more wholesome."

Sam gasped. He flinched under the words. Was he? He never thought. He didn't spend much time washing, but why should he? Flaxfield had never said anything.

"What shall we do with him?"

In his loft, Sam felt tired and sick. He wanted these people to go away and leave him alone. They had come into Flaxfield's house, his house, and taken it over as though they lived there, as though it was theirs, not his. And they were making plans for him, as though they were his masters. He wanted Flax-field to come in and turn them all out. For the second time since the old man died, Sam found himself crying, silently. Starback licked his face, which felt much nicer than you would think. Some dragons have tongues that are so rough they cut you, but the Green and Blue has a soft tongue, and Sam enjoyed the comfort the creature was offering. He missed Flaxfield now, more than he could have thought possible. Flaxfield had looked after everything for him, and Sam wanted him back.

"Send him back where he came from," said Caleb.

"We don't know where that is," Axestone objected.

"And he won't fit in, not now. Not once he's been an apprentice."

"He isn't, though," said Caleb.

Sandage tapped his fingers on the table, bit his lip.

"I don't like this," he said.

"What?" Khazib stared at the older wizard.

"Where was Waterburn?" asked Sandage.

"I'd forgotten about him," said Eloise.

"And Flaxfold," added Axestone. "She should have been here."

"She should," said Sandage, "but she was not Flaxfield's apprentice. It isn't so important. But Waterburn was."

"Have you heard the stories about him?" asked Eloise.

"Yes."

"Are they true?"

"Some of them are."

"Did he ever finish his apprenticeship? I heard he gave up."

"All I know for certain," said Sandage, "is that he finished with magic years ago."

"You never finish with magic," said Caleb.

"Sometimes it finishes with you, though," said Axestone.

"He disappeared," said Eloise.

"He disappeared," said Axestone, "just as the magic began to turn wild."

Sam strained to listen. *Wild magic?*

Caleb laughed.

"Wild magic," he said. "Nonsense."

"Be careful," said Sandage. "Those of us who are old have seen changes. There is a fire starting."

"What is that to do with Waterburn?" said Caleb, flicking his fingers against his sleeve.

"Waterburn was a favourite," said Axestone.

Caleb scowled.

"Flaxfield was closer to him than to most of us," Eloise agreed.

"He's not here now," said Caleb.

"No," said Khazib. "But why?"

"Waterburn disappeared," said Caleb. "That's right, isn't it? What matters is this boy. The one who pretends to be an apprentice."

"This is getting us nowhere," said Eloise. "I'm sure he's telling us the truth. Let us find out."

"How?" Caleb stared at her. "It's hot in here." He unfastened the beetle brooch at his collar and loosened his shirt.

"He will have signed indentures," she said. "That will prove it."

Sam had forgotten all about the paper he had signed six years ago.

"And if he really is, what shall we do? Flaxfield's death releases him."

"We will have a duty to the boy," said Axestone. "To complete his apprenticeship. One of us will have to take him on. If no one else will, I shall."

Sam shook his head. He could never serve this fox.

"And if he's not, he can turn the spit in a castle kitchen," Caleb predicted. "Or go down the mines."

"I have an apprentice already," said Sandage.

"He'll need a dozen baths first," said Khazib.

"He'll need a spell strong enough to clean out a town drain," said Caleb.

And so it went on. Sam had heard enough. He slid back up, doubled back, and on to the landing. Here, he made his way into Flaxfield's study.

It was a small room but, to the boy's mind, the best in the house. Three walls were books. Or it seemed that way. Every inch of space was covered with oak bookshelves made for the room. A huge iron grate with an oak chimneypiece provided heat in winter. A round oak table, with rush-bottomed oak chairs, and a few pictures on the fireplace wall completed the room. It was as functional as a kitchen or a laundry room, made for purpose, little added that did not contribute to its use. Here was the heart of Flaxfield's mystery. Sam had not stepped into it for the first three years he lived with the wizard. And then, the day Flaxfold left, the day they had signed the paper that Sam now knew was called an indenture, Flaxfield took him in there and sat him at the table. "Don't touch anything."

He nodded, eyes like moons, looking at the books.

Flaxfield opened a cupboard, part of the wall of bookshelves. He took from it a box and put the indenture in, replaced it and closed the door.

Turning to face Sam, he said, "Choose a book."

"For me?" he asked. More than anything else, he wanted to own one of these books.

The old man laughed.

"Not yet. Perhaps one day. Perhaps never. But, for now, chose a book you would like to read."

The boy looked hungrily at the shelves. Which one? There were huge books on the lower shelves, bigger than the wooden boards he chopped vegetables on, and heavier by the look of them. He would love to turn their pages and see what huge stories they held. But there were others, higher up, just above his head, with coloured leather spines, blues and greens and reds, with gold pictures and gold writing. He wanted to touch those as much as he wanted to tear into crusty bread and tangy cheese after a swim. Or the slender armies of matching volumes, all in the same livery, with numbers at the base of the spines. Some were so old they looked as though they had been buried in the woods. Others so bright and fresh they could have just been made. Which one?

"Or perhaps you would rather make up a medicine for me for a sick horse," said Flaxfield, "if there's nothing there to interest you."

Sam wheeled round, frightened Flaxfield was sending him out of the library.

"No!" he said. "I really want..."

The old man was smiling at him and Sam realized he was being teased. He had hardly smiled at Sam before today, hardly seemed to notice him.

"So many," said his master.

"I want to read them all."

"You shall, I think. But everything starts with one. Which one?"

Hastily, before Flaxfield changed his mind, Sam pointed to a book he had been considering. It was small, so he felt it would not be too much for him, old, because he liked to think of looking into something that had been there for years and years and that others had thought was valuable enough to read and to keep, and that had been here many years before he had, but not so old that the cover was dark and dirty. The leather was a dark green, with rich, gold letters, deepened by time, and a small drawing of [and this was what had made his mind up] a dragon.

"This one."

"Are you sure?"

He nodded.

"Very well."

Flaxfield showed him how to take a book from the shelf without damaging the spine. How to hold it gently. The boy laid the volume carefully on the table and looked at the wizard.

"Please begin. Read to me, boy."

Sam felt breathless and nervous. The way he did when he climbed the big trees by the riverbank and jumped into the water. It was frightening, but wonderful. So when he opened the book, the disappointment was like a slap. It was as though the branch broke just before he jumped and he tumbled down, through the tree, banging and bruising and scratching himself all the way to the ground. He couldn't read it. He scowled at Flaxfield.

"Why did you let me take that one?"

Flaxfield took it from him gently, smiled and said, "You chose it. Don't be angry. That's the first lesson today. Trust what you have chosen. There is a reason. Sometimes it has chosen you. What do you think of your book?"

"It's no good."

"Come closer."

Sam banged his chair across so that the two of them leaned over the book together. The old man smelled of herbs and oil; it soothed the boy and he reluctantly relaxed a little.

"See," said Flaxfield. "The page you opened has only writing. But look here."

He turned and there was a drawing of a dragon, a Blue and Green, in front of a small group of houses, and an inn, with trees framing the picture. Beneath it was a single word, in a script Sam had never seen before.

"Do you know what this says?" asked Flaxfield?

"No." The word came quietly, though still with a resentful tone.

"It is written in a language that no one speaks any more."

"Why?"

"The ones who spoke it are all dead, these many years, and all we have left are their books. But we can still read it well enough. The letters are not like our letters, as you have seen," he smiled, "but not so hard to learn."

Sam's anger had all transformed into curiosity and he forgot to sulk.

"What does it say?"

"Well," said Flaxfield. "That will have to wait, I think. But I will, soon, begin to teach you these letters, so that one day you will be able to read it. For now, let me show you something else about this book."

He took his eyes from the page with the picture, and he ran his finger down a column of words on the facing page. "Ah, here it is," he said. "So. Soot. Pepper. Salt. A snake's eye. One ash leaf? I thought it was elder. Never mind. And a blue plate. Of course. I remember." He spoke to Sam. Can you reach that ash tree outside? Through the window?"

He could.

"One leaf will do. Thank you. And that plate on the mantel-piece. Good. Sit down. And be quiet."

Flaxfield had taken other things from cupboards while Sam was leaning out of the window. He put the leaf on the plate and dropped the dried snake eye in the middle. Mumbling words from the open page, he made passes with his hands, sprinkled salt and pepper, as though about to eat it, then looked around the room. "Soot! We forgot the soot." He leaned back, took a pinch of soot from the cold fireplace and used it to trace letters on the edge of the blue and white plate. "There!" he sat back.

Sam looked at him. Then at the plate. Then at Flaxfield again. If this was books, he wasn't as interested as he thought.

"Oh," said Flaxfield. "Do you want to finish it?"

He nodded.

Flaxfield put his finger [one that wasn't sooty] on the page and said, "After me." Tracing each letter of a word he said, "S— t — a — v — k — a — r."

Sam repeated each letter.

"All at once."

"Stavkar!"

His eyes had been on the book, concentrating on the strange letters, but when he turned them back to the plate it was a boiling stew of colours.

Green and blue smoke hovered for a second and then,

contracted, gathered together over the plate and, in a moment, formed itself into a tiny green and blue dragon.

Sam sat back in fright.

The creature's wings flapped lazily, holding it in the air. Its head turned from side to side. Smoke dribbled from its nostrils. Its eyes, green as greed, flickered, focused, moved from side to side, then locked on Sam. The boy gripped the edge of the table, his hands hurting from the tension. The dragon flapped towards him.

"Don't move," said Flaxfield.

Sam held his breath.

The dragon came to a halt three inches from his face. Stared at him. Blinked and stared. He could smell the smoke, feel the heat of the breath, the waft of air from the wings, hear the soft swish of the tail. A tongue flickered, forked and slim. Sam shivered.

Without thinking, Sam joined his hands together, cupped them, held them beneath the creature and waited. The dragon stared. Sam smiled.

"So, it's a dragon, is it?" Flaxfield whispered. "Very well."

It was his first ever meeting with a dragon, and it was love at first sight. He knew then that he wanted his life to be about dragons. When the tiny creature had disappeared, he felt as though a part of him had gone as well. Flaxfield tidied the table [a job he would normally have expected Sam to do] and left the boy alone for a while. When he sat down again, the room was almost clear of smoke. Sam was staring at his hand. There was a small mark in the palm, smoke-grey and suggestive of a shape, though what was not quite clear.

Flaxfield closed the book and replaced it on the shelf. "Perhaps you would like to pick another."

The boy frowned. The rows of books didn't look so inviting now. They were a challenge as well as a promise.

"You choose," he said.

Flaxfield smiled at him and, astonishingly [it was a day of surprises], ruffled his hair. He had hardly ever touched him, rarely smiled. For three years he had been like a clock in the corner of the room. From time to time he gave the boy a reading lesson, or took him to the woods and fields to learn plants and animals, like striking the hour. Apart from that, the wizard might not have existed. He ate his meals, went out for walks, met visitors alone in the long room, mixed and ground and blended ingredients, bottled tinctures, stayed up all night sometimes making sounds, like conversations, or the rush of a river, or the grumbling of dead branches in the darkness. But he had nothing else to do with the boy. So this sudden attention, and the affectionate touch, were a mystery as well as a surprise.

"Good," he said. "Very good."

"I'm going to be a wizard," Sam whispered to Starback. The dragon climbed up his back and put his head on the boy's shoulder.

"I will. But not with those, those..."

He had no words for the hatred and fear he felt towards the company downstairs. Only the thought of Eloise made him pause. If she had offered. But not Axestone. Never him. He left the study and closed the door behind him.

"I'll find another way," he said. "Another master."

His lips moving all the while, he ran his finger along the edges of the door, not forgetting the side with the hinge. He breathed into the keyhole and he licked the ringed handle. Resting his forehead against the oak panels, he finished the spell and pressed his hands against the dark wood. It was done. Starback rubbed against him. Sam managed a pale smile. His face was lined with effort.

"I don't know," he whispered. "It's the strongest spell I know, to bind a door, but with a house full of wizards it may not last."

Starback put his nose to the door handle, licked it, drew back, breathed out and sent a ball of fire from his nostrils. The iron handle glowed red, then died down to cold black. Sam rested his hand on the dragon's head.

"Let's go," he said.

Ash took a small piece of wood from the table, scorched and twisted. Kneeling, she tapped it on the floor, rhythmically, in a repeated pattern. In the corner Bakkmann flinched and turned its face to the wall.

She scratched the end of the wood against the slate floor. One by one, then in a rush, black beetles prised their way up from between the slate slabs. They clustered round her, crawling over her hands and up her arms, getting lost in the folds of the grey robe.

"That's enough," she said, putting the wooden stick back on the table.

She shook herself and the beetles tumbled down till they were all in a group. She scooped them into her cupped hands. Their sharp legs scratched her palms, their shiny cases gleamed.

"Bakkmann, get a flame," she said.

The black creature clacked angrily at her.

"Do it."

It scuttled sideways against the wall and disappeared through the open door.

Ash laughed.

She dipped her head to her hands.

She opened her mouth wide and pushed the beetles in.

They scrabbled round in the darkness.

She raised her arms above her head, lowered them, leaned forward and, opening her mouth, let the beetles spill out at her feet.

As they fell, they burst into flame, popping and blazing, screaming and tumbling down. She stepped back and watched them die in pain.

When the flames had gone, she stooped, filled her hands with the ashes, stood, and breathed into them. The ashes puffed out, spread, hesitated, hung for a moment, then gathered into a dark shape.

"Good. That's it," she murmured. "Go on."

The shape resolved itself into a dragon, black, twisted, legs broken, wings snapped.

"That's fixed you," she said. "Now. Find him. Lose him. Make him mad."

The ash dragon flapped its damaged wings and half-flew, half-fell through the window and away.

She knelt again, pushed her thin fingers down into the cracks between the slabs, found and caught five more beetles. She popped them into her mouth and bit down, crunching them. She spat them out, smacked each one with the scorched stick and watched them flare up, bright, like nuggets of coal, then die back and crumble. She blew on them and they were remade, clacked open their wing cases, rose and flew round the tower room, bumping into the walls and ceiling.

"You know what to do," she said. "Off with you."

They flew out into the night.

"But you, boy," she whispered. "You're mine. Flaxfield escaped from me. You won't." ‖

Pages from an apprentice's notebook

SOME WELL-KNOWN FACTS ABOUT
MEMMONTS. Memmonts are, of course,
very tidy, or why would we say, "as tidy as
a memmont"?

It's also very hard to hold on to a
memmont. They only get here by accident and
are always trying to get back home, although
they are gentle enough and never bite,
unless they are attacked.

For some reason, they like weavers and
will always try to hide in a weaver's cottage
or workshop when they get lost here. The
ancient Cloude family of weavers, who made
tapestries for the Palace of Boolat, were

the first ever to find and keep a memmont,
which is why, to this day, every piece of work
from the Cloude workshops bears the figure
of a memmont somewhere in it. Sometimes,
as in the large tapestries, the memmont may
be a part of the scene; in smaller hangings
the memmont may only be climbing up the
side of the pattern, almost invisible; while,
in the scarves and handkerchiefs, it may be
embroidered into the piece by hand. But no
finished fabric leaves the Cloude workshop
without a memmont. It is said that the
family and the business will fail if a weaver
forgets to include the memmont.

The Cloudes would like it to be thought
that there is always at least one real, live
memmont in the workshop, and many people
believe that to be true, but, in fact, it is
many years since there has been one there.
Memmonts are pets to no one and will not

stay anywhere if they can get back home.

Wizards, of course, have more memmonts than anyone else.

A baby memmont makes a sound like a kitten. A full-grown memmont growls like a thuring. Thurings, however, will bite fiercely for no reason, so it is not good to get them mixed up. Three-fingered Vagan tried to stroke a thuring, thinking it was a memmont.

Every night, the roffles come looking for lost memmonts, to show them the way home.

✳

Wizards have ways

of knowing things. Sam didn't know if they would follow him, or if he could just walk away and they would forget all about the stupid, dirty boy who had lied to them and told them he was a wizard's apprentice. Why would they bother with him?

The road went two ways from Flaxfield's house, and then many ways. Crossroads and forks, side alleys and paths, the routes the animals took and the broad lanes of the drovers; two ways soon became ten, and ten twenty, and Sam had walked all of them for a short way and none of them for long. Whichever way he took, a wizard would be able to see his progress, unless he took care to hide it.

The sealing spell he had cast on the door to Flaxfield's study had been for a purpose. He did not trust the wizards to see inside that room. It was not for him, not to make his life easier. It was for Flaxfield. So it was allowed. But if he cast a spell to hide his path, would that be for himself? If it was, it would turn against him. If not, then he could slip away easily.

"Why is it so difficult?" he asked Starback. The dragon scampered ahead, then darted back, bumped against the boy's knees so he nearly tumbled over, then leaped high, wings brilliant in the moonlight. "It's all a game to you," said Sam. "But I feel sort of dizzy. I want to be sick and to run fast at the same time."

"He's a long time getting those puffballs," said Caleb. "Perhaps he doesn't even know where to look."

"If he comes back with a bag of mushrooms and agaric we'll know he's a fraud," said Khazib, his face darkened more than ever in the lamplight. "Then we can send him packing."

"That won't happen," said Eloise.

Caleb leaned back in his chair and looked around the room. "You're so sure," he said. "Why did Flaxfield live like this?"

"And what is wrong with it?" asked Axestone. "It's clean and sound. Only the finest oak furniture and honest clay pots."

"A peasant's house," said Caleb, absently smoothing the fine brocade of his jacket.

"Eloise is right. If we can find his indenture," said Sandage, who had been silently watching the others till now, "we'll know what to do."

The others looked at the ancient wizard, as though he had some seniority over them, some right to make decisions. He nodded at the desk in the corner. "Where would you keep important papers?" he asked.

✠

The moon had sunk below the line of the trees. Sam had chosen a drovers' road. Not too clear, not too smooth, but wide enough not to let him wander off into the fields and woods. By moonlight it was an easy path to see; now, in the darkness, it was a false friend, sometimes seeming to disappear, sometimes seeming to fork where no second road was. Sam sighed and looked around.

"I've never been this far before," he said.

Starback scrambled up a tree and looked down. His dragon's eyes could see the road as though it were broad day. Swooping down, he started off, leading Sam.

"And I'm tired," said the boy.

Starback waited.

Sam stepped five paces from the road, found cover and sat down. Starback stayed in the road.

"Come on. Let's rest here till morning."

Starback walked on.

You can ask a dragon to do something, but you can't tell it. So it was a night alone, or more walking. Sam waited for Starback to turn round and come and sleep next to him. Beech mast gave off night odours. The woods had seemed quiet and deserted as the two of them had walked along. Now, in the silence of stopping, the small noises and movements pressed on Sam. Did the branches sway in the breeze, or were they moved by something else? Did foxes and rats rustle in the leaves and mast, or was there a wizard, tracking them, circling him, drawing closer, ready to take him back?

Did robbers, used to these paths, even now grasp knives and clubs, ready to make away with him? His back pressed against the broad trunk of a beech, Sam stared into the darkness.

What was the use of magic if you couldn't use it? He grabbed a handful of the forest floor, leaves and dust, twigs and small stones, beech husks and old nuts. Flicking his arm, he tossed it into the air, and as it rose and sprayed out, every tiny part of it glowed silver, like stardust, lighting the small clearing just long enough for Sam to see around him, to reassure himself he was alone.

But he wasn't.

Back in the kitchen, Caleb undid the sealing spell on the desk.

"It doesn't feel right," said Eloise. "I never once looked in here when I was Flaxfield's apprentice."

"He wasn't dead then," said Caleb, over his shoulder.

Sandage stayed at the kitchen table, running his finger round the rim of his glass.

Khazib watched Caleb closely. "That's not an indenture," he said.

"But it might be important."

"It's in Flaxfield's desk," said Axestone. "So it is important. But it's nothing to do with us. Put it down."

Caleb's fingers left the papers slowly, his eyes remaining on them longer.

"Here," said Khazib, leaning across the brocade jacket. He lifted a sheaf of folded parchment tied with a black ribbon.

✠

Sam watched the sparkling debris fall to the ground and kept his eyes on the spot where he had seen the small figure staring at him. He had never seen a roffle before, but he had heard Flaxfield talk of them and had seen pictures in the books. In the half-light of the spell it was hard to be certain that the man was dressed all in greens and browns, but the strange, twisted hat, the pointy shoes, the bag shaped like a flat barrel, and most of all, the perfect, half-sized figure, all made it clear that this was a roffle. Sam kept his back to the trunk of the tree, crossed his legs at the ankles and bit his lip. He had used magic for his own comfort, and here, straight away, was a roffle. It had to be a bad thing. It had to be immediate revenge for his disobedience.

"Starback," he whispered.

The dragon had disappeared, far up the road, perhaps.

"What's that?"

The roffle's voice was deeper than Sam had imagined.

"Nothing."

"What do you mean, *nothing*? I know a nothing. Starback's a something. What's a Starback?"

The roffle had moved towards Sam, his pointy shoes picking up leaves and breaking twigs.

Khazib untied the ribbon. The folded parchments tumbled onto the glowing oak of the table.

"Here's mine," said Caleb.

"Mine, too." Eloise took hers.

One by one, each found his or her indenture, signed by Flaxfield in his strong hand, and then by them, in a childish hand, very different from the accomplished script each used now.

"It's as though I'm six again," said Eloise.

Sandage held his, turned it over and over in his dark hands, spotted with brown marks of age. He had been six once.

"Nothing for that boy," said Caleb. "I knew it."

Axestone, who had been holding his breath, sighed deeply.

"We'll make him fast when he comes back," said Caleb, "and take him first thing tomorrow to the mines. Get him a lodging and a job."

"He'll never survive," said Eloise. "Not after living here, with Flaxfield."

"They start them in the mines at twelve. He'll survive. Some old woman, glad of the money, will lodge him. Plenty of poor widows where the mines are."

Sandage pondered the reason why there were so many widows and nodded. "There will be better work than that for him," he said.

"He's too old to go apprentice to any other trade," said Khazib.

"And too dangerous," said Caleb. "After what he's seen here. Who knows what Flaxfield let him share? He was getting forgetful in his age. Some time down the mines will make him forget all this."

"And they don't last long down there," said Khazib.

Caleb grinned. "I'll lock him in under the stairs when he gets back."

"He's not coming back," said Axestone. "There's enough wizard in him already to know when to run."

They looked at each other, knowing the wizard was right.

"Then we must find him," said Caleb. "Before he does any damage. A half-wizard will harm us all." ‖

Pages from an apprentice's notebook

TAILORS AND TAILORING. Tailors are
best avoided, except when you need a new suit of
clothes or a waistcoat. They present themselves as
soft as cloth, but they are as sharp as needles.
Never trust a tailor. A tailor's job is to disguise
his customer. To make a fat man slim; to make
a weak man look strong; to take a peasant who
has found a fortune and to transform him into
a landowner or a merchant, until he opens his
mouth. Tailors are deceivers. And worse.

A tailor's shop is a very pleasant place to
spend the time, and a good tailor's shop is a joy
to the eyes as well as to the touch. Bolts of
worsted, linen and silk. Bobbins and shears.

A wide window set in a thick stone wall, to let the customers see the true colour of the cloth before they order the tailor to cut it to shape. And, most important of all, the table. A real tailor's table is made of cedar wood, as are all the shelves and the cupboards. Moths do not like cedar, so it protects the cloth from them. The table is long, at least three times as long as its width, and it must be wide enough to take a bolt of cloth.

The tailor's table has three purposes, but it is never used for food or eating at. Even a small amount of food or drink is enough to ruin a length of cloth worth a year's pay for a working man.

The table is for display. Watch a tailor seize bolts from the shelves and throw them onto the table, letting them unroll, and blaze with colour and ripple with rich folds. One, two, three, more and more lengths fill the table, until the customer thinks himself a king or a merchant prince. How people will respect him when he appears dressed in this. How they will listen to him when the tailor's shears and needles have worked their magic, snipping and tucking, lining and turning, hemming and cording.

The second use of the table is for the tailor to sit on. Slipping off his shoes, the tailor jumps onto the table, crosses his legs, picks up the cut pieces and, turned towards the big window, for light, begins to sew. It would be foolish to sew away from the light. The thread tangles, the needle misses its mark so that the seam is crooked or the tuck in the wrong place, the natural grain of the cloth is ignored and the coat seems twisted. Now, anyone with a thick needle can stitch a shroud or fasten a sack, even by lamplight, but that isn't sewing. The tailor's needles are thin and sharp and nimble and fast. And the finest tailors of all sew the cloth so that all the stitches are folded inside, hidden, so that the garment looks as though a needle has never touched it, as though it grew, like an ear of wheat or an orchid, complex, detailed, with shades and hues that blend and complement each other, yet never betraying a maker's hand. This is the sorcery of the tailor. This is what he conjures up, cross-legged on his cedar table.

The customer thinks he has bought a coat, as he would buy a horse or a cupboard, but it is not like that. For the coat, or the cloak, the worsted suit or the breeches have been made for him and him alone. Anyone can ride the horse, anyone can put his dishes in the cupboard as well as anyone else, but the clothes will only properly fit one man, so the tailor has entered into a pact, to transform him into whatever the clothes will make him. And it doesn't end when the customer walks out of the shop.

That's two of the three uses.

Memmonts don't like tailors. And tailors are frightened of memmonts. Memmonts are straightforward beasts, and they do not trust the skill of the tailor to transform the customer.

Tailors sometimes work at night, with the shutters closed. At two or three in the morning, there is a blade of light around the edge of the tailor's window as he sews a special garment for a particular customer, who needs it in a hurry, perhaps, or who has made a special request. This is sewing that does not need daylight.

Now, dressmakers are a different thing altogether. And weavers are another yet.

*

Sam looked around for Starback,

but the dragon had disappeared.

The roffle slipped his bag from his back and sat on it.

"Start at the beginning, but be quick about it," he said. "What's a Starback?"

Sam forgot about being punished for using his magic and he shook his head.

"Is it a book?"

Shake.

"A snake?"

Shake.

"A cake?"

Shake.

"Is it a long piece of string with a bottle on the end of it?"

"Why would it be that?" asked Sam.

"Why would it be anything?"

"It would be something sensible."

The roffle wriggled on his bag. "Ah, but why? You don't

look sensible. You look lost and dirty."

"Stop calling me dirty," said Sam.

"I've only just started. You see, you're not very sensible. I'm not going to bother with you."

He stood up, dusted the back of his trousers and hauled on his bag.

"Please stay."

"Why?"

"I'm alone. And I've never been here before. And it's dark."

"Three sensible things," said the roffle with a frown. He sat down again. "What's your name?"

"Sam. What's yours."

"Megatorine."

"Are you looking for a memmont?"

Megatorine crinkled his forehead.

"Who told you that?"

"Everyone knows that's what roffles do."

"No they don't. They think we come up for food."

Sam shook his head. "No, you've got lots of food. You look for memmonts."

"So," said Megatorine, "you're a wizard, then?"

"Who sealed this door?" asked Khazib.

They had each tried their strongest spells to open the study door, but each had failed.

Caleb had started, grabbing the handle without thinking to unlock it first, and he pulled his hand back, screaming with pain as the handle glowed red to his grasp, burning him.

Axestone smiled.

Caleb swore and said bad things about Flaxfield that an apprentice should never even think about his old master.

Sandage was more cautious, but used his best magic, and the door remained firm against him.

Khazib straightened his shoulders, held his head erect and pretended not to know that this was a trial of power between the five of them. Now it was a challenge, and the one who won would have gained in authority. He ran his fingers along exactly the same line that Sam had followed, moved his lips in a language none of the others knew, and commanded the door to open.

Eloise hung back, waited for Axestone to fail, which he did.

Her magic was softer, more intimate. She seemed to beguile the door into being one with her in the desire to open and, for a moment, it yielded, seeming to open, then slammed shut, fast as ever, locked against them.

Her eyes were wide and her breathing deep, but she gave no other sign of the great expense that the attempt had cost her.

"He had lost none of his power in his age," said Khazib.

"Indeed," said Axestone. "A spell as powerful as youth itself. Who would have thought he had such strength left in him?" And he walked away quickly.

"I'm not a wizard," said Sam, "but I will be one day."

"You are already, or you wouldn't know the secrets of the

roffles. That's wizard work," said Megatorine, in a voice so gentle and friendly that Sam told him everything, without stopping to think whether it was a good idea or not.

"Well, that's easily settled," said the roffle.

"Really?"

"You don't need a master," he said. "That's old-fashioned. You can go to a proper place to learn to be a wizard, with lots of others. Besides," he said, "there's lots of bad magic about these days. Magic that will eat you up if you're not trained."

Sam leaned forward, surprised to hear the roffle saying what the wizards had been talking about.

"How do you know that?"

"Roffles know lots of things. The tunnels in the Deep World link up all over the place. We move where no one sees us."

"Where does the bad magic come from?" asked Sam.

"Ah, now you're asking."

"And what's the answer?"

"Most things begin with one thing," said the roffle.

"What was the one thing?"

"A cat with a silver knife is one thing."

"No, it's two things," said Sam.

"So it is."

"A silver knife shaped like a cat is one thing."

"Is it?"

"What do you think?"

"It's a knife," said Sam. "That's one thing. But it's a sort of cat as well, and that's another thing. So it's two things."

"Two things can be one thing."

Sam thought about that.

"What was the one thing that started the magic going bad?" he asked.

"It was a wizard," said the roffle.

Waterburn, thought Sam.

"And that's why you've got to go to college, to learn properly. You need lots of wizards around you."

"But wizards live alone. They guard their secrets. They don't share them like that."

"Oh, it's secrets you want, is it?"

Sam wished Starback was with him. Somehow he seemed to know what to do when the dragon was nearby. This was the longest time they had ever been apart.

"Do you really want to be a wizard?"

"Yes."

"I'll take you, if you like."

"Is it far?"

"Day and a half. And if you see a memmont on the way, give me a shout."

"All right."

The night was so far on that the road was quite invisible, even the short path back to it through the trees had curled up on itself and hidden.

"We'll sleep here first, though," said Megatorine. "Make us a fire."

Sam had been longing for a fire, for warmth, and for

protection against any creatures of the forest.

"I can't. I've no flint."

"Magic one up for us."

Sam shook his head. "I can't use the magic for myself," he explained. "It would go wrong."

"That's all right. The fire isn't for you. It's for me."

"But..."

"No buts. No fire. No help. Find the wizard school yourself. I'm off."

Sam flicked his fingers and a crackling fire sprang up in the clearing. Megatorine gave him an orange grin. "That's more like it," he said. "I knew it was my lucky day. My own wizard, eh?"

And he curled up tight like a hedgehog and was snoring before Sam even had time to worry about who the fire was for.

Starback had flown back to watch the five wizards leave the house and search for Sam. They all set off in the right way, following the boy's footsteps as though they were glowing in the dark. Wizard sight sees what has been as well as what is there. But when they reached the first fork in the road the footsteps went in both directions.

"What's this," said Khazib. "Did he double back? Go both ways?"

Caleb ran along one path, then along the other, as far as the turn in each direction. "They go both ways for miles," he said. "He couldn't have doubled back, there wasn't time."

Eloise looked long and hard at each.

"I think this one," she said, pointing left.

Sandage put his hand on her arm. "Are you sure? Is there some magic we have not used?"

"No. I just think it," she admitted. "It could be the other way."

Caleb smashed his staff against a tree. All the leaves instantly died, curled up and fell crackling to the ground. Birds flew up from the branches, and a line of black beetles scrambled out from the roots and disappeared into the undergrowth.

"How is it done?" he shouted.

"If Eloise goes left, I'll take the right," said Axestone.

"I'll come with you," said Khazib.

"And I with Eloise," said Sandage.

"It is not possible," said Caleb. "The boy is no wizard, not even a proper apprentice. He can't have done this."

"But it is done, anyway," said Axestone. "So we must do our best. With us, or Eloise?"

"With you," said Caleb.

"I thought so," said Eloise, watching them set off. "Caleb will not follow a woman's lead."

"The more fool, he," said Sandage.

At the next fork in each direction, the footsteps disappeared altogether. Instead of two trails there were none. Sandage nodded his head slowly, "I begin to admire our young friend," he said. Eloise silently chose the left fork again, leaving Sandage alone. Over to the right, Caleb raged, and Khazib pointed at the two clear paths.

"The boy is clever," he said and trudged on alone.

"Not the boy," Axestone whispered to himself. "This is dragon magic."

"I'll beat him till his bones shake when I get hold of him," said Caleb.

Axestone walked steadily away. He left Caleb slumped at the base of an alder. "He may not be so easy to discipline," he predicted. But anger had closed Caleb's ears.

When he was sure that the five were separated, Starback flew back to the clearing and was not at all happy when he saw the fire and the roffle and Sam half-awake and frightened. He hid above him in the beech tree and waited for morning. While he waited the small shape of a black, broken dragon circled round, fell to earth behind Starback, found the rough bark of the tree and began to climb. Not a leaf moved as the dragon rose ever higher. He curled round them, like smoke. Then, when he had found a branch above Starback's head, he shimmered, lost shape, and drifted down onto the Green and Blue and folded himself round Starback's face and head. Starback blinked, shook his head, and shuddered as the smoke curled into his ears and disappeared. ‖

Pages from an apprentice's notebook

FINISHINGS. There is Up Top and there is the Deep World. People live Up Top. Roffles live in the Deep World.

Roffles are used to coming Up Top and it is easy for them. They are used to the way we do things here. Very few people have been to the Deep World and they find it hard to get on there. Things are different in the Deep World.

The first time that people go to the Deep World they often get ill. The food there is delicious, and different from food Up Top, and they eat too much too quickly so they spend the next day alone in the lavatory and come out with sore bottoms. This is why when anyone has

---

a runny tummy it is called "Taking a roffle holiday".

Then there are the Solstucks. These are small, green furry things. They can fly, but are not very good at it, so they waver about like bumble bees and they crash into things a lot. Roffles are used to them and they just laugh because it tickles. But most people find that if a Solstuck flies into them it hurts, like a wasp sting. They get a lump, which itches and then turns yellow and starts to ooze with a nasty fluid. The only way to stop this is to press some fresh cabbage leaves on the place. Roffles don't grow cabbages, so that's difficult. There are other things in the Deep World that the traveller comes across, which are not very nice, but which never trouble the roffles, because it is their world.

The only thing Up Top which troubles roffles is boiled eggs, so they never eat them.

*

Then, there is the Finished World.

There are many doors between the Deep World and Up Top. For people, there is only one door to the Finished World.

And they can only walk through it one way. No one knows what the Finished World is like. A wizard can see through the door to the Finished World, but he must not step through. A wizard must never follow through into the open door to the Finished World. Only a wizard can even see through the door. To walk through is to die, and to lose all hope of a final, safe journey to the Finished World, prepared and guided by a wizard.

Everyone knows the story of Glassmere, who fell in love with Skeltring. Wizards do not marry, and Glassmere went away to leave Skeltring in peace so she could marry an ordinary man. He returned after fifteen years and found that she had locked herself away, waiting for him to come back to her. She lived alone, in the Mill House where her parents had died. Her only company was the wild cats who came in from the forest and lived with her, sleeping in the beds and on the armchairs, dragging food into the house that they had caught in the forest, voles and rats, starlings and grass snakes. Skeltring had forgotten how to speak; she made noises like a cat and ate the animals they had killed for her.

When Glassmere found her he could see her cheekbones through her skin, her fingers sharp as sticks, her wrist bones wider than her arm. She had waited for him and now it was too late.

Glassmere cleared the house of cats and their stink. He made it as it had been, clean and fragrant, and decorated for a wedding. Taking Skeltring's hand, he summoned all his power and restored her to the lovely girl she had been the day he left.

Taking him in her arms, she kissed him, and died.

At Skeltring's Finishing, the village came back to her. They surrounded her house, bringing gifts and food and music.

Glassmere carried out the ceremonies, he gave her the Finishing Goods, led the procession into the forest and settled her on a grassy bank in a clearing. Then, when the time came for the Finishing Words, he saw the door open to the Finished World. Skeltring passed through. Just as the door was closing, she looked over her shoulder at Glassmere. He stepped through after her.

The people watching could never agree on what they saw. Some said Glassmere just disappeared. Others, that arms reached out and took him. Others said that he was still there and that he walked away in silence and was never seen again. Yet others said that when the air had settled and the door had closed,

Glassmere was no longer there, but where he had been standing there was a stone, slender and tall, and not in any way shaped like a man, with the base buried in the forest floor. To this day, people go to the stone when they are in need. Especially those who are wounded or lost in love. They leave flowers and gifts of food at the stone. Sometimes wine and oil. The flowers die and rot, returning to the earth. Wild cats come at night and eat the food.

A wizard must be prepared well to conduct his first Finishing and must always be assisted by his Apprentice-Master. Otherwise, to look through the door to the Finished World is too dangerous. To step through is death.

*

A weaver's cottage

stands open to the sun and a weaver's day begins early. Though it weave the most delicate fabric, a loom is a dangerous machine. Soft cloth comes from hard frames, and if you are going to make the shuttle fly and keep the warp and weft in straight lines with nimble feet and swift hands, then you need to see what you are doing or fingers will be snapped off as swift as bobbins twist. A green thread is as like a brown in the half-light as a frog is like a toad by moonlight, so a weaver's cottage has high, wide windows, walls more glass than stone. Weavers rise early and work as soon as it is light, and they do not weave when twilight comes, but sit and drink beer and tell stories.

Martin the weaver had been at work for two hours by the time he saw the boy and the roffle break through the line of trees and walk down the hill towards his cottage.

"He'll want food," he said. "And more." He pedalled a little quicker and made the frame dance, anxious to finish the next piece of the pattern before he was interrupted. The red yarn he was using was almost gone and he didn't like to finish before the last of it was woven into the design.

He broke off as they were halfway down the hill, stretched his legs and clattered downstairs before he had the chance to see Starback fly over the forest and settle on the tip of an ancient elm, watching the two small figures as they approached the cottage.

Axestone had taken every correct path and turn, but there was no trail to follow. Starback had cast a dragon spell over the way they had gone, and dragon magic is cunning magic. If he had only walked another half-hour, only taken one more turn, only cleared the forest and stepped out into the open field beside the weaver's cottage, Axestone would have seen Sam. But he didn't. He turned back, not knowing how near he had come to finding him. Eloise had taken a route that led her in a great circle, almost back to where they had begun, and then she returned home. Khazib? Well Khazib had cheated. He had used magic to try to stop Sam quickly and bring him back, and the magic had turned around and snared him in a fen with shifting waters and treacherous paths, where slimy creatures followed him with stinking scales and poison fangs. Because magic had trapped him there Khazib knew he had to be very careful not to use more magic to try to escape, or the creatures would grow in strength, with crafty eyes and hungry mouths. Sandage was the first to give up the chase, choosing to return to his own home and think of another way.

As for Caleb, Caleb lasted longest, tried hardest, walked furthest and grew most angry. His road divided and forked, and he doubled back and searched both ways, over and over, until he forgot which paths he had tried and which were new to him. He breakfasted on anger and went to bed on rage, meals which weakened his body as they strengthened his appetite for Sam. His hands were black from the study door. His face grew thin. His eyes bright with pain. He searched without purpose, advanced without care.

"I'm not having that boy in my house. Not like that."

Martin knew better than to argue with his wife. He shrugged his shoulders and looked apologetically at Sam.

"You can't blame her," he said.

Sam's face kindled and shone. He had never known he was dirty, now everyone said he was.

"What about it?" asked Martin.

"All right," Sam agreed. He was very hungry and he didn't want to be dirty any more. Mrs Martin tossed him the soap, a hard, yellow, lumpy, smelly stone, then she went inside, for modesty. Sam took off all his clothes and Martin made a fire of them, which burned up nicely, though with a nasty smell, not like the fragrant apple-wood fires that Sam made for Flaxfield in the winter. Many buckets of water later, and after making his eyes sting so much he thought he would go blind,

Sam found himself folded in towels and sitting at the kitchen table, hair damp and feet cool on the grey slate floor, eating toast and marmalade and bacon. He didn't like to say so, but he quite liked the feeling of being clean. He looked up from his plate and tried to work out what sort of people these were. Martin was an old man, at least forty-five, with grey streaks in his sandy hair and just the beginning of wrinkles around his eyes. Mrs Martin was about the same, but a little plump and with her hair tied back in a bun, except for the strands which had the nerve to disobey her and dangle down, sometimes falling in front of her face, which was stern, but not unkind. Even when he was sitting still Martin moved his fingers and his hands in a nimble, sweeping fashion, as though to emphasize what he said, but really in memory of the motion of the loom and the shuttle, which he missed whenever he was away from them. He smiled often, and laughed easily.

"This is a very tidy house," said Megatorine, between mouthfuls of bacon.

The Martins looked at each other.

"Very tidy. Do you have a girl who comes in to help?"

"How's your bacon, Sam?" asked Mrs Martin. "There's more if you like it."

She bent over the frying pan on the range and turned a thick, salty-sweet rasher.

"How far have you come?" asked Martin.

"Or do you do it all yourself?" asked the roffle.

"No, thank you," said Sam.

Mrs Martin forked the rasher onto her husband's plate, not offering it to Megatorine.

"I'm quite full, thank you," said the roffle, taking two more pieces of toast and spreading them thick with marmalade and butter in that order, getting marmalade in the butter dish and butter in the marmalade pot.

"I was travelling all night and half of yesterday," said Sam.

"Together?" Mrs Martin put the pan to one side.

"Very tidy," said the roffle.

"Do we still have any clothes?" asked Martin, keeping his head down and not looking at his wife.

"I should think it takes a lot of time, tidying and sweeping and scrubbing and suchlike," said Megatorine.

Mrs Martin nodded grimly. She disappeared through the kitchen door into a shady back hall, and Sam could hear cupboard doors and drawers.

"It's dangerous to sleep in the forest," said Martin, to Sam, but looking at the roffle. "You never know what might happen, or who you might meet."

"I looked after him."

"Did you?"

"And I'm going to look after him again, till we get him safely to school in Canterstock."

"Here," said Mrs Martin, emerging again. "Try these." She handed Sam a neatly folded pile of clean clothes. "Now," she said to the roffle, "we'll keep him here and look after him. You can be on your way."

Sam hurried out of the room to get dressed. There was a handkerchief on top of the pile and he blew his nose and dried his eyes. Where was Starback? And why had Flaxfield died like that, without telling him, without letting him know what to do? He had never been alone before. He pulled on the fresh clothes, enjoying the sense of being clean, the softness of the fabric, the sweet smell of the linen. His old clothes had been stiff with dirt and rough to the skin. Everyone wanted him, the wizards, the weavers, the roffle, and he didn't know who to trust, where to go.

"I'm going to be a wizard, though," he whispered.

A pair of green eyes opened at these words and looked at him through the half-light of the back hall. ‖

The important thing,

Sandage knew, was to find the boy. All else had to wait.

Sandage's house. So small it could shudder at a slammed door. So fragile it could seem about to fall down when the wizard burst in. Downstairs, a kitchen and a room where he saw those who came to ask his help. Upstairs, one room, with a bed, some cupboards, a shelf of books, a jug and bowl to wash in. His apprentice slept in a hut in the garden. People marvelled that Sandage, with all his power and reputation, could live so simply and in so small a space. He had been offered houses, in the grounds of great mansions, offered land to build a bigger house, offered men and materials to improve and extend his tiny dwelling, but he had refused them all. Because, in truth, his house was not his house, but only an entrance, to conceal his real home, a camouflage to confuse people. His home lay deep beneath the little house, and was reached by a hidden door in the kitchen. His study, his workshop, his library, and room after room stretched far beyond the confines of the small house that hid them.

Sandage cast an opening spell over the hidden door. It appeared, opened, swung shut behind him, and he made his way underground into the heart of his mystery.

He sniffed and smiled at the fresh, damp smell of the earth. He bent over and drew in the earth, eyes closed, head back, waiting to see what he would write, waiting to see where Sam was. He did not see the black beetle dig out of the soil, nor the way it moved the marks in the earth, nor the small hole it left behind when it burrowed down out of sight. ‖

Sam's blue eyes

gazed at the green ones. Green, with gold flecks, eyes twice the size of a cat's eyes, unblinking and intelligent. Sam tugged on the waistcoat and was dressed, which made him feel safer, less easy to attack. Raised voices the other side of the door told him that a battle was being fought and he guessed it was about him. He stepped back, away from the eyes, but the hall was narrow and his back brushed against the wall. The eyes drew nearer. Sam thought of a spell he could use to push the creature back, to hurt it, make it run away, kill it perhaps. His own eyes blinked while the green eyes stayed wide and watchful. With nowhere else for him to back into Sam saw the creature draw ever closer. He raised his left arm, pointed a finger and began to say something, when the door opened, light rushed in, and he made out, clearly, the form of the memmont, with glowing green eyes.

Mrs Martin looked at Sam, his arm raised to strike the memmont with magic. Her eyes filled with tears. Sam let his arm fall to his side. The memmont drew back behind a dark oak dresser, carved with intricate figures. Mrs Martin stepped forward and put her arms around Sam, folding him to her, his face pressed against the starched cotton of her apron. He remembered the day that Flaxfold had left and that she had hugged him, too. The only other hug he could remember. He wanted to push her away, but more than that he wanted her to hold him for a very long time.

When she finally let him go, he kept his head down.

"Was that really a memmont?" he asked, quietly.

"Shh." She wiped away her tears.

"I've never see one before."

She took him further from the kitchen, through another door and into a sitting room.

"Tell me," she said, "quickly. Who are you and where are you going, and why are you with the roffle?"

He hesitated.

"No time," she said. "Quickly."

Sam told her everything, from the day Flaxfield had died. He explained that he was learning to be a wizard and that he had no master now.

"These others," she said. "Won't one of them take you on?"

Sam paused and tried hard to explain why he did not want to go with any of them, why he did not trust them, but he didn't really understand it himself.

"They said I was a liar," he said. "That I was no apprentice. That I was making it up. But then at the same time, they seemed to know that I was telling the truth. I can't explain."

"Are you telling the truth?" She looked directly at him. "Or were you an odd-job boy who meddled with things you shouldn't know about?"

Sam glared at her.

"Don't take offence," she said. "The world is full of liars and cheats. I don't know you yet. But I think you are telling the truth. Help me to be sure."

"How?"

"Do some magic for me now."

"I can't."

She sat back and sighed.

"I can. But I mustn't. It's not there to play tricks or to show off with."

She nodded. "Good. You got that right. All right. This chimney smokes and we can't use it. You clear it for me, in return for your breakfast and your clothes. How's that for a wizard's work?"

Sam thought about it. It was the sort of thing that Flaxfield did all the time for the people who called on him, so it seemed all right. Of course, he wasn't a wizard, and strictly speaking could not take on work, but he had more than enough magic for this.

"All right," he said.

He took a candle from the mantelpiece and a tinderbox. Striking the flint, he made a flame. Lit the candle, placed it in the hearth and held his hands close to the stem, cupping the flame. He raised his eyes. The candle lifted, rose up the chimney and disappeared. All the air in the room seemed to gather into a fist and rush up the chimney, punching its way through. Mrs Martin gasped for breath. Outside, the chimney erupted into a volcano of soot and ash and smoke which paused, clenched and then swirled high, high above the house until it formed a small, black cloud in the shape of a fist. The candle hovered above the chimney stack, sank slowly down and placed itself neatly on the mantelpiece before sighing and giving up its flame, like a cat closing its eyes.

In the distance, Starback watched the smoke and ash, scratched a disappointed ear and waited. After a few minutes the air above the chimney began to shudder, as though heat was rising from a fire below. Starback waited for it to die down, but it continued. He watched carefully.

Sam's face was the grey of the dead ash in the grate. His fingers twitched, he breathed unsteadily. He stared at the ash and felt it was looking back at him. Mrs Martin sat in silence. He smiled uneasily at her, and she nodded.

"Are you all right?"

"Yes," he said. "Of course."

"You'd like a drink?"

He nodded. His eyes stayed on the grate, the ash. He took a poker from the fireplace and stirred the grey dust. He felt as though he had brought something into the house. The magic had called to it. He leaned nearer.

The roffle put his head round the corner.

"Very good fit," he said, pointing to Sam's new clothes. "Do you have a son, Missus?"

"Not now," said Martin, following him in.

"Tidy in here, too," said Megatorine.

"What's to do?" asked Martin.

Sam sipped the water, his hand trembling, still.

"Stay here, do," said the weaver's wife.

"You'll learn a trade," Martin promised.

"Not the right trade," said the roffle. "Let's be off, boy."

"You don't make wizards in schools," she said. "You need a proper master. You need to be an apprentice, not a schoolboy."

"Magic's magic," said the roffle. "He'll learn well enough."

Sam shrugged and gave Mrs Martin an apologetic look.

"It's all right," she said. "But if you ever need somewhere to go, this is the place. Remember?"

"Thank you."

Sam and the roffle made their way through the kitchen, back to the door. Martin took Sam's arm, half-turned him, and spread a cloak on his shoulders.

"Keep you warm at night," he said.

Mrs Martin gave him another swift hug and walked away quickly.

Sam turned his head at the bend in the road for one last look at the little cottage.

"You broke your promise," said the roffle.

"What do you mean?"

"I told you to let me know if you saw a memmont. I'll have to watch you."

In the tower, high above the field that stretched to forest, the slim, dark figure sat with closed eyes at a plain table. Her ash-grey robe flowed in soft folds from her shoulders. She leaned back, raising her arms and putting her hands to her hair.

"He's on the move again," she said.

She looked at the black figure which loomed by the closed door.

"Where?"

The question was no human voice, but a clacking as of snapped bones.

"I didn't see the place. He used loose magic, and I slipped in. I think he saw me, but he doesn't know yet. He's on the run."

The clacking noise indicated laughter.

"I have people ready," she said. "One of them will see him, soon enough. Then we'll know."

"Can I have him?" Bakkman clacked.

"Eventually. Once I have the seal from him and I can leave this place." ||

A kingfisher flashed across

the surface of the stream, dipped, splashed and flew up, a fish sparkling in its beak. Water boatmen skimmed across the surface, a single black beetle landed gently. Eloise lifted her arms high and tossed the bright shawl into the air, watching it spread like a tablecloth. Flashes of gold thread grasped at the sunlight and ran like veins in marble through the deep blue green of the silk. It hung, briefly, then softly floated down to the surface of the stream. Eloise held her arms out-stretched above it. Instead of being caught by the current it held in place, rippling with the motion of the water.

Eloise smiled. Her eyes were the colour of the silk. The blue of the water reflected upwards onto the white of her cheeks, and she seemed as one with the stream in its clarity and in its movement. The kingfisher dived again, upstream.

Lowering her arms slowly, she stepped forward into the stream. The water embraced her as one of its own. Waist deep, her full sleeves dipping into the stream, she leaned over the shawl and examined its surface. The veins of gold glowed and pulsed, as though flowing with blood. Eloise placed a slim, delicate finger to one side of the centre, then traced a line in the thread, which turned silver ahead of her movements. The silk background pattern moved and changed, as though in agreement with the movement of the stream, but as her finger traced its path along the thread, the patterns settled, fixed and revealed a landscape, with clusters of houses, forests, roads and rivers, a mountain and a coastline, a tower, a castle, a dark, high structure, perhaps a prison, perhaps a grim palace. Eloise frowned and brushed the beetle away from the cloth.

There were figures, too — a boy, a dragon, a wizard, a weaver, and more, many more. These figures were not quite fixed, as the other features were, but they moved, very slightly, but clearly, along the surface of the silk.

Eloise nodded, sighed and stepped back up the slope, back onto the bank, taking the shawl with her. She emerged from the stream perfectly dry, her clothes as elegant and as clean as before she entered the muddy edge, the clear water. Her lips, red before, were pale now and her hands trembled a little. The kingfisher dived, stuttered on the surface and came up, beak empty, seeking the safety of an overhanging alder.

"I see you," she whispered to the figure on the shawl. "And I am coming for you."

The beetle settled on the water, then dissolved and disappeared. ‖

Pages from an apprentice's notebook

A WIZARD'S NAME. Everything has a name, even down to the smallest singling, which is so small that no one has ever seen one. Most things only have one name. A wild pig is a pig, a beetle is a beetle and grass is grass. But the closer things grow to the world of people, the more interest people take in them, the more names they get. So, a pig is a pig but he may also be Snuffler, while another pig is also a pig, but she may be Snout. And a takkabakk is a beetle, but not a beetle. So it is with a mountain. This one may be Mount Marlew, while that one is the Peak of Terrim. Grass is always grass, but in a field of horses it is grazing, while once it is cut and stored it is hay.

People have this way of giving more and more names to the same things. But once you have given a thing a new word it becomes a new thing.

If you keep hens, for eggs and for the pot, never give a hen a name, because it is harder to kill and eat Clucker or Doofy than it is to pull the neck of just another hen in the yard when you want your holiday dinner.

When an apprentice comes to serve a wizard he has a name, the one his parents gave him. This is the name he will always be known by. It is what he writes when he signs a letter, or buys a piece of land. But one name is not enough for a wizard. Just as a pig may be a wild boar or a bacon pig, or a family pet, so there is more than one thing to being a wizard, and so a wizard needs more than one name.

It takes many years for a wizard to discover

the name of the apprentice, but it is the most important thing he will ever teach him.

There have been stories of wizards who have lost their way, turned to magic for their own gain, and tried to be greater than the magic itself. One wizard, Slowin, who tried to be greater than his own magic, stole the name of his apprentice. Slowin, whose magic name was Ember, had misused magic over long years. He started looking over his shoulder when he walked in the streets. At night he heard creaks and groans like floorboards and hinges. When storm clouds gathered and ordinary people took in their washing, Slowin locked himself in his tower and bolted the doors and sealed them with a spell. But his magic was growing weaker and weaker because he had not used it well, and the spells would not have kept a rat from getting in. Morning by morning, the magic he had wasted and had gained profit from was coming together.

All the tiny spells were joining up, and all the great acts of wizardry he had performed were gathering together, until they formed a mighty army of magic, ready for revenge on the weak and frightened Slowin. He blamed his name. He saw Ember as a sign of dying and weakness, the glowing coals of a fire that has once blazed away and is now still and sullen in the grate, waiting for more coal or wood.

He had an apprentice, a poor girl called Beatrice, who had come to him, as the custom is, as a small child. By this time Slowin was already abusing his magic, and he knew he had less and less to give, less to teach, so Beatrice, instead of learning, was little more than a slave. Slowin tricked her into using her magic to make spells for him to sell. She was a girl who deserved the finest master. She had a gift that few apprentices bring with them. Her powers could have been greater than Slowin ever dreamed of. He had been a strong wizard, once, but even then nothing to what Beatrice could have been. He saw the possibilities in her and was full of envy and spite, which made his laziness and his own weakness even greater, so he kept from her even the little he could have given.

The day came for her to sign her indenture and become his apprentice, for him to tell her what her name was. Her name was Flame. Slowin saw his opportunity to cheat the magic that was hunting him.

"You write Beatrice here," he said, "and there," he put his finger on the page, "your name in magic, Ember."

Beatrice looked straight into his eyes and he knew that she did not believe him.

"Hurry," he said. "Or you will never be a wizard."

So she signed, Ember, and he signed, Flame. When it was done it could not be undone.

Slowin had a new name, and new strength.
And Beatrice, who had come to him with such
promise, was now weak and spent, and the
revenge magic was turned on her.

That night, Slowin's house burned down,
and with it all his books and equipment and
ingredients, and the indenture that bound
master and apprentice together, destroyed by
fire. Slowin escaped, changed beyond change,
and was never seen again in that country.
Beatrice was dragged from the fire. Her hair
was burned off, her hands black from trying
to beat off the flames, her face, which
had promised beauty, would always tell the
story of the fire. She was half-dead, hardly
breathing. The magic had mistaken her for
Slowin. Another wizard saved her, turned
away the festering magic from Slowin's selfish
spells, and filled her dying lungs with new
air. She had lost the power to speak, could

no longer read or write, and kept her head shawled, the folds draped over her face to hide the scars. In taking her name, Slowin had taken nearly all she had.

A wizard is given a name at the very beginning of the apprenticeship as a sign of the trust between the child and the master, it binds them together in a secret companionship which is theirs for life.

For some wizards, two names are not enough, or even three.

*

Axestone's lined face gazed up

into the sky with the wide open eyes of a child. Spreading his arms, he let the wind catch his robe and fill it like a kite. The long sleeves flapped out and the loose robe billowed wide. Had he wanted, Axestone could have stepped forward and, with the help of just a little magic, let the wind take him, like one of his kites, and lift him up into the sky.

"Oh," he said. "Why not? It's not a game, it's medicine. I need a tonic after all that trouble."

With these words, he stepped up onto a non-existent stair and, in an instant, was carried the height of a high tower, higher even, up above the hilltop and into the cool, sweet air.

It was all air. Axestone breathed it in, filling his lungs, letting himself grow dizzy on the excess. The designs that the years had painted on his face were swept away and he was twelve again, an apprentice, bunking off from the work that Flaxfield had set him and escaping into the air where he felt most at home.

Leaving the clear air with more regret than he liked to admit, he made his way indoors.

A wizard's house is no accident of lodging. It reveals the wizard. Axestone lived on top of a high hill, with no other dwelling in sight. His house had been built for a miller and was long and low and spacious. It was built on the side of a cap mill, a stone tower with a wooden dome and wide sails. The windmill was his workshop, so that at all times he could tell which way the wind was blowing, how strong it was, how warm. Axestone always knew what the weather would be at least five days before it arrived. And the wind brought other news, too, to those who could hear it. It was a living thing, with moods and fancies and desires all of its own. And a history and memory. Axestone could sit in the windmill, listen to the creaking of the timbers, the flapping of the sails, the gusts on the round stone walls, and he could learn about what was happening in towns and villages over twenty miles away.

He set the sails in motion, not for more news, but for the pleasure of hearing them turn and for the satisfaction of the movement of something else while he worked on a spell to seek out Sam.

He took silk and linen and cord and laths of wood and needle and thread and he made a kite. Such a kite as a child would dream of. It was a shape and no shape. It was a dragon, a snake, a bird, a fish, a horse, a dog, a river, a tree. Even lying still on the table it moved and changed and shifted shape. But when Axestone took it outside and gave it to the wind and slipped it loose to the air, to lift into the clarity of the sky, it was all of those things and none of them. Axestone had poured his highest magic into it. Now, he held the cord and let the air complete the spell. He watched the kite bobbing and swooping. His skin tingled as he saw the shape struggle for solidity, watched it seeking Sam, scouring the skies for news of him, until, with an electric jolt of the cord, Axestone felt the kite settle into a shape and fix.

He reeled it in and studied it. It was shaped like a beetle, with teasing lines scribbled on its wing case, like roads and a stream.

"Clear, but not clear," he said. He silently paid tribute to Sam's skill, while at the same time hoping it was not the craft of another force which made finding him so difficult. ||

Sam felt Starback's absence like

a toothache, nagging at him, slowing his footsteps, a pain always there, hurting, but not enough to make him cry tears or shout aloud. Megatorine talked all the time.

"Do you see that bird? That's a flatterflit."

Sam knew it as a lapwing.

"In the Deep World we have flatterflits as big as badgers, and they can sing like moonerwards."

"What's a moonerward?" Sam flapped a hand at a blue dragonfly hovering in the heat in front of his face.

"Up Top you call them nightingales, but we don't have them in the Deep World because of the light down there. See that stream? You'll find tiddlers from the Deep World there, with seven eyes. They used to sell them at fairs and then they got into the streams, but we don't like Deep World stuff coming up here any more."

"What is the light like down there?" asked Sam, puzzled by the talk of the nightingales. He took off his waistcoat and put it over his arm with the cloak the weavers had given him. The fields shimmered in the heat, and the sun was baking the wheat on the stalks, filling the air with a toasty scent that made Sam hungry again. It was many hours since they had finished their breakfast.

"Now that's a very good question. A wizard's question, if you don't mind my saying so. Do you see that tree? The one with the horse chestnuts on it."

"How much further is it to Canterstock?"

"We'll just take a little rest here," said the roffle. He stepped off the path and under the wide branches of the horse chestnut. The shade folded over them and Sam smiled to be out of the sun. He spread his cloak on the ground and lay on it flat on his stomach while Megatorine leaned back against the rough bark. Propped on one elbow the boy looked at the roffle. To look at he was just like a little man. But his thoughts were roffle thoughts and Sam had found it difficult to know what was going on in his head.

"What's it like at the college?" he asked.

"Now, your horse chestnut is a good tree for shade, and for leaning against, but its fruit is not good to eat. Would you like a sandwich?"

Sam would.

They unwrapped the food Mrs Martin had prepared for them. Cheese sandwiches and ham sandwiches. A pork pie. Four meat pasties, two fruit pies, apples and raw carrots. Enough for three days, at least. There was lemonade for

Sam and beer for the roffle as well.

"Why didn't you tell me about the memmont?"

Sam looked down at his cloak and traced a finger along the line of the weave.

"I'll have to go back for it and take it to the Deep World."

"Why?"

"That's where they belong."

"They like to be with weavers."

Megatorine scowled into his beer.

"How did you know?" asked Sam.

"It was too tidy. I knew straight away."

"No, how did you know I had seen it?"

"I didn't," said the roffle. "But I do now, don't I? A wizard needs to be more careful than that. That's why you need that college, boy. Your old wizard didn't teach you very well, did he?"

Sam knew that Flaxfield would have been disappointed in him and he concentrated even harder on the weave of the cloak. Flaxfield was not two days dead yet, and Sam had lost his house, lost Starback, run away from the wizards and given a secret away to a roffle. He could see the old wizard's face frowning sadly at him, and he felt sick with sorrow.

"Canterstock will sort you out," the roffle promised.

"Tell me about it."

"It's not old wizards like your master was. Village magicians. It's proper magic. A wizard from the college gets respect in the towns."

"Why?"

"Because of their magic, of course. They can cast a spell to make a frog sing like a lark, make rancid milk taste like the sweetest cider, make a rich man marry an ugly girl before he finds out what she really looks like, too late."

The roffle sprayed pasty crumbs over his shirt front in his excitement. He bounced up and down on his flattened barrel seat.

"Oh, you should see the magic those ones do. There's nothing they can't manage. And it's because they've been taught properly at a college, you see."

"What's it like?"

"Like? What's it like? You've seen a castle."

"No."

"Well, you've seen the Palace of Boolat."

"No."

"No?"

"No."

"Everyone's seen the Palace of Boolat. Fathers take their sons there to see it as soon as they can walk and talk. It's the greatest marvel in the world. You have."

"No."

Megatorine sat back against the horse chestnut. "What sort of master was it you had? I can't believe it."

Sam was ashamed. Ashamed of himself for knowing so little, ashamed of Flaxfield for not teaching him more and showing him more.

The roffle scratched his head, hummed a little tune, then

said, "Anyway, it's the biggest building you can imagine, like a castle, like a palace. With halls and great rooms for lessons and demonstrations, with long, long corridors and dormitories and little rooms for all the students to sleep in. With gardens like you've never seen and can't imagine. It's the greatest place for a wizard to learn. And full of the most talented students."

Sam's sorrow had fled and he was full of wonder and excitement. He had never realized that Flaxfield was not a proper wizard, and he was grateful to have learned in time. But it could not be as simple as the roffle said. There must be money to pay, some sort of fee.

"How will I get in?"

"Through the door."

"No. Why will they let me in? Do you have to pay?"

"You just leave that to me," said the roffle. "I can square old Frasty."

"What's old Frasty?" Sam asked.

"Professor Frastfil is the principal of the college, and a very old friend of mine."

Sam didn't know that roffles were so well travelled or that they knew such important people. He made a resolution to add this to his notebook later on. For the moment he was more interested in the college.

"I'll have to change my name," he said.

"Sam's a good name." The roffle gave him a sly look.

"I like it," said Sam. "But they're looking for me. I need to hide from them."

"That's the cleverness of it, you see," said the roffle. "They'll never think of looking at the college."

"Why not? I'd have thought it was an obvious place."

"Ah, that's where you show how little you know."

Sam looked carefully at the cloak again, picking the edge with his fingers.

"Village wizards stay away from the college. They hate it because they weren't good enough to go there. They'll never think that a dirty kitchen boy like you would be able to go. And besides, they know you can't pay."

"I can't," said Sam, in despair again. "I told you."

"And I told you, that a friend of mine doesn't have to pay. Old Frasty will make some arrangement."

Sam discovered a small raised section of cloth on his fingers, near to the hem of the cloak. He traced it with his fingertips, looked carefully at the sun-dappled cloth and saw that the figure of a memmont had been woven into the fabric.

"Still," said Sam. "I'm going to use a different name."

Megatorine stretched and yawned. "If you like," he said. "What about your other name?"

"What?"

"You know. The name the old man gave you." He wrapped the left-overs in the waxed paper and started putting them into his bag, his back turned to Sam. "What was that?"

"Cartouche," said Sam, remembering a strange symbol he had seen in one of Flaxfield's old books.

"Cartouche?" The roffle raised his eyebrows. "What's

that, then, some sort of paper hat with fish in it, or a ribbon thing that you tie around roast parsnips?"

"I don't know," Sam lied. "It's just a word."

"Oh, nothing's ever just a word. A wizard should know that."

Sam knew that very well, but he didn't like seeing how much the roffle knew.

"Let's get going," he said.

"Sleep first."

"We need to get there."

"Why? They're not waiting for us, are they, with a big bowl of soup and a grey horse?"

"A grey horse?"

"Or a black one, then, if you like. Or a pig with a blue hat."

Sam wanted to slap him. He was bursting with jump, and needed to get on, to move around.

"It's too hot to walk now. A little nap in the shade and we'll be there by this time tomorrow. You'll see."

The roffle lay down with his head on the squashed barrel and was snoring almost before his eyes were shut.

He was right. It was too hot now, with the sun high on the clear sky, so blue that it looked like one of the pictures in Flaxfield's library. Walking was, if not impossible, then at least foolish. Sam stepped to the edge of the green awning of low branches and looked out at the fields around. The hedge-rows were neat and strong. The fields well-tended and full of crops. Elms soared up, majestic and beautiful, lords of the landscape. Sam could see, far away, in one of the great trees, perched high, a gleam of blue and green, scales shining like steel, the sun flashing off them.

"Starback!" he shouted. "Over here!" He ran out of the cover of the shade, waved his cloak in the air and called again. "Starback. Here!"

The dragon, who had been watching, stepped into empty air, spread his wings, dipped, swooped, flapped twice and rose up. Then, turning from Sam, he caught a current of warm air, rose again and soared high, high up, wheeled round in a full circle and flew off, leaving Sam with his cloak crumpled on the ground, his throat sore from shouting. Sam watched Starback until the dragon was less than a pinpoint of green against the blue sky, a memory in his vision, in eyes that stung with loss. ||

Khazib rinsed his fingers

in rosewater and dried them with a towel of fine damask. He had eaten and rested and was ready to begin his work. Almost ready. After his struggles in the mire he was enjoying the rest and tranquillity of his pavilion. The sides of the large tent were draped with costly carpets, reds and golds and deep brown, intricately patterned and woven by workers guided by magic so that the swirls and loops, the geometric shapes and interlocking lines were more than patterns, they were woven spells. No one but Khazib knew what these carpets could do.

Others would have a fire in the centre of the pavilion, the smoke, or most of it, snaking out through a central hole, but Khazib needed no fire here. The rugs were enchanted with spells that made the glow of their colours heat enough. The only flames came from the dozens of lamps, iron frames with thick glass windows, that cast their dancing light around the tent. A black beetle had flown in and was bumping against one of the lamps.

"Now," he said to the lamps and rugs, "the boy."

Care was needed here. Khazib was often too free with his magic, careless of the danger, but the rebuke about the willow and the mistake about the mire had made him cautious.

"The boy," he continued, "is in danger. We must find him, rescue him, bring him here where he can be safe." The lamps flickered, the flames sinking nearly to nothing, then flowered into light again. They did not trust his words.

"Mmm," Khazib pondered, "very well. We must question him, see that he has not betrayed Flaxfield. We must make sure he is what he says he is."

The lamps glowed steadily. There was more truth in this.

"Good. Questions it is, then. For Flaxfield's sake. Very well."

He chose a rug, big enough to lie on, small enough to roll up and carry without effort. Placing a lamp at each corner he observed the pattern. He held a fifth lamp over it, letting the light spill over the silk threads.

Murmuring in one of the dead languages of Flaxfield's library, one he had learned at the side of the old wizard himself, he persuaded the rug to reveal a landscape, concealed in the rhythm of the lines and colours, yet clear as day to the wizard. Khazib studied the contours of the map and frowned.

"You know many tricks," he said, "many clever disguises. But you are here," he pointed, "I think. And I am coming for you."

The lamps glowed gold on his brown face. The beetle circled down and settled on the rug, then burrowed through it and was gone. ‖

Starback wheeled away in the air

and headed towards Canterstock. The dragon's head dipped.
He felt a part of himself left behind in the forest. Dragons
can't cry, so they let their heads lean to one side and down. It
didn't help as much as crying helped. Nothing did. Starback
had seen animals in pain, animals frightened and lost. They
couldn't cry. So it hurt more, and the fear and the loss were
sharper, deeper. There was nowhere for them to go.

People aren't as big as bears, as strong as bulls, as fast as foxes, as clear-sighted as hawks. Animals are better than people in
every way, except one. People can cry. That gives them a way of
dealing with things that animals would never have.

So Starback spread dark wings to feel the sun burn away
the sadness. Dragons love to feel. They love the sun beat-
ing down on their backs. They love the icy water of the high
mountains. They fly higher and higher, till their scales
glow with the sun's heat, then plunge swift as swallows into
cascading ice, bursting into the waterfalls as they spill down

the rocky slopes. They love damp caves and dust-dry desert wastes. They love the green shade of cool forests and the smoke-sweet fires of autumn evenings.

Starback flew high today, till his head straightened up and he felt ready.

Starback's one thought was to look after Sam. Starback did not like roffles. Starback did not want Sam to go to the college. Starback did not want the other wizards to find Sam.

So far, Sam was with a roffle, and he was on his way to the college. Starback was not happy with himself for the way he was looking after Sam. He had thought that Sam would follow him, would leave the roffle behind and they could escape together. The dragon had spun a web of confusion behind them that had helped them to leave the wizards stumbling over false turns and dead ends and wrong roads. Without Starback's magic Sam would already have been caught. But Sam was walking a different way, and Starback was lost.

All afternoon the dragon spun in the hot winds and flew over the distant fields and forests. Once, far from where he had left Sam, he caught the flash of sun on sea and saw the green line of the horizon scratched against the blue of the ocean. Then he knew he had travelled too far, flown too high. He wheeled round, lost height and made a straight line for Canterstock.

The sun was low when the dragon's eyes caught the first roofs and towers breaking over the landscape. Dragons' eyes see further than a horse can ride in a day, so he was still far off. By the time he hovered over the town it was dark. Lights glowed in windows. Smoke rose from chimneys. The college stood grey and hunched in the square.

Starback circled lower and lower and came to rest outside the gate. He kept his back to the college and his eyes on the road into town. He would see Sam arrive and he would stop him from going in. Roffles are not good in towns. They prefer the open road, the lonely house, the field and forest. In town, Sam would come back to Starback. He would not go inside the building.

The clock in the square counted out the night hours. Starback needed no clock. A horse whinnied in the stable of the inn. Rats scuttled across the square, foraging for scraps from the market stalls. They kept their distance from the dragon. Green and Blues do not eat rats, but rats know better than to go near. The dawn still needed several hours when Starback felt the square jolt to one side. He reeled back, startled. The square twisted out of shape, then shimmered, settled back and rested. The rats shrieked and scurried away. Starback felt dizzy, sick, for a moment, then he lifted a cautious leg and moved one step forward. He braced his back legs, pushed hard and ran, and, without thinking he was going to do it, he rose up, spread his wings, flapped them briskly and was flying.

All thoughts of keeping Sam from going into the college had disappeared. He rose up higher and higher. Before it even shaped itself in his mind as a plan, he swooped round and set himself in the direction of Flaxfield's house. He needed to know if the wizards were still there, and, if not, where?

They would be looking for Sam. They must not find him.

Starback knew where to lead them. His wings caught the night air. His tail was a splinter of silver in the sky. It was two days' journey to where he was going and he would be there before dawn, ready. ‖

That night, Sam dreamed

that he was Starback.

His claws scratched on a cobbled street. The bulk of a huge stone building reared up behind him, grey and grim, like a prison. The strangest thing, at first, though many more strange things followed later, was the way he could see. His eyes were sharper than ever Sam's eyes had been. They could see the tiniest creatures, whose lives were lived between the cracks on the cobbles, scuttling in the dust. Yet when he lifted his head, he could see the very top of the towers that crowned the grey edifice. There were beetles, scratching their way against the stone, clinging to the lichen, so far up that a stone dropped from there would take many seconds to reach the earth. Yet Starback's eyes could see the smallest detail.

But he was not interested in high or low. His eyes searched the streets which met in this square in Canterstock. He was waiting for someone, waiting to warn him, waiting to keep him out of the grey, grim gaol.

Sam wanted to feel more. He wanted to test this body, see what it could do.

He lifted a cautious leg and moved one step forward. He was strong. He felt that he could carry many times more than his own weight. The muscles were like pistons. Rearing up, he moved his head from side to side, eyes searching. The power and precision of his vision startled him. His mind was agile, sharp. He had seen every detail around him in an instant, and he could recall it instantly.

Sam thought of himself, dreaming he was Starback, thinking of Sam. It was like falling from a very high place. His mind couldn't hold all the thoughts at once. He was falling, turning, arms flailing, trying to get himself upright and stop the ground rushing up at him. He steadied himself, thought very hard, and felt a terrible sadness, a longing to see Sam, a sick feeling that he had been sent away. It was like the feeling he had when Flaxfield died, like being empty of everything, it was like fear, with nothing to be frightened of, but still very frightened. He stopped thinking of Sam. It was just too difficult.

What else could this body do? He moved again. Walking was a constant decision of whether to use two legs or four. Either was comfortable, but one was clearly better than the other, depending on the sort of ground he was on and how fast he wanted to go.

He wanted to go very fast, so he braced his back legs, pushed hard and ran, and, without thinking he was going to do it, he rose up, spread his wings, flapped them briskly and was flying.

He gasped with the beauty and wonder of flight, mounting ever higher, riding the rolling steady air beneath him.

Before it even shaped itself in his mind as a plan, he swooped round and set himself in the direction of Flaxfield's house. He needed to know if the wizards were still there, and, if not, where?

Sweeping round like a skate's heel on a bend he set his course for home, transported by the ecstasy of striding the air. So this was what it was like to be a dragon. How much better than being a boy.

The river, then the willows, then the house itself. Sam circled the house. Below him seethed with magic. Then, as he stooped down, he woke, and was Sam again, and his heart in hiding broke, rebuffed by the wind. ‖

Pages from an apprentice's notebook

WANDS. A wand is a bendy stick. That's it.

I've been told I have to write more on this page.

Well, a wand is a stick. Not just any stick that you might pick up. A wand is straight and slender. Willow trees make good wands when the branches are young.

Wands have many uses.

An old man may use a wand when he is walking, or an old woman. Or someone who has had a fall and hurt their legs and needs some way to help them balance.

Some teachers use wands when they want

---

to point to things. Some teachers think that
new learning goes in, not through the eyes or
the ears, but through the backside, so if a
pupil is slow they beat his backside with
a wand to make the knowledge go in better.

But a teacher must always remember when to
use the wand and when to withhold it. Tug
Turner was very fond of flicking his pupils
with his wand. He used to make the class
chant as he whipped the naughty boys. Each
time the wand flicked the boy the class would
call out — THAT'S. THE. WAY. TO. MAKE.
HIM. LEARN. One day, he told Beakerton to
come and be whipped for not learning his sums.
Beakerton said, no, he wouldn't. Tug Turner
pulled him from his seat and flicked the wand
across his legs. He started to bend Beakerton over
and shout, "Come on, class," to make them chant,
when Beakerton, who had grown more than Tug
Turner had noticed, grabbed the wand and

pushed Tug Turner over and flogged him with it. The class all yelled out — THAT'S. THE. WAY. TO. MAKE. HIM. LEARN. — ten times, till Beakerton let him go. Beakerton walked out of the classroom and never came back. After that Tug Turner used the wand a lot less.

Wands are flexible because they are cut when they are young and the sap is in them, so they are still wet. This makes them useful for making all sorts of things.

Wands can be woven together to make a basket. If you weave wands in straight lines you can make a hurdle for a fence. Or you can weave a wall of wands and cover it with a paste made of clay and mud and cow pats. This is called wattle and daub.

A wand can be used to make a horse ride faster, but it is cruel to whip a horse with a wand. A horse that is whipped too hard can throw its rider and kill him.

The secret of a wand is that it is flexible.
It bends. It can be made into something else.
Sometimes, as with the horse or the pupil, the
wand is used on its own. Other times, as with
baskets or hurdles, wands are plaited together
with other wands to make something bigger.

If it does not bend, it is not a wand.

Wands make good fishing rods. A thick stick
that does not bend is no good for this. You
need to feel the wand move in your hand
when the fish bites. There is a connection
between the fish and the fisher, and it is
the wand which makes the connection. Just
as there is a connection between the teacher's
hand and the pupil's backside.

The wand used for fishing is sensitive and
springy. It draws the fish to it, and it helps
the fisher to play the fish, to land it safely.

The wand used to punish the pupil or urge
on the horse, flicks more painfully than a

hand would. It gathers the pain into a single point, to sting.

This is why a wizard may use a wand. It makes a connection between the wizard and the object of the spell. It concentrates the magic and makes it stronger, sharper.

Whenever a wizard uses a wand to help with a spell, he should always remember Tug Turner and be careful that whoever the spell is working on can't turn around and make the magic hurt the wizard.

There's nothing very special about wands. A wand is a bendy stick. That's it.

A wand does not make a wizard. A wizard makes a wand.

A wizard's staff is a different thing
and needs a page of
its own.

✳

Part Two

WIZARDS
EVERYWHERE

It was a moment

of contrasts. Sam had never seen a building as grim and grey as Canterstock College. And he had never met a person as twinkling and friendly and welcoming as Professor Frastfil.

As they were entering the town Sam wanted to turn around and run away. The college was vast and grey. Hard stone, small windows, great iron doors with cruel spikes. And Frastfil was small and plump, with a round, open face, spectacles and a smile, and the longest hooked nose Sam had ever seen. His clothes were loose and shabby, and he jangled his money in his pocket all the time, whether he was speaking to you, or trotting happily along the long corridors, or mumbling a spell. No situation was too solemn or too simple to stop him jingling his pockets.

"Welcome, welcome. I'm so glad to see you. Come along in, dear boy, come along in."

He jingled and smiled Sam through the iron door, and into the college.

"Good morning, Trelling," he sang out to the porter in his little lodge.

The porter nodded to Professor Frastfil.

"Letters for you," he said.

"Splendid. Splendid."

Trelling lifted his arm. A stack of letters on a high shelf fanned up and formed themselves into a line like a skein of geese in flight and swooped down in formation. They came to rest in the air just in front of the professor, who took them and put them into a deep inside pocket in his baggy jacket.

Megatorine pushed open the door into Trelling's little office and sat down on his barrel. He poured himself a cup of tea from a pot on the bookcase and settled in for a chat, old friends.

Sam blushed to see magic used for such a little task.

As they hurried into the quad he tugged at Frasty's sleeve.

"Couldn't he have handed you the letters?" he asked.

Frastfil jingled and smiled and pretended to box Sam's ears in a jolly way.

"Got to use the magic," he said, "or it gets rusty."

"Does everyone know magic here?"

"Oh, indeed, yes. Yes, yes, yes. Got to have magic all around the place. It's what we're for."

"Even the man who watches the gate?"

"Trelling? The porter? Oh, yes. One of our best pupils was Trelling. Could have gone on to do anything, but he loved the college so much he didn't want to leave. Everyone who works here, cooks, gardeners, everyone was once a pupil."

They stepped into the building and plunged into a world that Sam never believed could have been. Frastfil led him along highly polished wooden floors in a long corridor, with classrooms off to one side. It was lit by globes, floating in the air, that bobbed and drifted and glowed. As they passed each door Sam could see and smell and hear the business of magic going on in the classroom.

Sam wanted to rush in and stop them and at the same time he wanted to burst through a classroom door and see what they were doing, join in the magic and show them what he could do as well. For years Flaxfield had made him dig the garden, rather than use magic to turn the earth over. He had made him clean the floors, rather than flick his fingers and send the dust flying through the door. He had stopped him from floating in the air, prevented him from lighting fires, not allowed him to be free to use his magic whenever and however he wished.

They climbed a narrow, winding stone staircase, up, almost to the top of the building. Professor Frastfil waved his hand and the door swung open. He flung himself into an armchair and pointed to another for Sam to take.

"This desk," he said, "belonged to Cosmop, my third cousin twice-removed, and one of the greatest and most respected wizards there ever was.

Sam thought it was just a desk, whoever else had sat at it. Sitting at a great man's desk didn't make you a great man.

"Our friend the roffle speaks very highly of you," said the

professor, with an encouraging smile, "but I really need to see for myself that you are a serious candidate for a place at the college. You are also, well, a little older than most students when they arrive, and perhaps you will need to be put with younger pupils than yourself, to catch up."

Sam was annoyed at this and his eagerness to prove that he was as good as any other twelve-year-old took away some of his caution.

"What do you want me to do?"

"Let's test you in your recipes," said Frastfil. "What are the ingredients of a charm to keep a man free from colds all winter?"

"That's not the thing to do," said Sam. He quoted Flaxfield's words exactly: "Colds keep a man sensible. Never try to stop them coming or he will walk about in winter without a woollen coat and die of stupidity."

"The correct answer," said Frastfil with a frown, "is goose fat, dried mandrake root, the hard snot from a butcher's handkerchief and seven drops of lemon juice." His money jangled louder than ever in his pocket.

Sam laughed, thinking it was a joke. Then realized it was not.

The professor made his face merry again and twinkled at Sam.

"Never mind. Let's try this one. What spell would you say to rid a house of all its spiders?"

Sam couldn't understand why he was asking these questions, except to test his understanding. They had nothing to do with magic as far as he could see.

"Why would you do that?" he said.

"Just tell me the words of the spell."

Sam could only tell the truth. It was all he knew to do.

"You would never drive all the spiders out of a house," he said. "They keep down flies and other insects that are dirty and cause diseases, and the spiders do no harm to anyone."

"Ladies are very frightened of spiders," said Frastfil. "Sometimes they ask us to get rid of them. What spell would you say?"

Sam shrugged his shoulders and looked away through the window. A kestrel hovered, wings trembling. Sam admired the fire of its feathers, the freedom of its flight. How much better to be a bird than to be sitting with Professor Frastfil smiling at him and jingling the money in his pockets.

"I won't say it now," said the professor, "or it will drive all the spiders away from the college and then where would we be?"

Just where I said, thought Sam. *Infested with flies.*

"But even a beginner at the college would be able to tell me how to do that," he carried on. "I really don't see how we could think of taking you on here. I'm sorry."

Sam's dream of the freedom of the falcon melted away. He was alone and without friends or money. That was more of a prison than a freedom.

"Where shall I go, then?" he asked.

"I'm afraid," said the professor, "that I really don't know." He smiled happily and jangled. "I would offer you a job in the college, but, as you have seen..." His smile was broader than ever.

Sam nodded again. Even the kitchen staff were old students here. Every one of them a wizard.

"Sorry, sorry." Frastfil jumped and jangled to his feet and started to show Sam out.

"I don't do spells and potions," said Sam.

"Quite so," said Frasty. "All the roffle's fault. He must have misunderstood."

"I do magic," said Sam, standing up.

"Rabbits out of hats? Card tricks? Jolly good stuff for children's parties, but not for us, I'm afraid." Frastfil gave him another encouraging smile. It was the smiles that had begun to annoy Sam and make him want to demonstrate what he could do, just to show this man.

"Proper magic," said Sam. "Not tricks."

Frastfil was eager to get rid of Sam and waved him to the door. Sam stood firm where he was.

"I'll show you."

"We really must go. I have to, er, that is, er..."

Sam knew that Frastfil had nowhere else he needed to be, but that he wanted to end this interview and put him out in the street. He forgot all his fears and uncertainties about the college, forgot how grim and grey it looked, forgot how the sheer volume of magic tumbling around the classrooms had made him worry about Flaxfield's warnings, forgot how irritating the smile and the jangling were. All he wanted was to prove that he was as good as anyone else who was there, that he was good enough to be a student at Canterstock College.

He clapped his hands. The door slammed shut, wrenching itself away from Frastfil's hand. Frastfil found himself swept back into the room and forced down over the silly desk that his whatever had owned and into the armchair. The chair spun round and round and round and lifted into the air, Frasty holding on in terror of falling out. All the books jumped off the shelves and formed a cloud of paper and boards around Frasty's head, spinning in the opposite direction from him, like a dust whirl in hot summer.

"Put me down. Put me down."

Sam dropped the chair to within an inch of the floor, jolting Professor Frastfil but not hurting him. Still it spun. He turned the books into crows and had them break out of the circle and dart at the Professor, jabbing their orange beaks at him, cawing and flapping and diving till he was dizzier from dodging than he was from spinning. Sam clapped his hands again and the crows became books and roosted on the shelves, the chair came to a rest exactly where it had begun, and Frasty sat, gasping for breath and fumbling for a handkerchief to wipe his forehead.

"I'll go, then," said Sam, picking up his bag and opening the door.

"Wait! I think we can find you a place." ||

Tim Masrani walked on one side of Sam

and Smedge on the other.

These were the pupils that Professor Frastfil had summoned to take care of Sam and to show him round.

"Best to get you straight into lessons," he smiled. "Throw you in at the deep end."

Sam was so relieved that he didn't have to go out friendless from the building that he was glad to agree to anything.

"Whose lesson are you in, boys?" asked Professor Frastfil.

"Miss Peggofry's," said Tim.

"Splendid," he jangled. "Couldn't be better. Run along now and look after ... er..."

"Cartouche," said Sam, feeling a little foolish with a name that didn't fit him.

"We'll have to get you kitted out," said Tim.

"Can't have you looking like that," Smedge agreed.

"Aren't we going to lessons?"

"Later."

"I don't want to get into trouble," said Sam.

"Old Frasty meant us to get you kitted out first. He just doesn't think of it. No good at all on practical things."

"What is he good at?" asked Sam.

"So," said Tim. "First off, uniform."

He ran shrieking with pleasure down the corridors, followed by Smedge, who tried to sound the same, but didn't seem as comfortable with the noise as Tim was. Sam had to run as well, to keep up, but he didn't shriek at all, just in case, though he wished he could, Tim was enjoying it so much.

"Come on, Vengeabil," Tim called. "Wakey, wakey. We need some kit."

The storeroom was a long, low-ceilinged room that ran underneath the corridor on the ground floor. Lit by the same bouncing globes, though dim and weak down here, it was full of dark corners and suspicious nooks. Row after row of shelves ran along the walls, piled high with cardboard boxes, painted tins of all shapes and sizes, bottles and flasks, wicker baskets, cages and glass cases. Some of them were labelled with words like, *trousers — outsize* or *portable cauldrons* and seemed harmless enough, but others squatted on high shelves or scowled through the gloom and seemed to be watching the boys as they shouted out for the storekeeper.

"Vengeabil!" Tim shouted. "We'll help ourselves!" He prodded Sam. "Vengeabil is past it, really. Sleeping in a corner, I shouldn't wonder. Should have retired ages ago. We'll just have to help ourselves."

He jumped over the counter and started to look through a pile of pullovers with the Canterstock crest on them.

"You should wait for Vengeabil," said Smedge.

"Give me a hand," called Tim.

Sam watched the two boys. Smedge was a little shorter than Sam. He looked as though his uniform had been ironed on him. There was not a crease or a loose button, and everything fitted him perfectly. He smiled a lot, but seemed to think about everything before he did it or before he spoke. Nothing came rushing out.

"I think we'd better just stand here," he advised Sam. "Frasty said I should keep an eye on you."

Tim Masrani, though clean and tidy enough, was more ragged round the edges. He looked as though he might just have had a fight, or have run away from a farmer. His clothes looked a bit lived in. Just now, as he was rummaging through the pile of jerkins, one of them wound itself round his head and turned into a bat, its wings covering his face. Tim grabbed it and tried to pull it off. Another jerkin slid down, turning into a snake as it fell and wrapped itself around his legs. Then a third leaped from the shelf and, becoming a jellyfish in mid-air, splatted onto Tim's own school jerkin and slithered down to the floor with a wet flop.

"Ugh," mumbled Tim. "Ugh, disgusting. Urrgh." He was tugging at the bat and trying to kick away the snake, and flailing about, getting more and more tangled up.

Sam shuddered. He lifted a hand to send a flash of magic to help his new friend.

"None of that," said a quiet voice.

A dry, wrinkled hand settled on Sam's shoulder.

"Save your magic," he said. "He'll be all right."

"Vengeabil, you old fraud. Get them off," Tim gasped.

"Can't you work it?" said the old man. "Try *Book Two of Charms for Beast*s."

Tim groaned.

"Forgotten already?"

Tim nodded as well as he could with a bat wrapped round his face.

"You?" Vengeabil asked Smedge.

The other boy took a wand from his pocket, a slim twig of elm, brown and worn, and, waving it at Tim, chanted a quick spell and the bat and the snake and the jellyfish turned instantly back into jerkins with the college crest on them.

"New boy?" asked Vengeabil.

"Yes."

"Name?"

"Cartouche."

Vengeabil, who had been grabbing shirts and jerkins and socks and trousers, paused, looked hard at Sam and said, "Really?", his eyebrows raised.

"Leave him alone, you," said Tim. "I'm looking after him and I don't want him to end up in some dusty storeroom after he's finished here."

The jerkin which had been a jellyfish slid across the floor and up Tim's leg, leaving a soggy trail on his trousers.

"Oh, Vengeabil, that's not good," he complained.

Vengeabil laughed and gave Sam his uniform, which was mostly just the College jerkin.

Smedge gave him a hand, while Tim made a drying-off spell which more or less worked, though his shoe was still soggy and squelched when he walked.

"You need to pay a bit more attention to your work, young Tim," said Vengeabil. "Goodbye, Master Cartouche. Come back and see me for a chat when you haven't got that idiot with you."

"I will," said Sam. He looked at Tim and blushed. "Not that, I mean."

"That's all right," said Tim. "Vengeabil is a dry old fossil," — the storekeeper raised an eyebrow towards the slimy jerkin — "but he's not far wrong about me being an idiot."

"You'll do," said Vengeabil. "Off you go."

They clattered up the stairs.

"I'll show you to our dorm," said Tim, "and you can get changed."

"Someone should teach Vengeabil a lesson," said Smedge. Sam wondered what sort of lesson he meant, and looked at Smedge. The boy's face was set with an idea. Sam felt it, and it was as though he had eaten something disagreeable, his stomach protesting. Smedge caught Sam's expression and his face changed. He smiled broadly.

"You know. Let him see he's here to help us, not to throw his weight around."

"Oh, he's all right," said Tim. "Knows what he's doing,

really." He shook his wet foot. "Horrid smell that thing's left, though. I'll change my socks while we're up there."

"Up there" was a dormitory, right up at the top of the stairs, with little dormer windows that jutted out like mountain peaks on the roof.

Sam felt silly in his new uniform. He didn't like looking like everyone else.

"Thank you, Smedge," said Sam

"Are you hungry?" asked Tim.

Sam was.

"If we mess about here for a bit we can go straight to lunch and miss the end of Peggofry's class," said Tim. And he floated up to the roof and perched on a crossbeam.

"We should go back," said the other boy.

"It's boring," said Tim.

"I'm going back."

"If you go, we all have to go," Tim complained.

"That's up to you," he said. "I won't tell."

"You won't have to." Tim floated sadly down and landed gently on his own bed, which was next to Sam's. "What do you want to do, Sam?"

"I don't mind. I'm a bit nervous, so I wouldn't mind waiting to go to my first class."

"There you are," said Tim. "We'll wait till after lunch."

Smedge came and took Sam's arm. "You have to go," he said. "You don't want to get into trouble on the first day, do you? Rules are here to help us. The sooner you get into the swing of things the easier it will be."

"I'll do whatever I'm told to do," said Sam.

"Then you will do very well," said Smedge.

"We'll see," warned Tim. "We all start off like that."

Smedge gave Tim a friendly punch. "We don't all end up being idiots," he said.

"What happens to people when they leave the college?" asked Sam.

They were clattering back down the spiral staircase.

"That's what Duddle's class is all about," said Smedge.

"You can be anything you want," said Tim. "Court wizard to a great prince. Local wizard in a small town. Personal wizard to a rich businessman. Set yourself up as a wizard and let people come to you and pay every time. You can stay here and teach. You can do anything you like."

"If you go to classes," said Smedge. "Otherwise, you end up an idiot and have to take any job you can, and hope you don't mess it up."

"You mean you can end up here in the kitchens? Or in the storeroom?"

"Exactly," said Smedge. "You don't want to do that."

Tim looked embarrassed.

As they passed one of the higher landings Sam saw a door, half-open, and eyes watching them. As soon as he caught the glance of the one beyond the door, the eyes blinked, the door slammed and he heard footsteps running away. Sam had a sense of fear on the other side of the door, and he felt that there was also something for him to fear there. He stopped, put his hand to the door knob.

"No," said Smedge, "Leave it."

"Who was it?"

"Nothing," said Smedge. "Come on."

"It was something," said Sam, "and it was looking for me."

Tim took his arm, reassuringly. "It can't have been. No one here knows who you are."

"Who was it?" Sam repeated.

"It was just Tamrin," said Tim, giving Smedge a sideways look. "Forget it."

"Come on." Smedge led him further downstairs.

"What do you mean, mess it up?" asked Sam, going back to their conversation.

"If a carpenter makes a bad chair, you fall off it," said Tim. "Not much harm done."

"But if an incompetent wizard, one who doesn't know what he's doing, makes a bad spell," said Smedge, "there's no knowing what the end of it will be."

"Magic that doesn't stop when it should, that doesn't get the job done properly, can go on and on getting more things wrong," said Tim. "And then you need a really good wizard to put it right."

This sounded more like the sort of thing that Flaxfield said, and it comforted Sam.

They were back in the classroom corridor, with its stinks and sounds.

"Where have you come from?" asked Smedge.

"Oh, a fair way off."

"You're old to be starting here," he said.

Sam blushed.

"Leave him alone," said Tim. "It's none of our business."

"OK," said Smedge. "How about your friends? Are you going to miss them?"

Before Sam had the chance to reply a bell rang.

"Lunch," said Tim. "Excellent."

"We'd better introduce Cartouche to Dr Duddle," said Smedge.

"No way," Tim argued. "We're going to eat. Come on!"

He grabbed Sam and whisked him off again. Across the quad and into yet another part of the college. Sam felt he would need to be there for most of the rest of his life just to find his way around. Flaxfield's cottage and the weaver's house were the only other buildings he remembered ever being in.

When he saw the dining hall he just stopped still and gawped. It was enormous. Long wooden tables with benches ran along the sides and centre. At the far end another table ran at right angles to the rest. Boys and girls, dozens and dozens of them, perhaps hundreds, surged forward like marbles spilling out from a bag carrying Tim and Sam before them until the two boys were rolled up near to the top of the room and sat down.

Tim Masrani sat to one side of Sam and Smedge to the other.

Lunch was soup and bread and roast lamb and mashed turnips and mint sauce and gravy and runner beans and jam sponge and custard.

Sam ate it all in as much silence as he could escape with. He knew there were lots of people in the world. All the books showed him that, and there had been a number of people calling at Flaxfield's door for his help, but they never came in more than threes or fours. The wizards who had come when Flaxfield died, thirty or forty of them, were the most people that Sam had ever seen at one time. Now there were hundreds, all in the same room at the same time.

And they talked. They talked all the time and to everyone. They talked to the person next to them. They shouted across to people three tables away. Sam saw one boy, trying to catch the attention of another, finally grow impatient and wrap all his words in a paper napkin and make it fly across the room and blow open over the boy's head so all the words could tumble out and he could hear them quite clearly.

There was magic everywhere. No one asked for the mint sauce to be passed to them, they used magic to bring it. And how they showed off. The ones who couldn't be bothered just let it slide over the table to them. Others made it float. One had it up in the air and spinning, not spilling a drop, and then pouring itself over his lamb. Another, a joker, made the dish grow legs and waddle across the table to him, complaining that it had a sore knee.

There was a time for letting off steam after lunch, before the bell went for lessons, and Tim and Sam slid off their bench quickly and went into the garden, ignoring the others who preferred to go to the school yard and play Folop or Trangik.

"Does everyone do magic all the time?" asked Sam.

"Pretty much."

"Doesn't it come back and harm them?"

"Why should it?"

Tim pulled the head off a blue and red painted daisy and started to strip it of its petals. As each one fell it turned into a tiny dragonfly and flew around Tim's head.

Sam wanted to talk but didn't know how much he could trust Tim. The roffle had made him ashamed of Flaxfield and he didn't want to appear a country wizard, a figure of fun.

"I was told never to use magic unless there was really no other way to do something."

"But," said Tim, "that's like saying don't use a bucket when you can scoop up water in your hands. It takes so much longer. Or don't dig with a spade when you can scrabble away the earth with your fingers."

Sam thought about this.

"That's not the same," he said.

"It is."

Sam brushed away a couple of dragonflies that had deserted Tim and seemed to prefer him.

"Can you actually do any magic?" asked Tim.

This was what Sam had been dreading. He already wondered what harm would come to him from showing off in front of Frasty, now Tim wanted him to do something. And soon he would be in a class and be expected to do more. It was all so difficult.

"Who was that we saw on the stairs?" he asked.

"But can you? Why are you here?"

Tim's open, honest face confronted Sam's, and Sam knew that he looked shifty and dishonest by comparison. How could he not? He was carrying secrets. He wanted to trust Tim, but it was too soon.

"I've never seen so many people before," he said. "I don't know what to say to them."

"What about your friends back home?"

Sam shook his head. He thought of Starback, his only friend.

"No friends?" Tim punched him gently. "We can't have that."

Sam smiled.

"Am I really your first friend?" Tim beamed with delight.

"I've never seen another boy before," Sam told him.

Tim whistled and the tune turned into pink paper streamers that floated up out of sight.

"Who was that on the stairs?"

"I'll tell you what. I'll be your best friend, and I'll tell you who it was, if you show me some magic. How's that?"

"Isn't Smedge your best friend?"

Tim thought for a second.

"Smedge doesn't really work like that. How about it?"

Sam blew on the dragonflies that still danced around Tim. Each one of them turned into a tiny dragon, yellow with red stripes. They formed a perfect circle, all looking in towards

Tim. Then they opened their mouths and blew smoke at him, making him cough and his eyes water.

"That's not friendly," he laughed, coughing away the smoke as the dragons flew away in a line and settled in the bushes. "But that was wonderful. We don't do dragons for another year. They're very tricky. You are good, aren't you?"

"Who was it?" asked Sam. The question had grown in his mind every time someone refused to answer it or dodged away from replying.

"It was Tamrin," said Tim.

Sam waited for him to say more. And waited. "Who is Tamrin?" he asked at last.

"She's just a servant," said Smedge.

They hadn't heard him approach, didn't know how long he had been near, listening.

"She cleans the dormitories and takes out the rubbish to the midden, and washes up in the kitchen."

"I thought all the people who worked here were wizards?"

Smedge linked arms with Sam and led him towards the college.

"They are. Even Tamrin, in a way. But she never finished properly. Professor Frastfil took pity on her and gave her a job, even though it was bending the rules. He's a really kind man."

"Time for Duddles," said Tim.

"Your first lesson," said Smedge.

Sam felt sick.

"Come on." ||

No one seemed very interested

in Sam, which was a great relief to him. Even Dr Duddle didn't really seem bothered when Tim and Smedge introduced him.

"It's not usual," he complained. "But I suppose we'll have to let you stay. Catch up as you can, will you? Boys, you'll have to keep an eye open for him."

"We will," Smedge and Tim agreed.

It was very dull stuff. Sam could still hear the bangs and squawks and rumbling from other classrooms, but nothing like that went on in here.

Dr Duddle didn't seem to like magic at all. All he wanted to talk about was how the pupils could make money from it when they left the college.

"A wizard is no different from anyone else," he said.

Some of them groaned, some of them seemed to like the idea.

"Being a wizard is just a job," said Duddle. "Like being a blacksmith or a farmer. A wizard has some special powers;

that's what you're here for, to learn those special powers, but at the end of the day, you just go out there and do a job."

Sam knew that farmers were tired at the end of the day, and he knew that a blacksmith needed a strong arm and a steady hand and a good eye, but he had seen Flaxfield after working some strong magic, he had seen Eloise when she had been at Flaxfield's Finishing, and he knew how he felt after he had worked at a new piece of magic and it had drained him of all the strength he had. He didn't think that farmers and blacksmiths felt like that. He remembered the way people had treated Flaxfield, with respect, and with not a little fear. He didn't think that they felt that way about blacksmiths and farmers. Most of all, he remembered the way Flaxfield lived. His silences and his solitude. His devotion to his books and his herbs and his apparatus. He remembered the way that Flaxfield had taken people's problems to himself and laboured over them to make sure the right magic was worked. He didn't think that farmers and blacksmiths, hard-working and skilful though they were, took their work into themselves the way a wizard did. And he thought Duddle was either a fool or a cheat. There was a lot to understand about this college.

His thoughts took him back to the five wizards he had left talking about him in Flaxfield's kitchen. He hoped they had all gone away and forgotten all about him, but somehow he didn't think that was likely. There had been the feeling, in the weaver's cottage, that he was being watched. That had to be them. He remembered the threat of taking him to work in the mines, and he wondered if his parents were still living somewhere and why they had given him to Flaxfield to look after. A rap on his head brought him back to the classroom. Dr Duddle stood over him, glaring down. Some of the other pupils were nudging each other and grinning.

"I said," Dr Duddle said, "perhaps you could tell us how you think you might earn a living after you leave this academy. What are your ambitions, Mr Cartouche?"

No one had ever called Sam "Mister" before, and he didn't know that Duddle was only doing it to mock him.

"Oh, please," he said. "There's no need to call me Mister. You can call me —" and he nearly said Sam, and remembered just in time. "Cartouche."

Dr Duddle was a rather strict teacher, whose punishments were unpleasant, and he was not used to what sounded like cheek. He drew himself up to his full height, which was not very much, tugged at the lapels of his neat suit and barked at Sam, "Don't think you can come here and try to make a fool of me, young man."

"He was only trying to be polite, sir," said Tim. "He's not used to it here."

"Silence, Masrani. I'll deal with you later. Let's see, then. You must have impressed Professor Frastfil at your interview. Show us what you can do and we'll tell you where we think your talents lie. Then we can guide you to a proper occupation. A Court Wizard to a King, I'm sure, or the Official Wizard to a great city. A keen and talented young man like you could do anything. Let us see a taste of your powers."

Sam stared ahead, refusing to look down in apology or to look up at the teacher.

"Go on," whispered Tim.

Sam stared, silently.

"Nothing?" asked Duddle. "Nothing at all?"

The class began to giggle.

"A beginner? In this class? Some mistake, I think. One last chance. Show us, please, Mr Cartouche, what you can do."

Tim trod on Sam's foot, but he still stared ahead. He would not use magic for a man like this.

"Very well. I shall ask Professor Frastfil to remove you from this class and put you with the beginners. It will be best for you and for all of us. In the meantime, class, please. Three minutes' break. Make free with any demonstrations you wish for our new boy."

The air filled with flashes of colour and light. Fireworks and fanfares. It was not like Duddle to give them a rest and they took full advantage of it. Most of the class just enjoyed themselves with magic games, creating flying swords and fencing with each other above their heads, sending Folop balls flying across the room, filling the air with grasshoppers and bats. But some of them decided to make fun of the new boy. A personal rain cloud appeared over Sam's head and began to pour on him. Tim made him an umbrella. Frogs pushed their way out of his desk and flopped onto his lap. Tim turned them into hamsters.

"You do something," he said to Sam. "Protect yourself.

You have to or it will get worse."

Sam had never been bullied before. One of the good things about not being with many people is that there's no one to be cruel to you. He let it happen, allowing Tim to do what he could to stop it.

He looked at Duddle and waited for him to tell the others to leave him alone. Duddle looked away and wrote something on the blackboard.

Sam's desk turned into a tub of hot soapy water with dirty washing in it that slopped over the sides and drenched his new clothes. Tim was distracted by a side attack on him by a swarm of wasps.

Duddle finished writing on the board, and, with the chalk, he drew a circle in the air, called out, "Finish, furnish, fly!" All the wasps and swords and balls and every other last piece of magic in the room swooped through the circle and disappeared. All except the wash tub and the soapy water, which stayed in place.

"Oh, dear," said Duddle. "Never mind. Some magic always remains behind. Just your bad luck, I think. You pop off and find somewhere to dry yourself while we continue, Mr Cartouche. We'll manage without you. Off you go."

Sam and Tim stood up.

"Not you, boy," said Duddle.

"Go to the dorm," Tim whispered, sitting down again. "I'll see you there later." ||

Sam unpacked his bag

and spread out everything he owned on the narrow bed in the long dormitory.

He had towelled himself down, and, because there was really no other way and it was not just to make things easier, he had hung his wet clothes from the crossbeam of the ceiling and dried them with a warm summer breeze. Dressed again as a pupil of this strange college, which was like nothing he had expected, he looked at his property. He did not include any of the uniform that Vengeabil had given him. He did not think of that as his.

A bottle of lemonade, half a pasty, three spare handkerchiefs, two spare pairs of socks, the clothes and the cloak from the weavers, a shirt that had been mended many times, a piece of string, a knife and his notebook.

Sam had made the notebook himself, on Flaxfield's instructions. They made many books when Sam was just a small boy, and he coloured in them and practised his letters.

Rough and ready things, they fell apart easily, the stitches not being tight enough or the gum not strong. They practised making better gum, neater sewing, straighter cutting. The books lasted longer, fell apart less often.

After he was properly signed up as an apprentice, Sam was sent off to make another book.

"Make it a good one this time," said Flaxfield. "Put some magic into it."

"Really?"

"The best you know."

Kid's leather, still marked with the black and white pattern of the young goat's skin. Two stiff boards, paper, strong thread, gum.

He cut and folded and stitched the sheets of paper. When there were enough pages, he covered the boards with the leather, using the gum to stick it down. At every stage, Sam was careful to pour magic into the making. He cast a spell on the leather to make it supple and not to crack. He conjured a spell of sturdiness on the boards to stop them from bending and buckling. The paper he protected with a spell against damp and mould. He boiled the gum himself from horses bones and hooves and other stuff, and he made it proof against the tiny creatures which love its sweetness and chew away at it. He cast a spell of binding on the thread so that no pages should ever work free and escape. And he prepared himself every day to cut and fashion the materials, adding to his skill with the tools a magic ability to construct the book.

When all was done, he went to Flaxfield.

"Let me see."

The old wizard turned it over and over in his hands. He smiled. He lifted it to his face, to enjoy the scent of the new leather, the fragrance of the gum. He stroked his hands over the thick pages, as though he could feel writing on their blank faces.

"Good," he said. "You have made well."

"Will you finish it?" asked Sam.

"Why?"

Flaxfield had always finished everything for Sam. He made sure that any magic that had been used was sealed off and could not escape into mischief.

"You must finish it yourself," said Flaxfield.

He watched while Sam cast a spell of finishing, teaching the book to know itself, and to be fit for its work. Finally, he sealed it, so that if anyone else opened it they would not be able to read what was there. Flaxfield watched carefully.

"I could add one thing, if you would like," he offered.

Sam handed him the book again.

Flaxfield held it and traced the cover with his finger. Where he had written, letters of gold glowed with the words:

An Apprentice's Notebook

"This is yours," he said, "to use as you see fit. Whatever you write in it is for you to decide. And never let it leave you. Ever."

He handed it back to Sam. The letters faded, then disappeared.

Sam held it now, wondering if he would ever write in it again.

Days with Flaxfield were shapeless, sprawling. There was supposed to be a lot of book learning. Flaxfield would start Sam on a lesson about frogs, or steam, or the shape of sparrows and, just as Sam was about to settle to it, with a book, in his seat in the window, Flaxfield would call him over.

"Look at this."

Sam would close the book, not sadly, and trot over to Flaxfield.

"See this penny?"

It was just a coin. Quite old, with the pattern very rubbed and smooth.

"What can you buy for a penny?"

"I don't know."

Sam hadn't been to shops. Money meant nothing to him.

"String? Sausages? A long ribbon?" asked Flaxfield.

Sam waited for him to get to the point. It was better than studying.

"You're quite right," said Flaxfield. "You can't buy much for a penny. Here." He tipped more coins onto the table. There were silver thruppenny bits, shillings and sixpences. More pennies. A big coin that Flaxfield said was half-a-crown, and two gold sovereigns.

"Put them in order," said Flaxfield.

Sam lined them up, biggest on the left, smallest on the right. The half-crowns were the biggest, then the pennies, then the shillings, then the sovereigns, then the six-pences, then the thruppenny bits.

"That's one way," said Flaxfield. "Do it another."

Sam thought about it. He pushed the coins around, let-ting them slide on the smooth surface of the table.

"What are they worth?" he asked. Flaxfield explained the dif-ferent values of each coin. As he did, Sam put them in line. First the gold sovereigns, then the half-crowns, the shillings, the six-pences, the thruppenny bits and, finally, the big pennies.

"Well?" said Flaxfield.

"It doesn't look as neat," said Sam.

"Indeed not. Do it again. A different way."

Sam put them in line again. Pennies, sovereigns, thrup-penny bits, shillings, half-crowns, sixpences. They were all jumbled up for size and value.

"What sort of order is that?"

"The ones I like best first, then the others, all the way down to the end."

Flaxfield smiled.

"The pennies are worth the least."

"But they look so nice and they're smooth and interesting. See how big they are, but quite thin. I like the darkness of the metal and the feel of them in my hand."

"And the sovereigns?"

"The only gold ones. They're so heavy, it's a surprise when you pick them up. I like that."

"Poor sixpences."

"I know."

"Do it again."

Sam made a circle with the pennies at the centre.

"Again."

He spelled out an S, for Sam.

"Again."

He found that each coin had a date on it and he put them in a line, oldest first.

"Again."

"You do it," said Sam.

Flaxfield made them hover over the table and sing a song about blackbirds.

"That's cheating."

"It is."

But it was very funny and they laughed till they hurt.

"Again," said Flaxfield.

Sam tossed each coin in turn and put them in two piles, heads and tails. He did this three times and, of course, it was different every time.

"Very good," said Flaxfield. "Again. Take your time and think."

Sam took the half-crown and closed his eyes. He let the coin rest in his hands. He waited for it to unfold and tell its story. He saw a tree and two men and an argument. He felt damp earth on his fingers, heard the noise of a spade. Darkness and time and silence. He opened his eyes and put the coin to his left.

The first sovereign filled his nose with the fragrance of baking bread. He put it to the right. The next was a moon behind the clouds, the sound of sea breaking on the shingle, a dull noise of a sharp blade running into resisting flesh. The left side. The sixpence brought a child's laugh and the taste of sweetness in his mouth. Right side.

When all the coins were in place, in two groups, right and left, Sam sat back and looked at them.

"Well?" said Flaxfield.

"They have stories. These are sad stories, pain and death. These are happy."

Sam's face was pale. He kept looking toward the door, as if waiting. His arms hung by his sides.

"A good arrangement," said Flaxfield.

"Again?" said Sam.

"I think not."

Flaxfield scooped up the coins and poured them into a leather bag.

"Shall I go back to my work?"

"No, go and play now."

Sam went off, tired, but delighted that he had got away with a whole morning with no work and no study. Flaxfield watched the boy and the dragon running down to the river together.

Sam turned to the page: *Coins.* As he started to read he caught a movement on the edge of his vision. Looking up, he saw the same eyes that had watched him earlier. Snapping the book shut, he rushed forward and through a door he had thought was a cupboard. A narrow, dark staircase led up. He ran, two steps at a time, and just managed to grab another door before it slammed shut. He ran through it so fast that when he emerged into the light he shouted with fear and threw himself back, banging his elbow and scraping his knee.

He was on the roof, and had nearly thrown himself off it, hurtling down to certain death on the cobbles below.

The eyes had a face now, and a body. A girl, about his own age, and a little shorter, with straight, blonde hair, a squarish jaw and the look of a mad dog stared at him. ||

Frastfil's round, trusting face

was painted with the colours and patterns of worry and uncertainty.

"I only want to do what's absolutely best for the college and for the students," he said.

"Of course," said Smedge," that's what we all want, sir."

"It seems very harsh," said the Professor.

"Well, it may be difficult for him, but if it's in his own very best interests and the interests of all the other students, then of course it's the thing to do," said Smedge.

Frastfil paced up and down in his study. His worry was pouring out of his ears in the form of purple and blue bubbles that rose up and popped on the ceiling, sprinkling light showers of purple dust all over the shoulders of his crumpled jacket, and staining his hair and nose.

Dr Duddle stood by the fireplace, not quite tall enough to lean against the mantelpiece. He kept putting his elbow up then frowning and taking it away again when it wouldn't reach. His unhappy face turned to each speaker in turn.

"You remember the trouble we had with Tamrin," said Smedge.

Frastfil remembered very well. So did Duddle.

Tamrin had arrived at the college in the same week as Smedge and Tim Masrani. They were the same age and were put in the same class. As beginners, they knew nothing at all of magic, or hardly anything. Just as some children can already read and count when they start school, some of the pupils at Canterstock College could already cast a few simple spells when they arrived. A bright child often pestered the local wizard to show them a spell or two. It was not encouraged, and the college preferred pupils to know no magic at all; that way, they could be trained in proper discipline, and they made fewer mistakes. Magic is like a knife: useful, but dangerous, not something to give to a child. So the magic that the young pupils learned was like a pair of small, round scissors, or a soft ball. The entrance test was more a matter of reading and counting, so the pupils could learn the spells later, rather than testing them on magic itself. That could be learned soon enough.

Tamrin had been brought to the college by her guardian, a tailor from Cawthwaite, who paid three years' fees in advance and told them to make sure she behaved herself.

Tamrin struggled a little with the reading and counting and was nearly not accepted. The tailor offered to pay extra fees and promised she would catch up. Even then, they were thinking of not giving her a place when Tamrin, upset that she was struggling with the reading, made the book turn into a flock of miniature doves and fly out of the window. It was much more powerful magic than anyone had ever seen in a child that small and she didn't seem to know how she did it. No one had ever taught her a spell. They asked the tailor, but he refused to talk about it.

"Just make sure she's good when she leaves, that's all," he said.

When they asked her to do more, she soon showed that she was better than pupils four or five years ahead of her. So she started, and soon was reading and counting as well as the best child in her class, better even.

The trouble was in making her stop doing too much magic. She caused chaos in the classroom and disrupted the lesson. If she grew bored, and she often did, she would make magic friends to keep her company, or she would make the teacher's words turn into trumpets or teacakes. Then the class would be laughing so hard that by the time the teacher had sorted it out they were too wound up to get any work done.

Tamrin was often punished for her naughtiness. As time went by, the teachers found it harder and harder to keep control. When Tamrin disrupted a class, the teacher's magic wasn't strong enough to stop her. Then, on her sixth birthday, she lost her temper in a lesson and flooded the classroom. Water gushed out of inkwells, fountains sprang up from the desks. A river of blue water burst out of the book cupboard and poured into the room. It was Dr Duddle's class. He tried some spells to divert the water, to dry up the torrents, but it overwhelmed him and swept him away with its force. He was like a rabbit fighting a wolf. The other pupils were thrashing about, trying to stay on the surface as the water filled the room. They made magic lifejackets and dinghies, they flailed about in the swell, but nothing could turn the tide. Just as they were about to lose the battle and drown, Tamrin released the spell. The waters sucked back and the classroom was exactly as it had been, save for Dr Duddle, who was stranded on a high cupboard, panting with terror.

That was her very last lesson. Duddle had demanded that she be removed from the college and Frastfil would have agreed, but Smedge, though only six himself, persuaded them to let her stay.

There had always been something special about Smedge. He seemed a small man, rather than a little boy. He talked like a grown-up and didn't seem to enjoy the running about and playing that the other children did.

"If you let her stay," he said, "she may get better and come back to lessons. And if she doesn't you will be able to keep an eye on her."

Frastfil and Duddle watched the little boy trot away after he had said this.

"He makes me uncomfortable," said Frasty.

"Yes," Duddle agreed.

"He's right, though. She could be dangerous somewhere else."

"She's dangerous here," said Duddle.

"Is there any way we can keep her under control?" asked Frastfil.

"She's too strong for us. But we could do something about that. We can take her down a peg or two. That will weaken her. And if she stays here, there may be ways we can use her magic later on."

Frastfil jangled his money in his pocket with fearful agitation. "But will she do it?"

"We'll give her no choice. Do as we say, or the tailor will be sent for to take her away."

They thought about the tailor. There was something about him that told them that Tamrin would not want to be sent back to him as a failure. There was something else about him that made Frastfil unwilling to tell him that the college had failed with Tamrin.

"It might work," said the professor. "But what about her? Will it hurt her?"

"It's for her own good," said Duddle. "And the good of the college."

"That's right." His face brightened up. "Ah, well. It's a shame, but she'll be able to bear a bit of unhappiness, if it's for her own good."

"Oh, it is." Duddle patted the professor's arm.

So they set her to work in the college, cleaning and helping the cooks. Since the day of the flood no one had seen her work any magic at all. Not even a single spell. It was as though she had used it all up in that single act of defiance and she had no more. Because she never went to lessons, she didn't learn school-magic either.

Sometimes, Frastfil had asked her to come and talk to him, to show him some magic, but she answered his questions in single words and did no magic at all. Gradually, they forgot that she once had some power and they hardly even noticed her. Except for Smedge, who watched everything.

And here they were again. With Sam this time.

"Well, if he turns out like her," said Duddle, "we may as well throw him out now. Be done with it. We don't want another lame dog hanging around the place."

Frastfil jangled. "He's very powerful," he said.

"I haven't seen it," said Duddle. "Have you?"

Smedge nodded.

"I watched him in the garden. He's strong."

"All the more reason to get rid of him now," said Duddle. "Before there's any more trouble."

Frastfil looked across at Smedge. It was strange how much the Professor seemed to rely on what was, after all, only a boy still, twelve — and one of his own pupils.

"He's got a point," he said.

"Oh, he's got a point," said Smedge. "Dr Duddle is very clever and our best teacher, I think."

Duddle was not bright enough to recognize flattery. He loved to hear well of himself.

"But," Smedge continued, "I think Dr Duddle would say that it has done Tamrin good, keeping her here. She's calm now and no danger to anyone. Untrained magic is very dangerous indeed. If we let Cartouche go now, his magic will grow even stronger, I think. And then he will be a threat to properly trained magicians, the sort that Dr Duddle works so hard to prepare."

"He's right," said Duddle. "But what shall we do?"

"I have an idea," said Smedge.

He explained it to them and Duddle thought it was a very good idea. Frastfil, who found it difficult to disagree with one person, had no strength to disagree with two, and jangled his consent. ||

There was nowhere for her

to run to. Tamrin and Sam were together on a small turret over the dormitory. The roof was steeply pitched, with grey slates and slippery sides. The only way back out was through the door, which Sam was blocking with his body. Of course, there was always magic to escape with, and the people here didn't seem to mind how often they used it. So Sam guessed that this girl didn't have enough magic, if any, to help her to run up the side of the roof and escape.

No magic, then, but enough anger and ferocity to do something else. She looked as though she might leap at Sam and bite him at any second. Her hands were trembling and Sam didn't think it was just fear. Her lips were parted, showing small, white, sharp teeth. Her hair was damp from sweat, clinging to her forehead.

Sam leaned against the door, slid down and sat looking at her.

"You're Tamrin."

She was wearing work clothes, not the uniform. A thick

apron, coarse shirt and heavy boots. Her hands were grimy and her face smudged where she had rubbed her cheek and wiped her hand under her nose.

"And you're Samfire."

"What?"

She laughed at him.

"Why are you watching me?"

"Why are you here?"

"What do you want?"

"The same as you."

"Why did you call me Samfire?"

"Isn't it your name?"

"No."

She laughed again.

"I suppose you have lots of names," she said.

"Have you been looking in my book?"

"What book, Samfire?"

"My name is Cartouche."

"If you like. Why have you come here?"

The kestrel Sam had seen from Frasty's room was circling overhead. It was hot on the turret. The late afternoon sun pooled in the small space with the high roof around it. Sam could feel sweat beginning to trickle down his face.

"Why are you watching me?"

"I'm not watching *you*. I'm just doing my jobs and you're there."

Tamrin sidled across the turret and found herself a patch

of cool shade. She squatted there, feet tucked underneath her, and smiled. She was trapped. But she was comfortable and Sam was baking. The kestrel swooped and perched on the rim of the turret wall, head turned sideways, one eye fixed on Sam.

Sam felt that it was important to keep Tamrin there. He felt he needed to know why she had been following him, who she was, and what she could tell him. And he could only do that if he stayed in front of the door.

He frowned. The lines from his forehead knitted together, left his face and formed a network of darkness that spread and thickened and cast him into its shadow. At the same time, a breeze tumbled down the slate roof and cooled him, drying his hair and lifting it slightly from his brow.

"You were a pupil here once," he said. "What happened?"

Tamrin undid the knots in her bootlaces, retied them and undid them again, winding the cord in her fingers over and over.

"It's my first day," said Sam, though he knew that Tamrin knew that anyway. "What's it like?"

"How much magic can you do?"

The kestrel stepped off the parapet, opened lazy wings and soared down out of sight.

"I don't know," said Sam.

She nodded.

"They have books here," she said. "So you know how much magic you can do by what book you are on. Every book is harder than the last one. Book Three is stronger magic than Book One."

"How many books of magic are there?"

Tamrin stared at him.

"How many do you think?" she said.

Sam thought about it. There were several answers to this question, and he wondered which one to give her. He could say "twenty", or whatever number he chose, and she could say "right" or "wrong". But then there were three real answers.

"How many years does it take to finish school here?" he asked.

"Twelve."

"Then there are twelve books of Canterstock Magic," he said.

Tamrin smiled.

"That's right," she said.

"How many books of magic are there?" he asked her again.

"How many do you think?"

"There is no end to the number of the books of magic," said Sam.

"That's right," she said.

"How many books of magic are there?" said Sam.

"How many do you think?"

Even under his shade Sam felt the closeness of the air on the turret, the captured heat of the sun, the caged atmosphere.

"I have answered twice," he said. "You answer this time."

Tamrin stopped playing with the bootlace. She tied it for the last time, thinking as she did. Then, as though she was stepping off the parapet after the kestrel, trusting herself to the empty air, she said, "Magic is not to be found in books, only the echo of magic, only its footprints where it has trodden, only the traces it has left behind, only the signposts it places for those who follow, only the map for those who travel."

Sam stood up, moved away from the door and sat down in the shade next to Tamrin. His cloud dissolved and the breeze moved with him to cool them both.

"You were a pupil here once," he said. "What happened?"

Pages from an apprentice's notebook

TREES KNOW MORE THAN YOU THINK.
The poplar knows how to bend in the wind.
The oak knows how to plant itself wide and
deep so that the wind has to go around it.
But even the oak lets its furthest branches, its
slenderest shoots, bend to the wind. The trunk
of a willow is so slight that only a little
damage will destroy its strength. A willow that
has been damaged will live, perhaps, but it will
be twisted and stunted. An oak can live and
spread even after the trunk has half-rotted
away, leaving a cleft big enough for a man to
walk into.

Many oak trees are entrances to the Deep

World. Roffles carve away at the openings and burrow down, finding the tunnels that connect the Deep World to Up Top. The entrance to a roffle hole in an oak tree is always sideways, never straight down. Otherwise, a boy could step into a hollow oak tree, and fall through. And no boy, and few girls, can ever pass a hollow tree without seeing if they can get inside.

Megatolly the peddler had oak trees where he stored his goods. He used to ask people which part of the oak was the tree. This is known as Megatolly's Question and has never been answered.

*

Vengeabil had other affairs

to tend to. His world beneath the college was so much more than the pupils ever guessed at. The old man who ran the stores, who gave them their uniform when they arrived, provided exercise books and pencils, replaced their broken flasks and retorts, made sure they had enough ink for their pens. This was Vengeabil. A bit of a college joke, old, scruffy, bad-tempered. He had a reputation for being absent-minded, but no one ever wondered how anyone so forgetful could lay his hand immediately on any item you wanted from his crowded, higgledy-piggledy stores. Nor did they ever wonder how he could make such strong magic against them when they cheeked him. They treated him with a cheerful contempt, encouraged by Frasty and Duddle, who always laughed when they spoke of him, and called him Old Vegetables.

"He's safe enough out of the way down there," the professor used to say. Duddle sometimes said it was time for a new person to take over the stores, that Vengeabil probably had a load of old junk down there and it should be made more efficient. Recently, Smedge had started to say that it needed a clear-out, that Old Vegetables wasn't up to the job any more. Perhaps he should be made an assistant in the sheds where the odd-job workers lived and worked. It would be a big demotion but the college had to move on with the times.

"I wonder," Frasty had begun to say, "if we shouldn't take Vengeabil out of the stores and put him in the sheds. It would be easier for him. He needs a rest and the stores would work better with someone else in charge." Frasty was very good at forgetting that someone else had suggested something. He liked to think it was his own idea, when, in truth, he never really had any ideas of his own at all. He took the shape of the last person who sat on him.

But Vengeabil knew what they said. Vengeabil knew more than most people thought.

"That new boy," he said to Tamrin.

They walked past the first part of the stores, where all the uniform, and everyday things were piled high, down the corridor and round a corner. There was a heavy velvet curtain across the passageway. Anyone who tried to look behind it would see only a wall, but, when Vengeabil pushed it to one side, it revealed a further passageway, wide and clean and fresh, and light. It was sealed with a hiding spell, a very powerful one. Tamrin followed him, letting the curtain fall behind her.

Many doors led off from this passage. They took one on

the left, letting themselves into a big kitchen, with a deal table and chairs, hooks from the ceiling with ladles and spoons, pots, pans, and posies of herbs and wild flowers. There were baskets of fruit and fresh vegetables, bowls of flowers and racks of bottles and jars. A scent of fresh bread floated from the oven and Vengeabil took out a large crusty loaf and laid it on a metal rack to cool.

Tamrin helped herself to a glass of fresh lemonade from a jug on a marble slab.

"What about him?" she said.

"You tell me."

"All right," she agreed. "I know he is."

"Does he know?"

"No. No idea at all."

Vengeabil cut a slice of cheese and chewed thoughtfully. He sprinkled crumbly fragments onto the floor and seven honey-coloured mice scampered from nowhere, snatched them up and scampered back. Vengeabil smiled after them.

"He'll have to get out of here soon," he said. "Before Frastfil realizes."

Tamrin finished her drink and wiped her mouth with her sleeve.

"Where will he go?"

"It doesn't really matter," said Vengeabil. "He'll just have to keep going until it starts to make sense to him."

"When will that be?"

Vengeabil pulled a small cupboard away from the wall and

opened the door to a pantry. He ducked his head out of the way of hams and sausages that hung from the beams.

"What sort of wood?" he said. "It must be right." He clattered a pile of lengths of timber, rough-hewn and dusty.

"Willow?" He handed one to Tamrin.

"I'm not sure. Give me something else."

He found an elm branch and one of ash. Closing the door and pushing the little cupboard back, he watched Tamrin as she tried each stave in turn.

"Willow has strong meaning for him," she said. "But it's not him. Someone else. I think the ash."

"Take your time."

Tamrin banged the elm branch on the red-tiled floor. It rang like a deep bell, warm and confident. She did the same with the ash. It boomed like a fretful sea hurling itself with anger and pain against the rocks. Doubt and concentration carved themselves on her face.

"This one."

She handed him the ash.

Vengeabil took it sadly.

"You are right," he said. "Help me to do it."

It took them four hours, more. When they had done, the ragged branch of ash was smooth and almost straight. The bark shone. The end curved a little. It was as tall as Tamrin.

"You can't go," said Vengeabil.

"I know," she said. "I hate this place."

"You never knew what it was like here before."

This was an old conversation between them. One they would have many times again.

"Why do things get bad?" she asked.

"So they can get better again. Give it to him when I tell you it's time." ‖

Tim found Sam

in the corridor leading from the dining hall. He grinned and
gave Sam a soft punch on the shoulder.

"Ready for Duddle?" he said.

"I'm not allowed back in lessons," said Sam.

Tim whistled.

"That's not fair. Why not?"

"Dr Duddle said he won't teach me."

Tim made a face. Little copies of Duddle poured out of his
mouth and fell to the floor, their arms flailing helplessly as
they fell. They made a little popping noise when they landed
and disintegrated. Sam laughed.

"Complain to Frasty," said Tim.

"Sh."

"Eh?"

"It's all right," said Sam, in a loud voice. "I don't mind."

"Old Frasty will make Duddle take you back. He's a bit of
an old fool, but..."

Sam blew a little puff of air towards Tim, who, to his surprise, found himself singing the college song.

"Good," said Frastfil, drawing up behind him. "Well done, Tom. Teaching Cartouche our song."

"I thought he ought to know it, sir," said Tim, giving Sam a grateful look. "And I'm Tim."

"Of course you are. I'm going to have to take him away from you, I'm afraid," said Frasty. "We're on our way to the library. Off you go to your lessons, Tom. Follow me." He beckoned Sam and set off down the long corridor.

"No one ever uses the library any more," said Tim.

Sam shrugged.

"I've got to work there till Duddle will take me back," he said.

"I'll come up later," said Tim.

"Thanks."

"Come along, boy," Frastfil's voice echoed back to him. Sam trotted off, curious to see what a library looked like.

The library was upstairs. Sam found Professor Frastfil rattling the door handle and frowning.

"It seems to be locked," he said. "I don't know why. It shouldn't be. There's nothing in there."

"Are there lots of valuable books?" asked Sam, putting his hand to the door.

"Oh, yes. Yes indeed. The library is one of the treasures of the college. A very precious place."

"Don't you have a key?"

"I used it. Look."

The key was in the keyhole.

Sam could feel that the door had a locking spell. The key was useless.

"Is there something else locking it?" he asked.

"Ah. Very good. Well done. Yes."

Frasty jingled the coins in his trouser pocket.

"It must have a spell on it," he said. "Let me see. Er, yes. I know."

Frastfil mumbled some words and waved his hand over the lock. He rattled the handle again. The door was locked as tight as ever. Sam moved a discreet hand over the hinge, then drew a line with his finger towards the handle. The door swung open, nearly taking Frastfil with it, head over kneecap.

"Got it."

He grinned at Sam.

"See? That's what magic can do for you. Take that lesson to heart and use your time here to learn."

"Yes, sir."

Frastfil looked around.

"There's a librarian," he said. "Somewhere."

He stepped through the door. Sam followed. The boy's eyes lifted and fell, looked left to right. He gasped. Bookshelves soared up as far as he could see. Thirty, forty floors of them. Far more than the building could possibly hold. Yet the room was small, circular, only fifteen paces from side to side. An iron staircase led up to the next floor, and an iron gallery ran round the edge of the room, allowing access to the books on that level, then another staircase, another gallery, and another, and another, and another, until Sam lost count.

"Yes?"

Vengeabil stepped out from behind a bookcase. He held a book in one hand, his finger marking the page he was on. He scowled at them both.

"Oh, Vegeta... I mean Vengeabil," said Frastfil. "You're here?"

"As you can see."

"Yes, of course you are. I'm looking for the librarian. You know, the old man, I can't seem to remember his name."

"Jackbones."

"That's it. Jackbones. Of course. Is he here?"

"You gave him the sack," said Vengeabil.

"Did I? Why did I do that?"

"I expect you had your reasons. I look after the library now," said Vengeabil. "What can I do for you?"

"Do you? The library? As well as the stores? Oh, well. Who appointed you?"

"I did."

Frastfil jingled the coins louder than ever.

"Oh dear," he said. "Can you do that?"

"Do you want to use the library?"

"This boy here does."

"Then it's a good job someone's looking after it, isn't it?"

Frastfil jiggled from one foot to the other. He felt in his pocket and produced a sheet of paper, which he handed to Vengeabil.

"Dr Duddle has set this boy some work to do, to catch up. Please can you make sure he finds the right books and gets on with it?"

"I know just what to do," said Vengeabil. "Thank you for calling in, Professor. Goodbye."

Frastfil was out of the library before he quite knew how it had happened. The door was shut behind him. He put his hand to it, to give Sam a last warning to work hard, but when he tried, the door was locked again. He frowned, jingled his change and walked away, beaming.

Sam waited for Vengeabil to tell him what to do.

"What do you want to do?" the man asked.

"Professor Frastfil gave you the work I've been set," said Sam.

"Oh, yes. So he did."

Vengeabil tore the paper into little pieces and threw them into a wicker basket.

"So," he said. "What do you want to do?"

"I don't know."

"Well, I'll just leave you alone until you do know," said Vengeabil. Then he went back to wherever it was he had appeared from. Sam moved over to see. There was a desk, with a rubber stamp and an ink pad on it. Behind that, to one side of a bookcase, a small door that Vengeabil had disappeared through. He turned and faced the library again.

For just a moment he was frightened, afraid that he would be in trouble for not doing the work he had been set, then, looking at the library, he forgot all about the fear and just smiled.

He walked all around the circle of bookshelves, then walked back again. He crossed over through the centre four times then sat on the bottom stair of the iron staircase and looked around and up and down. He tried to count how many different levels there were going up, but he kept losing track. He wanted to look at a book, but he wanted to take his time. He didn't want to choose the wrong one. He closed his eyes, raised his arm, pointed his finger and moved the arm from one side to the other and back again. When he was satisfied, he stopped, opened his eyes, peered along the line of his finger and found a book. It was small, green, with gold letters, and about the level of his head when he stood up. He kept his eyes on it, crossed the floor and put his hand out to take it from the shelf.

It wasn't a book. Nothing was. The whole shelf was made of wood, carved and painted to look like books. Sam stroked his fingers over it to the end of the shelf. The next bookcase along on the left had real books on it; so did the one on the right. The shelves above and below his book were just wooden as well. He stepped back. Looking now, he could see that one whole section of bookshelves was false. He made another circuit of the library. There were fourteen sections of book, shelves, without gaps in them, but seven were real and seven were false. He made his way back to his book.

Putting his hand on the book, he felt that the section was a door. He pushed the book and used a small unlocking spell. The door moved, opening smoothly, silently. He stepped through, into a small, square room, with a low ceiling. The walls, like the other part of the library, were all books on shelves. An iron hoop suspended from the ceiling lit the room with six candles. There was a table, with two chairs to it, and a ladder, to reach the high shelves, and two armchairs, not close to each other. A candle burned on the table next to an inkwell, a pile of paper and a tray of pens.

Sam left the room and closed the door. He went and sat back on the iron stair.

"Vengeabil," he called out.

The man appeared, before Sam could draw breath for a second summons.

"Yes?"

"What am I supposed to do?"

"What do you want to do?"

"I don't know."

"Very well," said Vengeabil, and he left.

Sam thought he might go back into the small room, and find a book and sit at the desk, or even in an armchair.

He pushed the green book again, stepped through and closed the door behind him.

"Yes?" said the man sitting at the table.

He was thin, small and had a savage mouth.

"Oh, sorry," said Sam. "I'll go."

"As you wish."

Something about his mouth was wrong. It was wide and had more teeth than it should have done. As though his great-grandfather had been a shark.

The man carried on writing. Sam pulled the door. It wouldn't open. He made a stronger spell. It still wouldn't move. He was locked in the small room with the man. ‖

Vengeabil looked at Tamrin's notes

and pointed a finger at the paper.

"That should be 'breadcrumbs'," he said, "not 'pig vomit'."

"Sorry," said Tamrin. She drew a neat line through the word and changed it.

"That would make a big difference," she said.

Vengeabil smiled.

"It's not like you to make mistakes," he said.

"No."

"You may as well stop now. You're not concentrating."

The room was very like the one Sam had found. It was not so tidy. As well as the table there was a small desk and a couple of extra chairs. It was more like a schoolroom. Tamrin had the desk, Vengeabil the table. Both were covered with papers and books and other bits and pieces.

"How's he doing?"

"He found the first room straight away."

"I knew he would."

"He's in there with Kafranc now."

"Oh," said Tamrin. "That's frightening."

"Yes."

Tamrin chewed the end of the wooden pen. She had ink on her fingers and a smudge on her cheek.

"What was the library like?"

"When?"

"Before."

"Before Frastfil?"

"Yes."

Vengeabil perched on the edge of his table and folded his arms.

"You should have seen it then," he said. "It was a market garden of magic. Everything you could want grew here. And it was tended and cared for, nurtured and nourished. Busy, but never loud; full of life, but never out of order. Look at it now."

"Was that when Jackbones was in charge?"

"Jackbones was a man to meet," said Vengeabil.

"Tell me about him."

Vengeabil smiled.

"He was the sort of wizard who made magic look so easy, so elegant, so," he searched for a word, "so perfect. As though there was nothing else."

Tamrin pulled her legs up and wrapped her arms round them, her chin on her knees.

"I wish I'd met him," she said.

"You never know."

"It's too late now, he's gone."

Vengeabil flapped his hand and the air around his finger ends turned an angry red and black.

"Why did Frastfil sack him?"

"He didn't. Not really. I just said that to annoy him."

"You said I should never tell lies."

"And I was right. And I shouldn't have said what I did. And mark my words, it will come back to hurt me one day. Anyway. He wasn't sacked. He left. Forced out."

Vengeabil stood up and paced the small room.

"He loved this library. He loved the college. Then Frastfil came and changed everything."

"When was that?"

"You should have seen the college then," said Vengeabil.

Sam tried the best unlocking spell he had and the door was still shut fast.

"Where did you come from?" asked Sam.

"What do you mean?"

The man put down his pen and stared at Sam.

"I was here a minute ago. The room was empty."

"How do you know?"

"I didn't see you."

The man stood up and slammed his hand on the table. His mouth gaped and the teeth glistened.

"Say that again," he said.

Sam squared up to him, his fists clenched, ready.

"I didn't see you."

"You said it," said the man, "you really said it."

His face crumpled up and Sam thought he was crying. He howled and stamped his foot. He fumbled in his sleeve and drew out a big red handkerchief. He wiped his eyes with it, blew his nose with a very loud sound and wiped his eyes again. He shook the handkerchief and a cabbage fell out and rolled over to Sam's feet. Sam looked down, the cabbage grew short, thick legs and waddled back to the man, who picked it up, held it in his hands like a pigeon, then threw it up into the air, where it exploded into a shower of rose petals that fluttered down, settled on the carpet and his shoulders and in his hair.

"Oh, dear," he said. He wiped his eyes again. "Oh, thank you, that's the funniest thing I've heard for years." He shook his head in pleasure. "You didn't see me so I wasn't here."

"I don't see what's funny about that," said Sam.

The man sat down and indicated the other chair.

"Sit down," he said.

He held out his hand to Sam.

"My name is Kafranc," he said.

"I'm Cartouche."

"It's a pleasure to meet you, Sam," he said, shaking hands. Sam blushed.

"I'm sorry I laughed," said Kafranc. "But I do like a good laugh and there's not much to make me laugh here, these days."

"It's not very polite."

"Indeed not, but I've said I'm sorry, so there you are. Now, let me see. Do you really believe that something's only there if you can see it?"

His face was solemn now, no trace of laughter. Sam felt he was being tested.

"Close your eyes," said Kafranc. "Think of somewhere else."

Sam closed his eyes and thought of Flaxfield's house. He was in the kitchen. Flaxfield was at his table, scribbling on a sheaf of papers. Cold, spring sunlight fell through the window in bright patches.

"Have you thought?"

"Yes."

"Can you see it?"

Sam squeezed his eyelids together to stop himself from crying.

"Yes."

"Can't hear you?"

"Yes."

"Good."

"Is there anyone there with you?"

Sam nodded.

"Keep your eyes closed. Are you there or here?"

Sam could smell the wood smoke from the fire, feel the warmth, see Flaxfield, his head down, concentrating.

"I'm there," said Sam.

"Are you here?"

"Yes."

"Can I see you?"

"Yes."

"Can you see me. Keep your eyes closed!"

"No."

Kafranc lowered his voice.

"This other person. Can he see you?"

Sam concentrated. Flaxfield lifted his head and looked around the kitchen. He scratched his cheek, then went back to his work.

"Can he see you?"

Sam shook his head.

"You can open your eyes now," said Kafranc.

Sam kept them closed.

"It's all right. He'll still be there the next time you look. Open your eyes now."

Sam opened his eyes and was alone in the room. He tried the door and it opened easily.

"Sam's leaving the room," said Vengeabil.

He slid a little door which closed the peephole to the library.

"What do you think happened?"

"It's up to him whether he tells us or not."

"How could one person spoil the whole college?"

"A college is like a family, or a farm with lots of workers, or a village. Everyone brings something to it, but there's always one person, the mother, the farmer, the headman of the village, a grandfather, someone, who in some way is the one who sets the standards. In a family it can be either the mother or the father, or even someone else, the family decide; on a farm it's the farmer, which is why some farms are prosperous and happy and on some farms the animals are neglected and the fields give hardly any grain. Some people are chosen to be the one who makes things good or bad and you can change them if it doesn't work. In the college, the principal, once he's appointed, is in charge. A good principal makes a good college."

"And is Professor Frastfil bad?"

Vengeabil had another peek into the library. Sam was sitting on the bottom stair again, his head in his hands.

"That's the terrible thing," he said. "Frasty isn't really bad. But he's weak, and bad people are making him do bad things."

"How will it end?" she asked.

"I've got to go back and see Sam," said Vengeabil. He smiled. "Get on with your work."

Sam heard Vengeabil approach. He kept his head in his hands while he wiped his eyes. Vengeabil ignored the red rims when Sam looked up.

"How are you doing?" he asked.

"All right."

"What do you want to do?"

Sam shouted at him.

"Stop asking me that. Why do I have to decide what to do? Aren't you supposed to tell me?"

Vengeabil eased next to Sam, who had to shuffle up so that there was room for two of them on the step. It was narrow, so their shoulders touched.

"That's a start," said Vengeabil. "Is that what you want? You want to be told what to do? Do you want to do the work that Dr Duddle set for you?"

"You ripped it up. I can't."

Vengeabil whistled, as though summoning a dog. The pieces of paper rose up from the basket, swirled round in the air, joined together again, folded themselves into a paper bird and flapped across to Vengeabil, who let it settle on his hand then passed it to Sam.

Sam smiled and stroked it. Vengeabil changed his whistle to a bird song and the paper bird grew heavy in Sam's hand, fledged and fluttered, and became a greenfinch.

"No," said Sam, "I don't want to do his work."

He opened his hands and the bird flew up, circled the library, hovered over the basket, broke into twenty scraps of paper and fell like a flurry of early snow.

Sam looked up at the rows of galleries disappearing up for ever.

"How many floors are there?" he asked.

"No one has ever found out."

"How do they all fit in? The college isn't that tall."

"There's always a way."

They sat in silence for a while, then Vengeabil asked, "What do you want to do?"

"I don't know why I'm here," said Sam. "I don't mean in the library, I mean in the college. I don't know what I'm doing here."

"Why did you come here?"

"I was running away and I met a roffle and he said I should."

"You mean someone else told you to come here?"

"Yes."

"And now you want me to tell you what to do?"

Sam stood and crossed to the door he had been through. He put his hand on the false books and let it rest there.

"Are all the false bookshelves doors?" he asked.

Vengeabil stood up and went to the librarian's table. He took a sheet of paper, dipped a pen in the inkwell and wrote. Sam looked over his shoulder.

Why am I in the college?
How many floors are there?
How do they all fit in?
Are all the false bookshelves doors?

"And are there any more questions?" said Vengeabil.

"What am I supposed to do next?"

"You mean today?"

"No. I mean next, for ever."

Vengeabil wiped the nib on a piece of blotting paper.

"Five questions," he said. "Do you want to answer them?"

"Yes."

"Now?"

"If you like."

Vengeabil smiled.

"It's up to you," he said.

"Where should I start?"

Vengeabil handed him the pen.

"You make the list."

1. How many floors are there?
2. How do they all fit in?
3. Are all the false bookshelves doors?
4. Why am I in the college?
5. What should I do next?

"Very good," said Vengeabil. "Now you have to decide. This is a library. Do you want to find out by reading in books, or by looking for yourself."

"Both," said Sam.

"Good answer. Let's make a start."

The door handle rattled. Someone bumped against the door, trying to open it.

"Who's that?" said Sam.

"You'd better open it and see."

Sam remembered the shark-mouthed Kafranc as he put

his hand to the door, and he held himself tense, ready to fight or run from whatever stood behind it.

Tamrin couldn't concentrate on her work, and Vengeabil and Sam were busy, so she left by another door and went to wander the corridors of the college. She knew places and passageways that had been forgotten since the old teachers and the old college workers had left. The people who had come since Frastfil arrived had not bothered to find out what the college was like. They taught their own lessons and went to their own rooms, but they didn't look around the way Tamrin did. Apart from Vengeabil, Tamrin knew more places in the college than anyone else, and she was still discovering new ones.

First of all, she went down a crooked staircase that led to the kitchens. She was supposed to be working there, but no one ever noticed when she didn't turn up. If she wasn't there to wash up after a meal or to wash the cabbage and peel the parsnips then they just made a spell to do it. Tamrin did her work in the kitchens, not because she liked it, but to stop them using magic to do it instead. She never used magic herself to get out of a job and she felt guilty when she let others do it. Since Sam had arrived she had hardly been in the kitchens at all; she wanted to watch him, see what he was doing.

She sneaked in, grabbed a piece of bread and folded it round a slice of chicken, pocketed an apple and sneaked out again, all before the cooks had time to notice she had been there.

She chewed on her meal and dodged back upstairs. If the hidden corridors and passageways went all through the college, Tamrin hadn't discovered their secrets yet. She had to cross an open corridor to get through to the stairway to the roof, where she wanted to sit and eat her meal. She looked both ways to see if the coast was clear, stepped out and, just as she was making her way to the next hidden entrance, Smedge turned the corner and saw her.

"Tamrin," he called out. "Hey. How are you?"

He smiled and waved.

Tamrin couldn't dive into her secret corridor because she didn't want to give it away to Smedge. She either had to run away from him or stop and say hello.

He was smiling at her in a friendly way. Tamrin scowled.

"Where are you going?" he asked her.

"Nowhere."

Smedge laughed.

"That's where you always are. I'll come with you. I've never been nowhere."

Tamrin stood still. She held the bread and chicken to her side, not wanting to eat while he was there.

"Do you remember when we first came here?" said Smedge. She nodded.

Smedge looked up at the ceiling and blew a puff of air from his mouth. It began to form into a canopy of tree branches, green leaves and sun dappling through. He smiled and started to make a bird to sing to them. Tamrin frowned. The tree cover trembled. Smedge smiled harder, tensing himself, he held his breath and for a moment the tree started to blossom. Tamrin clicked her tongue. The bird shifted shape and became a snake, curled round a dry branch. The leaves withered, shook and began to fall around their feet. The sunlight faded. The bare branches were grey against the gloom.

Smedge tried to pretend he was not panting with effort. He smiled with his mouth at Tamrin. His eyes glared.

"Shouldn't you be in class?" she asked.

He fought to find enough breath to answer her. The dead tree swayed over their heads.

"It would be nice if you were in lessons as well," he said. "We miss you."

"I'm not allowed lessons."

"I think that could be changed."

Tamrin leaned against the wall.

"I don't want to go to lessons."

The smile never left Smedge's face.

"You could learn more magic if you came to lessons."

Tamrin kicked at the dry leaves underfoot. She gave him a half-smile.

"Really?" she asked.

"I think Professor Frastfil would let you go back, if I asked him. I could help you. You could fit into college life again."

Tamrin realized that he was serious. That he was

threatening her. She had the free run of the college and only as much kitchen work as she bothered to do. If she went back to classes, then she would be trapped.

"I don't think Dr Duddle would have me in his class," she said.

"Oh, I think people can be persuaded," said Smedge. He smiled. "I'll do what I can to help."

He picked up a dry leaf and rested it in the palm of his hand. It uncurled and grew green and glossy. He folded his hand and held it tight.

"It would be for the best," he said, "if you fitted in more."

Tamrin coughed. Smedge shook his shoulders. He opened his hand and saw, where the leaf had been, a bright green gout of snot. He looked straight at her. The air around him shimmered. Tamrin felt a surge of something sweep over her, cold and clenched. She swerved her body, to allow it to pass. Smedge took a handkerchief from his pocket and wiped his hand. He smiled at her.

"I'll see what I can do."

Tamrin watched him walk away. She found a dustpan and brush and swept up the leaves. The snake had disappeared. Then she went up to sit in the sun. It was hot on the roof. She picked pieces of chicken from her bread and held them in her hand for the kestrel. It swooped and snatched them, not resting. The apple was sweet in her mouth. She tossed the core over the parapet and sat in the shade, looking up at the clouds. ||

Sam's hand was moist

with anxious sweat. It slipped on the door handle. He wiped
it on his sleeve, then turned the handle, made a swift spell of
opening and got ready to act.

"Hello," said Tim. "That door's a bit stiff."

"Ah, Master Masrani," said Vengeabil. "Come on in. I'm
sorry there's not much here for you. Perhaps when you learn
to read without moving your lips we'll see more of you."

Tim gave a shy grin.

"Hello, Vengeabil. You here, now? He's always like this,"
he said to Sam. "Has he been giving you a hard time?"

Sam looked at Vengeabil, who was waiting for an answer.

"No," said Sam.

Vengeabil lifted an eyebrow.

"Well, yes," said Sam. "He has."

"I've brought you some food. Snaffled it just before the
hall opened up for lunch."

He put a bundle of cloth on the librarian's desk and opened

it out. There were meat pies, bread, apples, plums, a corner of cheese and three broken biscuits.

"It's a bit battered. I had to be quick. We can make it go three ways," he offered Vengeabil.

"Take it away and eat it," he said. "I'm busy. And I don't want sticky fingers on my books. Make sure you wash your hands before you come back."

Tim laughed.

"Your books," he said. "Are you stocktaking? Counting them? You'll have a long job. It's not like your stores here, you know."

Sam gripped Tim's arm.

"He's..."

"I'm just making sure they're all here," said Vengeabil, in a clear voice and with a look at Sam.

Sam helped to wrap up the food and they ran off, slamming the door behind them.

"I know a place," said Tim.

The place was a room, a perfect cube, three times as tall as the boys, with a ridge running round the wall about two thirds of the way up, and a couple of squarish protrusions in two diagonally opposite corners. It was empty, save for some wooden packing cases and a clumsy bookshelf stacked with jars, filled with something Sam didn't much want to look at too closely.

They spread out the cloth on a packing case, sat on smaller boxes and laid into the food.

"What's old Vengeabil doing in the library? What have you

been doing all morning? Are you counting books with him? I got a detention from Duddle for giving him some cheek. And Smedge wasn't there, either, was he in the library with you?"

Sam chewed his pie while Tim poured out his questions.

"What is this place?" he asked.

"It's the old brickotelle court," said Tim. "No one uses it now. They say Frastfil stopped people playing it because he's no good at it. What have you been doing?"

"Duddle set me some work to do," said Sam, which was not a lie, but he didn't feel very happy at not really telling the truth.

Tim groaned.

"I bet it's really boring," he said. He broke off a piece of cheese and ate it with the bread. "What do you think Smedge is doing?"

"I don't know. He wasn't in the library."

They ate in silence for a while. The mention of Smedge had stopped their conversation.

"I've got to go back," said Tim. "Or I'll be in more trouble."

"What did you do to cheek him?"

"I asked if you could come back to lessons."

"Was that all?"

Tim threw an apple in the air. It bounced off the ceiling, skidded down the wall, then bounced from side to side, covering court, deflecting at crazy angles when it hit the ridge or the lumps in the corners. Tim put his hand in the air and caught it, taking a bite just as it turned back into an apple.

"Brickotelle," he said. "Of course, I cheated. In real brickotelle you're not allowed to use magic. That was a demonstration.

"I thought no one played."

Tim blushed.

"Vengeabil taught me." He jumped up. "See you tonight?"

"Yes."

"Good."

They raced back to their places. Tim just got there in time to avoid another detention. Sam put his hand out to open the door when it swung open of its own accord.

"Looks like you're expected," said Vengeabil. "Books or explore?"

"Please show me some books," said Sam.

Vengeabil nodded.

"Try this for a start."

He handed Sam a book. Sam smoothed his hand over the covers. They were silver-blue, with ridges and bumps. He looked at the spine. The title was in raised letters, gold and black.

The Seventeen Varieties of Dragon

Sam's hand trembled.

"What's the matter?"

"Nothing."

"Don't you want to read about dragons? I can get you something else."

"Yes, please. Something else."

He drew his sleeve over his eyes.

"You don't like dragons?"

Vengeabil searched the shelves for a different book.

"It's not that."

"I see."

He gave up the search.

"What do you want to read about?"

"You choose."

"I chose. It's your turn."

"I want to know how many floors there are in here, and how they all fit in."

"Well. There are books for that, but I don't think you'll understand them. The only way is to go up there and count."

Sam shook his head.

"I don't want to explore any more today. I want to read."

"Well, that's good," said Vengeabil. "At least you're telling me what you want at last."

"I want to know why you taught Tim how to play brickotelle," said Sam. "I want to know whether you're the librarian or the store keeper. I want to know what Smedge is like and what he's doing. And I want to know why I'm so unhappy."

"Is that all?"

"I want to know how I can be happy again."

Vengeabil put his hand to his face and considered all this.

"Where do you want to start?"

"Who are you?"

"That's a long story," said Vengeabil. ||

The light had gone

by the time that Sam was free from the library and Tim had finished his detention.

"I'd like to cast a slime spell on Duddle," said Tim when they met in the garden.

"I don't think I'm staying here," said Sam.

Tim looked away from him.

"I wish you would," he said.

"It's not the right place."

"I know. Have you made up your mind?"

"Not yet."

"Look at the stars," said Tim. "Don't you ever wonder what they're for?"

The night sky was an open book of constellations.

"They're for the same as everything else," said Sam. "They're just themselves."

The stars silently agreed.

"Why did you come here?" asked Sam.

Tim brightened up. He liked to talk about himself.

"I just did magic," he said, "when I was little, and I wasn't any good at anything else, so they thought I should come here. Learn to be a wizard. And that's what I want to do."

He brushed his hair back from his face and grinned.

"Are you doing well here?" asked Sam.

Tim didn't stop grinning when he admitted that he wasn't.

"I'm never going to be top of the class," he said. "That's Smedge."

"Is he the best at magic?"

Sam lay back on the grass and looked up at the sky, his hands behind his head.

"He's the best at the sort of magic they like here. He's the best at pleasing people."

"I don't want to be like that," said Sam. "I just want to be the best wizard I can be."

"That's right," said Tim. "So do I. That's why I don't work hard enough at the magic they want. Book magic. I like the magic I came here with."

"Is it just that?"

"Not really. There's something else. I don't know what it is. A lot of the magic here is just games. It's all over the place. But there's something else. There's a sort of magic within the magic. I can't explain it. It's as though Smedge and Duddle, and a couple of other teachers, are doing a different magic. I don't like it."

He frowned, struggling to understand what it was he was saying.

"Do you know," he said, "when you walk into a room and the people don't stop talking, but they seem to change the subject and have to catch up quickly, to pretend they were talking about that all the time?"

Sam shook his head.

"I haven't really had a lot to do with people."

"Oh. Well. It's like that. Sometimes one of them will be doing some magic, and I'll see them, and they'll change it just in time. I don't know what they were doing before, but it feels wrong."

"I learned a lot in the library today," said Sam.

"What was Vengeabil like?"

"What do you think?"

"He teases me," said Tim, "but I like him. He's odd, but he seems to know what he's doing."

Sam let his eyes leave the stars and he turned his head to the college, brooding over them to his left. He could make out the oriel window to Frastfil's study, the column of bowed bricks that marked the spiral staircase to the dormitories, the turret where he had confronted Tamrin, the rows of windows of classrooms and studies and practice rooms. He could tell, without seeing him, that Smedge was in the window, three along from the principal's study, the light off, his head half-hidden by the frame. He was watching them, thinking himself unobserved. Sam knew he could hear them. He wondered how long he had been listening.

"What did you learn, then?" said Tim. "In the library."

"Oh, you know," said Sam. "Book stuff. Let's go in. I'm tired."

Smedge watched them disappear through the small door by the kitchen.

"What do you want to do today?" asked Vengeabil.

It had been the same question for three days now and Sam was used to it. He smiled.

"I want to go up there," he said, pointing to the staircase.

"Off you go, then."

Sam was startled.

"Isn't there anything you want to tell me before I go?"

"No."

"Is it dangerous?"

"Would you still go if it was?"

"Yes."

Vengeabil shrugged his shoulders.

Sam put his foot on the first stair. It was iron, pierced with a pattern of leaves and slim branches woven round each other. He looked back at Vengeabil.

"Is there anything I should be careful of?"

"Yourself," said Vengeabil. "Off you go."

Sam looked up. The stairway ran round and round, up to the next level. He climbed it at a normal pace. The floor of the gallery was made of the same ironwork as the stairs. It ran all the way round the library so Sam could lean over and see Vengeabil. He was disappointed that the man was not looking up at him, but sitting at the desk, writing. The books on this level were all bound in green leather. He looked at some of the titles. They were all about herbs and plants.

On the next level, the books were bound in scarlet and were all about grinding and mixing compounds. Level three had blue books, with titles that mentioned clouds and skies and winds. By level four Vengeabil was looking small at his table. Level five had books bound in aquamarine and the leather was smooth and glossy. Sam sat for a while, in a niche set into the bookcases at a small desk, and turned the pages of a book he had taken at random from the shelf. It had pictures of whales and mermaids, a sea monster with a long neck, a fish that seemed to be all teeth and no head.

He stopped counting levels after that and just climbed till he was out of breath. Vengeabil had left his desk and gone, perhaps to his room, perhaps to one of the other rooms behind the false bookshelves. Sam had been in four of those rooms now.

The levels above him seemed no fewer than when he had first set off. The levels below spiralled down, almost out of sight. The floor of the library was no bigger than the half-crown Sam had ordered once with Flaxfield.

"What are you looking down at?"

Sam grabbed the rail of the gallery to stop himself from falling.

He looked over his shoulder.

"Who are you?" he asked.

"Well," she drew herself up to her full height, which was about the same as Sam's, "I've been here a long time, so I think I'm entitled to ask you that first."

"I'm..." Sam hesitated, trying to remember the name he was using here. "Oh, I'm Sam," he said.

"So you are. Are you going on up or staying here?"

She put on a pair of spectacles, round, with tortoiseshell frames and silver earpieces. Her hair was cut shorter than any woman's he had ever seen, much shorter, even, than his. She looked about forty, for a woman, which meant she could be any age if she was a wizard.

"I'm going to rest for a while. Then I'm going up."

"How far?"

"All the way to the top."

She laughed. She was slim, and moved with an easy grace.

"Tell me what you find," she said. "On your way down."

"Haven't you been up there?"

"There?" She raised an elegant hand and gestured up the staircase. "I've been up higher, but not to the top. No one ever goes all the way up there."

"Why not?"

"They've all given up, long before."

Sam looked down, over the gallery rail, then up. The distance down was further than he could calculate. The distance up, more still.

"How high are we?"

"It's easier to see from outside. Come."

She led him round the gallery a little, then found a door in the bookshelves. He followed her through, into another of the endless rooms that branched out from the central well. She pointed to a window.

"Look out there."

The town square lay before him. It was market day and the stalls covered the cobbles. The buildings on the other side of the square faced him, and, guessing from the levels, he thought he was on the third floor of the college. He crossed the room back to the gallery and looked down. Level after level stretched beneath him. He went back to the window. Third floor up from the ground.

"How does that work?" he asked.

"Sorry. I have to go. Ask one of the others."

"I haven't seen any others. You're first."

"Just because you didn't see them it doesn't mean they weren't there. I thought you'd learned that. Close the door behind you."

She left the room, and when Sam followed her onto the gallery, she had gone. He looked over the rail.

"Isn't there anyone who can tell me what to do?" he asked.

As far as he could see, up and down, round every railing, people started to appear. They gathered at the rail, silently, till every space on every level was filled with people. They looked at him, and he knew that every one of them was a wizard, and that every one of them would tell him something if he asked. All the books, all the wizards, all the learning in the library was spread out before him and behind him. All he had to do was choose.

"No," said Sam. "Thank you, but no."

The people drew back, receding softly like the sea on a shallow shore.

Sam found the staircase trickier to walk down than up, something about the turn of the tread and the effort not to fall.

Vengeabil was at the desk again when Sam reached the ground.

"What do you want to do?" he asked.

"There's too much here. Too many books. Too many people. I want to leave here and find a new master. I want to be an apprentice again. I want to learn from one person."

"It's late. You shouldn't leave today. And a message came while you were up there. You're to go back to lessons tomorrow. To Dr Duddle."

"I won't go," said Sam.

"You should," said Vengeabil.

"I'm not staying here."

"I know. But it might be fun. Leave them something to remember you by."

He smiled, and Sam couldn't help grinning back at him. ‖

That night,

when everyone was asleep, Sam found his way back to the turret. He stared into the fear-black night. There was no moon. The stars, as ever, had many messages. Sam tried to read them. They whispered to him, many voices, many words, many thoughts. He could not make out what they were saying. Except that he knew that they spoke to him of Starback.

It was cold now. The turret did not hoard the sun's heat, but let it go as soon as the light faded. Sam drew his cloak around him. He had lost count of how many days he had spent in the college.

He did not hear Tamrin arrive. She slid silently down the steep slope of slates. The first he knew of her being there was when the stone top of the turret bloomed into a glowing line of jasmine, that illuminated his face and breathed a mist of delicate perfume into the night air.

He smiled, not turning his head.

Green and blue and silver-grey lizards crept silently from

the jasmine. Each as small as a fingernail. They darted among the dark green fronds and rested on the white flowers, licking black tongues across their cheeks, reflecting beauty in the starlight.

Sam joined in, weaving forget-me-nots between the jasmine blooms, the blue against the white.

Tamrin stood close to him, their shoulders touching. Sam allowed the pressure against him, welcomed the closeness, returned the touch. He was warm now. His cloak fell open and his hands reached forward to brush against the jasmine, enjoying the tickling sensation of the lizards as they scurried around, unafraid, running between his fingers, surprisingly warm.

Without moving, Tamrin caused the jasmine to grow and tumble more branches down the wall, falling at their feet, then transforming into meadow grass, sweet with its own greenness and rich with every sort of wild flower. The scent of jasmine blended with the fragrance of the summer fields. For the first time, Sam felt the power of magic in someone else, his shoulder to her shoulder. No movement, but an awareness of something active, something working.

He filled the meadow grass with harvest mice and shrews. He conjured up dragonflies and wrens and lapwings.

He knew, as he worked the magic, that Tamrin was aware of him as he had been of her.

He felt remade, more at rest than at any time since he had found Flaxfield lying dead.

They stepped away from the wall and looked at the place they had made. The grey-grim college glowered around it in the darkness.

"You have to leave here," said Tamrin.

"Yes."

"Soon."

"Come with me."

"I can't leave. Not yet."

"I'll send word," said Sam.

"I'll find you."

"Yes."

Tamrin handed him the staff she and Vengeabil had made. It felt like the missing part of his body he never knew he had lost. ‖

Smedge didn't like

pen and ink. They were old-fashioned and messy. He always seemed to get ink on his fingers and he hated that. There were a hundred easier ways to send a message. Even simple magic could come up with about twenty, but he had been told always to use pen and ink for these messages and he knew better than to try even to cheat and magic a letter. She would know.

He dipped the nib into the ink and continued writing.

The girl, Tamrin, is not as stupid as I thought. As soon as the boy arrived she watched him and waited for an opportunity to be alone with him to talk. They were together on the turret, twice, but one or other of them sealed it and I could not listen to them, or see what they did. I must have been wrong when I told you that her magic had withered away and was finished. She has been hiding it, I think. And there must be someone here who is helping her. I will look into it.

Duddle is working for us now. Frastfil is a fool and I have him under control.

The boy calls himself Cartouche. At the moment, if we tried to get the better of him he would beat us. Frastfil is going to trick him into using his magic every day and to make him work more magic than he can control. The boy is already confused and frightened and he will get angry when we taunt him. He will work magic to make himself feel better and then it will turn against him. Then, when he is weak, I can seize him and bring him to you.

There was more. When he had finished, Smedge folded the paper in an intricate design, blew on it and threw it into the air. It unfolded itself into a moth, with a fat, black body and grey powdery wings. It fluttered in a circle, dipped, turned and flew through the window and into the night. ||

Sam decided

not to wear his uniform even for his last day in class. He dressed in the clothes he had travelled in. He put the cloak over his shoulders and grasped the ash staff.

"You can't go to class like that," said Tim. "You'll be banned again."

Sam left the uniform on the bed and ran downstairs.

Dr Duddle hesitated, then pointed Sam to his desk, ignoring the clothes. He had his instructions.

"Professor Frastfil has persuaded me to give you another chance," he said. "So, if you'll please be so good as to just let us see how much catching up you need to do?"

Sam ignored him.

The class looked at him with growing interest and excitement. It was going to be another amusing lesson.

"If you'll all open your text books at page seventy-three. Orgletray, will you perform the third spell, please?"

It was a spell to make a very bad smell in a very small space.

Orgletray's plump face crinkled up in a smile. He stood up, cleared his throat and started to say the words. From the other side of the room a girl jumped up and started to cough and wave her hands in front of her face.

"No, please," said Duddle. "It's Mr Cartouche who needs to be made a part of the class. Direct the spell at him, if you would."

Orgletray looked apologetically at Sam, who smiled grimly back. The stench was terrible, but only he could smell it. A hum of malicious pleasure charged the classroom. This was better than work.

"Number five on page eighty, please, Lynsorm. For Mr Cartouche."

A slender girl with auburn hair stood and cast a spell of headache that swept across Sam's mind for an instant before he brushed it aside like a wasp, sending it spinning, and grown with anger, at Duddle, who gasped with pain and fell to his knees, white-faced and breathless.

The class became silent.

Sam stood up and looked at his fellow-students.

"He can be as stupid and mean as he likes," he said, indicating Duddle with his staff. "But you don't have to join in. You can stand up to him."

Tim's face was red with emotion. Smedge watched, silent, attentive.

Sam tapped his staff on the scrubbed floorboards. The air in the classroom thickened, grew dark and still. Duddle still crouched in deflected pain. All the light in the room gathered into a ball and disappeared, leaving the blackest night. Not a glint of light, not a fragile pulse, broke through the complete darkness. The pupils began to call out in terror. Sam tapped his staff again and silence embraced darkness. He looked around the room. To his eyes, all was as in starlight, stripped of colour, yet clear, distinct. The others sat, as though asleep with open eyes. Sam laid a hand on Tim's shoulder. He looked up and saw as Sam saw.

"I'm leaving now," said Sam.

"I wish you'd stay."

"You know I can't."

"No. Will you come back?"

"I'll see you again," said Sam. "I promise."

Tim looked at the others.

"What will happen to them. Us?"

"I'll leave it like this for an hour. They'll be none the worse."

Duddle groaned.

"What about him?"

"It's a bad headache," said Sam. "But he asked for it in the first place."

"You can't leave him like that."

"It will wear off," said Sam. "Eventually."

He settled Tim back in his seat, took his hand from his friend's shoulder and left him, blind and still as the others, until the spell wore off.

Duddle was too wrapped up in his own dark pain to hear what had been said or to see Sam leave the room.

As Sam crossed the courtyard, towards the gate and the porter's lodge, Sam felt the cloak reach out to him, become one with him and make a decision of its own. Without having made any attempt to do it himself, Sam became invisible. Trelling did not move his eyes as Sam passed him. When Sam opened the gate and passed through, the man turned his head, gave an exasperated click of his tongue and moved to close it again.

Tamrin watched him from the turret. She saw him walk through the old town, past the high walls and the ditch, and out onto the road to the north before an agitation in the air around him told her that the cloak had released its hold and he was visible again.

"Where now?" she asked.

The door of the castle was always open to visitors. She was the only one who could not pass through. Ash welcomed them. Few left.

She greeted the newcomer with pleasure.

"You've come back," she said.

"Have I been here before?"

His expensive clothes were ripped and dirty. He was thin, unshaved, confused. His hand fiddled with the black and silver clasp at his neck. His fingernails were bitten and bleeding.

The beetle jewel moved under his touch, as though alive.

"Let me look after you," she said. "You must be hungry."

He followed her inside.

"Have I really been here before?"

"Oh yes."

Her fingers went to his throat, to the brooch.

"I gave you this. Remember?"

Bakkmann's laugh was like twigs cracking.

"Your hands are burned," she said. "And you need sleep."

"Yes. I've been trying to get something. But I couldn't."

He explained to her as she watched him eat.

"You'll sleep tonight, Caleb," she said. "And then you'll go back, quickly. Find it. For me." ||

Part Three

WIZARD WAR

It had reached that time

when the day was just more dark than light, the houses scattered down the slope like the bones of a long-dead sheep. Beyond them, humps in the ground, tall mounds, more houses, closer together, squat and sullen. Sam walked past three, to show he was free to choose, then knocked on the door of the fourth.

Evening scents crept into the small garden in front of the house, fragrances that concealed themselves from the sun. the dying scents of summer, the new, mustier scents of autumn. He knocked again and leaned against the door-jamb. There was no light in the window, but Sam had heard noises from inside as he approached, so he knew they were in. He could try somewhere else, but, having chosen, he decided to stick with his decision. What was it Flaxfield had said? *Trust what you have chosen. There is a reason. Sometimes it has chosen you.* He tried to call to mind the old man in the study, his face glowing with the joy of magic, his hands moving swiftly to create the tiny dragon, but he could only see his face with the herbs around it, the hands unable to reach out for the bread and figs.

Sam sat down, his back against the door, hugging his cloak to him. Letting his head loll to one side against his ash staff he fell asleep, the sounds from the house still in his ears.

He was not woken so much as pulled to his feet, and the face that confronted him was not friendly.

"This is no time to come calling," she said.

The woman had just arrived and was carrying a bag.

Sam tried to answer. He moved his lips and he made a gesture with his hand, the sort people do when they want to add to the words. But there were no words. He had not drunk all day and his mouth was too dry.

The sky was black now. He did not know how long he had slept. The stars told him to stay where he was.

Someone inside the house opened the door. A small face looked at them.

"Wait," she said. It slammed shut.

The woman looked long at Sam.

"How old are you?" she asked.

Sam held up fingers, ten then two.

"Can't you talk?"

"I'm thirsty," he croaked at last.

He watched her face as she made a decision.

"Come in. But don't be afraid and don't get upset."

Sam nodded.

She put her hand to the door. Hesitated. Then she turned her face back to him.

"What's your name?"

"Sam."

"My husband died today, Sam," she said. "He's in here now. All right?"

He nodded again.

It was a small room — kitchen, sitting room, scullery all in one, but you could only look at one thing. A dead body attracts attention. It was a little time before Sam's eyes took in the two figures who stood near to the range. The boy was a little taller than Sam, the girl a little shorter. The boy looked like his mother. A face is so different in death that Sam could not tell whether the girl looked like her father.

"I've got the things for the Finishing," the woman said, setting down a bag, "but there's no sign of her."

She scooped water from a tank, poured it into a mug and handed it to Sam.

"Sip," she said, "don't gulp."

"We can't wait all night," said the boy.

"She's not here," said his mother.

The girl was emptying the bag; herbs, apples, a rock, the rounded heaviness of a small iron pick, more herbs, a small posy of marigolds.

"It has to be done tonight," the boy insisted.

"I can do it," said Sam.

They looked at him.

He finished drinking and held out the mug for more.

"I can do it."

"Don't play tricks, boy," the woman warned him.

Sam unfastened the cloak and spread it on the back of a chair, shrugged off his bag and put it on the seat of the same chair, rush-bottomed, ragged. He leaned the ash staff in the corner. Moving the girl to one side, he arranged the herbs and other things on the table. He held the rock for a few moments before deciding where it went. He took longer over the iron pick. The flowers were easy to place, and the herbs always went in the same order.

"I need oil," he said, "and water, hot water, and salt and soap. And you must all wash."

The boy jostled Sam away from the table and stood too close to him. His breath was sour in Sam's face.

"Just stay away from him."

Sam moved back one step.

"If you like," he said.

His mother took the boy's arm. "It's all right," she said. "That's why he's here."

"December should do it," said the girl.

"Let's get washed."

Sam washed first, set aside a bowl of hot water and clean cloths and soap and started while the others washed.

It was just over a week after he had signed his name for Flaxfield that Sam trotted off behind the old man to do this for the first time. It was raining. Sam never did this now without remembering the fresh scent of wet earth and feeling the cool breeze on his face. They walked all morning, stopping often to select herbs, Flaxfield explaining what they were looking for and letting Sam find them.

"Rub it between your fingers," Flaxfield said.

Sam lifted his hand to his nose.

"Well?"

"Sweet" or, "like the ground" or, "lemony". Sometimes Sam didn't know a word to describe a herb.

"That's because there isn't one," said Flaxfield. "It smells of itself, and nothing else smells quite like that. Parsley's like that. It smells of parsley."

That first one was a woman, not much more than a girl. She had drowned when she slipped from a muddy riverbank while she was looking for irises for a vase in the kitchen.

Flaxfield spoke softly to the family first, then went to her, took her hand and said, "Hello."

Sam waited by the door, half-in, half-out.

"Come on, Sam. Say hello."

Sam stepped forward, took the cold hand.

"Hello."

"Now sit there."

Sam sat while Flaxfield did everything. He cried when Flaxfield put the irises next to her.

They slept in a neighbour's barn and left before anyone else was up. It was a quiet walk home.

"Why do you do that?" asked Sam.

"It has to be done."

They walked on. Flaxfield pointed to a herb, almost as tall as Sam, dark green leaves, and purplish-red flowers.

"We'll have some of that."

Sam brought it to him.

"Clown's woods," said Flaxfield. "Nothing better for bruises, or inward wounds."

"Why do *you* do that?" Sam asked again, making himself more clear.

"Someone has to do it."

Now, that someone was him. He was ready and not ready. It was not apprentice work. He had done it so often he knew he would make no mistakes, but he had never done it in his own right, without Flaxfield standing near to him, to seal it. He knew he shouldn't, but he knew the woman was right. Her door had chosen him. He felt a fist of fear in his stomach.

Every time, since the first, every time, Sam had done one more thing. The second was an old farmer, and Sam had washed the man's hands. The third was a builder, and Sam had arranged the arms and straightened the head, just before the last things. There had been twin boys, his own age, and Sam had taken all their clothes off them and washed them, before dressing them again, ready for the herbs. A soldier had been wounded many miles away and died on his way home, brought by a comrade who had promised he would not let him lie in a strange land. Sam washed his wounds and sewed them up with a steel needle and twine.

"Please tell me his name," Sam said.

"Bearrock."

Sam took his hand.

"Hello, Bearrock," he said.

The woman laid a gentle hand on her son's arm.

"Tremmort, tell them it is time," she said.

The boy glared again at Sam. He closed the door silently behind him as he stepped into the night.

The girl slipped onto her mother's knee and they cuddled each other as Sam prepared Bearrock.

It was hard for Sam to know what he had washed and what was still to do, the body never seemed to get any cleaner. Bearrock was a big man. Not tall, but broad. The muscles in his arms were like his name, hard and solid. His legs and shoulders, too, were like a landscape of gentle hills. His body was all-over black-lined. At first Sam tried to clean the black away, then he saw that it was under the skin itself. Thousands of tiny cuts had healed with the dust and dirt of the mines under the skin, there for ever. Sam had thought the body was dirty, but now he looked at his basin of warm water in surprise. It was hardly darkened, though the washing was complete.

The woman caught Sam's look.

"Miners are clean men," she said. "They like to leave the darkness behind, save where it has scarred them, and there's nothing to be done about that."

Sam smiled at her and, for the first time, she smiled at him. The first unfriendliness at the doorway had been left there, or somewhere between the door and where she now sat. Sam and Flaxfield had always been received kindly at the houses of grief. He wondered where the person was who should have been doing this.

He stepped past her and took the herbs from the table, and the other things. He left the pick where it was.

While he said the words and arranged the herbs he heard the door open and the soft movement of people entering. He did not turn his head, not needing to know, not wanting to pause.

When all was done, he looked round. Silent men looked at him, their faces blank. The same black lines. The same broad shoulders and thick arms. The same weight and strength. Tremmort, the boy, stood in the centre.

Sam moved from Bearrock, faced the boy and said, "Do what is right."

The boy did nothing.

Sam nodded.

"Do it," he said.

The men's attention had left Sam and now they all waited for Tremmort to act. Sam knew how he felt.

"You know what to do," he said.

Tremmort did nothing. Sam could not help him. Not with these men watching. He had to do it for himself.

One of the younger men stepped forward.

"I'll do it," he said.

"No," the woman stood, letting the girl take her place

on the chair. "No one but Tremmort is to do it. Not you, Brakewood."

Sam waited. The men looked at Tremmort, then looked away.

"It has to be done," Brakewood said.

"And Bearrock's son will do it." The woman put her face close to Brakewood's.

"Then let him do it."

Sam looked again at Tremmort. The boy was now out of reach. The body of his father, the small room, the crowd of strong men, the anxious face of his mother. It was too much for him. He could not move.

"No?" said Brakewood. "Then I shall." He shouldered past the man next to him, moving towards the table. Sam put his hand on Brakewood's shoulder. A flash of anger and dislike crossed Brakewood's face, then he stood as still as sand.

"You can do it," said Sam. He stared at the boy. "You know what to do."

Tremmort looked around the kitchen. All the figures were silent and still, save Sam, his mother and himself. No one blinked. No one moved so much as to shift from one foot to another or scratch a nervous chin.

"Tell him," said Sam.

"You can," she said. "Don't let someone else do it. Please."

"Look at the table," said Sam.

The boy's eyes searched for something to understand. As he looked, his shoulders relaxed, his hands, which had been clenched into fists, unfolded. He nodded.

"Is it right?" asked Sam.

"Yes."

Sam took his hands from Brakewood's shoulder. He tottered forward, nearly losing balance, then Tremmort pushed past him and grasped the pick. A murmur of approval came from the men, and an angry shove from Brakewood. Tremmort stepped away, unclasped his father's hands and folded them round the pick.

"Dig deep," he said. His voice was low and clear. "Dig through to the finish."

A sigh of satisfaction held the small room for a second, then, with a hollow clap, two men handed planks of wood over the heads of the crowd. Hands went up, passing them forward. The body of Bearrock was lifted onto them. The crush of men parted and Bearrock was borne through the space, out into the darkness and the star-sharp night. ‖

The first after Bearrock

was Tremmort, then his mother, holding his sister's hand. The three of them walked, heads high, looking straight ahead. The men followed, the oldest first, then in order, which left Brakewood last. Sam held back. Now that he had finished the preparations for Bearrock he felt dizzy. His head hurt, a pain that started somewhere in the centre of his forehead and spread all down the left side of his face and into his teeth.

He had walked for five weeks. The food soon spent, he had foraged when he could for berries, the roots of safe herbs, tender shoots of plants Flaxfield had taught him were good to eat. He had followed the path of a stream, drinking whenever he was thirsty, but it had taken a course through thick undergrowth and he left it to follow a dry road. Flaxfield's words about summers getting hotter came often into Sam's head as he walked mile after mile, not knowing where he was heading, content so long as the college was ever further behind him. He started by carrying the cloak over his arm, the waistcoat looped through his belt, until he discovered a strange thing. Resting beneath a tree the first afternoon, he had left the cloak over his legs by mistake. His legs were cooler than the rest of him. Hitching the cloak around his shoulders, it was as though an autumn breeze soothed away the dense heat. After that he kept the cloak over his shoulders as he walked, and found the heat did not trouble him. Only the sun on his uncovered head made him dizzy sometimes.

Fields and hedgerows, coppices and ponds turned to scrubby land and dry stone walls. The streams and fresh grass gave way to heather, gorse and rocky escarpments. The heather was sweet and soft to sleep on, but no good for food. High trees, with shade for soft plants, herbs and berries became spiked bushes, low shrubs. Green and gold, deep blue and soft pink, the colours of countryside, disappeared. The moorland purples and greys were picked out against the green-black leaves and dark-red thorns. Springing bracken whipped round Sam's legs, and the thousands of tiny ticks and mites that lived in its fronds bit him, sucked his blood and left spots and sores.

He reached a prominence, scrambling up a dry, shiny slope of hard stone, just as the sun was at its height. No shade to shelter him from the worst of the day. No water to cool his thirst. He had not drunk for over two days now. His tongue was big in his mouth. His throat was sore. The pain down the side of his face made him half-close his left eye for relief. He needed to rest, but if he sat down before he drank he might not get up again.

Half a day's walk away, half of another day without water, Sam saw the small town. He knew it without knowing what it was. For a moment he thought he would rather lie down where he was and leave himself to the sun. Behind him lay the college. Somewhere, he knew, wizards were looking for him. He had escaped them both. But only to walk, as if by choice, perhaps by some decision made for him long ago, into the very place he feared most. He had walked for weeks, only to come here.

Below him, in the middle-distance, hunched like a wounded wolf, lay the mines.

He hugged the cloak to him, moved his ash staff forward, and his feet followed, into the oven of the afternoon, towards whatever waited for him there.

It had reached that time when the day was just more dark than light, the houses scattered down the slope like the bones of a long-dead sheep when he walked past the first few houses, too proud to knock at the first door and beg for water. He knocked at the fourth. It had chosen him.

Now, thirsty no more, but aching with hunger still, he watched the procession wind its way into the night. Knowing that he had not yet finished, he followed.

The faces that stared at Sam were not hostile, but nor were they friendly. It seemed to Sam that it was more that they were afraid of him. No, afraid was too much. They looked at him with wary eyes. Hundreds of eyes. More people than had been there for Flaxfield's Finishing.

The crowd parted to allow the procession to move forward. As they left the house behind them, music started. Sam had never heard music, more than a single voice singing, or a penny whistle from a shepherd come for a remedy for the bloats.

It was a single fiddle at first, low and slow and sad. Bearrock's body moved down the slope, further into the town. The crowd turned itself into a line of followers, not tidily two-abreast, but sometimes three, sometimes a small group, families together, sometimes a single person choosing a space around himself. They waited for the leaders to pass before joining in, so every eye regarded Sam as he passed, every face asked the same question. Some whispered to themselves, and he caught the same word over and over again: *December*, and a shaking of the head.

There is very little magic in the preparing of a person for the Finishing. Sam had done more than an apprentice should, but there had been no one else. It was the Finishing itself that was the test.

The single fiddle was joined by another. Their voices sang different notes, but they blended like butter and sugar in the bowl, each bringing something new, something needed.

They were in the town itself now. The streets closed in on them. The houses moved nearer for comfort and reassurance.

Doors opened and closed, discharging people from their rooms.

The men at the front stopped, moved aside in turn and

gave their burden to others. They stepped away, rubbing their shoulders. The planks weighed more than the heavy man they supported.

Sam saw that Brakewood had stepped forward to take his share of the weight, but had been firmly kept aside. Tremmort was too small to carry. The planks would have tilted to one corner. He still led the followers.

There were shops now, a market square, a broader street leading away, torches burned on high, iron stands, orange flames caged in black against the night sky.

The men rested the planks on a stone ledge beneath a clock tower. They stepped back and a semi-circle formed around the bier.

The fiddlers were joined by a drummer. A shallow circle stretched with goatskin in his arms, the drum was struck with a short stick. Sam marvelled that even this simple instrument could be made to sing different notes, as the drummer struck near the rim, or close to the centre, touching the skin with his fingers sometimes to change the pitch. The drum shared the weight of the solemnity of the fiddles, and it took to itself some of the sadness.

It was Sam's first real music and he heard in it a magic of its own, like wizard magic, but more elusive. He wanted to walk into the tunes.

The crowd shifted and surged, like leaves on a great tree in the wind, held in place, yet ever moving. Sam found that its momentum had carried him to the very front and he stood now between Tremmort and his mother. He made to step back, but hands kept him there.

The music closed in on itself. The crowd waited. To Sam's left a gap appeared in the crush of bodies. Four roffles walked through and went straight to the front. Just as all attention was fixed on the roffles, the crowd to Sam's left parted, a noise of whispering broke into the magic of the music, and the most frightening woman Sam had ever seen stepped into the space. ‖

Caleb was asleep when

Flaxfold found him, slumped against the door of the study. She moved his cloak, the better to cover him. It was morning, early and still cold.

The house stank. Flaxfold opened windows, swept the kitchen floor, gathered up rotting food from the table and put it in a sack to take out for the pigs.

She lit a fire in the range. The sweet smell of the smoke helped to freshen the air in the house. She took eggs, butter, milk and fresh bread from her basket. While the fire settled and the range heated up she went to the larder and carved slices of ham from a joint that hung from a hook driven into a black beam. The sharp knife stripped the meat easily from the bone and it fell, cool and heavy into her open hand.

Flaxfold sliced the bread and spread it thick with butter. She scrambled eggs and cooked them on the range, adding salt and the cream from the top of the milk.

She woke Caleb and led him downstairs. Caleb looked at

her with blank eyes, saying nothing. Flaxfold sat him at the table and put the food in front of him, his arms resting on the grained wood.

She cut a corner of the buttered bread, spooned on some egg and held it to his face. He opened his mouth, chewed, and swallowed with some effort. He made no move to take more. Flaxfold cut another piece of bread, added egg, fed him again. She put a mug of milk to his lips, to help him swallow. Milk spilled down his chin. Caleb put his hand up to steady the mug and winced as it touched. Flaxfold turned his hand over in hers and saw that it was marked with raised blisters where he had burned it. His other hand was the same.

"I'll see to them later," she said.

He stared at her, as though he had just noticed she was there. He shivered. Flaxfold closed the window and wrapped his cloak around him. The colours were faded and the silk scuffed and singed. He smelled stale and scorched.

It was a slow business. Flaxfold fed him until the food was finished and the mug empty. He showed neither pleasure in eating, nor any resistance to her.

When all was done, she led him to a deep chair in front of the fire, covered him with a blanket and he fell asleep immediately.

Flaxfold washed the breakfast things. She never left dirty washing-up to be done later. She made a small pot of strong tea, more scrambled eggs and bread and butter, and ate her own breakfast while Caleb slept.

The sun burned off the early mist. The range breathed out

black heat. The kitchen relaxed into a rhythm of work under Flaxfold's hands. Caleb did not stir as she returned it from the mess he had made of it back to its customary calm and order. Only one unpleasant reminder persisted, a smell. But as that came from Caleb himself there was nothing she could do till he woke.

She made her way to the study and examined the door. The beautiful oak was now marked with deep gouges where Caleb had attacked it with an axe. It was scorched and blackened. Flaxfold traced her finger over the burn marks. Had Caleb tried to burn it down? Or had he tried more magic to open it and been driven back by fire from the sealing spell? She pressed the palm of her hand against the surface. The wood was cool and composed. It had been the battlefield of a war of magic between Caleb and the sealing spell. It had withstood iron and spells and had held firm, keeping its secrets. And now it was wounded, scarred.

Flaxfold found wax and oil and a fresh cloth. She smoothed the oil into the scorched scars. She rubbed wax into the deep wounds of the axe marks. She sang, soft and slow as she worked, a song of forests and of green shade, a song of sun on leaves and wind high in the branches.

The door began to gleam with ancient light. When she was done there was no sign that it had ever been marked. Flaxfold smiled. The iron handle was unchanged. It had burned Caleb's hands when he wrenched at it trying to force the door open. The fire had saved it from attack, and it hung, strong and round as ever. Flaxfold put her hand to it, turned it, opened the door and went in.

It was two days' journey to the castle, and dark when Eloise got there. She wore the silk map as a shawl.

Khazib travelled on horseback, his rug rolled and tied to the saddle behind him. He moved as naturally on a horse as on his own feet, feeling himself and the animal as one. They rested briefly overnight, stopping after the moon had risen and starting again before dawn.

Caleb's sleep was troubled with the vision of a dragon circling high above him in the sky. He ran to escape from it, down tree-dense paths to a riverbank. He broke through the cover to the waterside and the dragon swooped down on him, swift and deadly. Caleb raised his arm to protect himself. The dragon drew near, the blue scales changed to feathers, and it was a kingfisher, plunging into the water and sweeping up and out, a fish caught in its beak glancing silver in the sunlight. He stumbled, fell, and his hands sank into the river as far as his wrists. The cold water hurt and he pulled back. The quick movement woke him and he found himself in the chair, Flaxfold on her knees at his side. His hands were, as in the dream, wet. She was rubbing lotion on the palms. At first it stung, then, as she stroked, it became soothing, taking the pain of the blisters.

"How's that?" she asked.

He looked at the range. The flames had all gone, leaving

the steady glow of the hot coals.

"We need to do this four times a day," she said. "You'll soon be better."

Sunlight caught colours from the uneven glass of the windows and striped the walls with bands of colour. Caleb watched them shimmer as Flaxfold finished anointing his palms. Her head was bent to see his hands. He could not see her face. Her hair, white and wound round into a knot. Her neck brown at the back, from the sun, and the skin crinkled with age. She looked up and their eyes met. He remembered her from somewhere long ago but he couldn't think where.

"Sleep again, now," she said. So he did.

Another day, and Khazib needed rest in the afternoon. The pace was too fast. Khazib balanced his urgency to get to Sam with his care to be strong and ready when he arrived at the castle. If he tired himself with the journey he would be too weak to deal with the boy. He rested by a stream, unfastened the rug, slipped the tack from the horse. It shook its head, snorted and walked delicately into the water, to drink and to cool down. Unrolling the rug, Khazib ignored its intricate secrets and gave himself to sleep. By the time he woke, the stars were already telling their story.

The sun was low in the sky when Caleb woke in the kitchen, long shadows from the trees stretching towards the house in the late afternoon sun. Flaxfold was sitting under the willow up from the river bank, watching the sunlight decorate the water. As soon as he stirred she stood up and made her way to the house. As she entered he opened his eyes and blinked away the sleep.

Flaxfold had left a tin bath ready for him in front of the range, and water heating on the top. She poured the water, tested that it was not too hot, gave him two large towels and soap that she had made herself, scented with bergamot and other fragrances that were good for healing.

"Take off your clothes and leave them on the chair," she said. "I'll fetch you some others."

She wrapped dock leaves around his hands and fastened them with slim shoots of willow she had plucked from the tree that had given her shade.

"Don't get your hands wet," she warned.

Flaxfold was short, not much taller than Sam, and she tilted her head back to look at Caleb.

He licked his lips.

"Are you thirsty?"

She poured him water from the earthenware jug into a clay beaker. He had to hold in it in both hands to drink because of the leaves. He didn't spill much.

Flaxfold unfastened the silver and jet clip at his neck, opened his shirt collar and pushed back his hair. She turned the brooch over in her hands. The jet was carved into a delicate black beetle, smooth and shining, perfect in detail. She clipped it to his jerkin, not to lose it.

When she returned, he was wrapped in towels, staring at

the range. Despite the warm afternoon sun, the fire, and the hot water, Caleb was shivering. And his hair was dry and still smelled of smoke and sweat. Flaxfold leaned him over the tub and washed his hair carefully. She used fresh water from a jug to rinse the suds. While he dried himself and put on the clothes, Flaxfold prepared a potion for him. She was not slim, but she moved with a delicacy and a lightness that made her seem more graceful than she looked. And she carried herself with assurance. Her hands moved confidently over Flaxfield's shelves. She measured by eye, rather than with a spoon or cup, dribbling some liquids frugally, allowing more generous amounts of others.

Although she had removed the dock leaves from Caleb's hands he was too burned to fasten his clothes himself and she had to help him.

"These were ready for Sam," she told him. "To grow into."

He looked down at them and when she handed him the potion he drank it without hesitation.

"Better?"

He didn't answer, or even nod his head. She took the beaker from his fingers and checked that it was empty.

"You shouldn't sleep again yet," she said. "That should help."

His shivering grew less. Flaxfold led him to the kitchen table and sat him down.

"You won't nod off if you're sitting upright."

Caleb rested his arms on the table. He looked at his hands.

"Do you remember me?" she asked.

He looked at her, then away.

"I'll tell you a story," she said. "You used to like stories."

Eloise drew the silk shawl around her face. It covered her shoulders and hair, her throat and mouth, leaving only the eyes exposed. To an ordinary person she was now invisible. To a wizard, perhaps. These things were a matter of strength and experience. She hoped that Sam would not be able to see her. She watched Khazib approach the castle. Still she held back.

Sandage left the road and slept at an inn. His dinner was a dish of rancid meat in thin gravy and a hunk of bread which was two days old. The bed creaked all night. When he woke, his skin was dotted with red where the bugs had bitten him. The innkeeper asked him for three florins. Sandage put them carefully on the counter.

"Do you think that a fair price?" he asked.

"There's no other inn."

Sandage pondered the problem. If he cast a spell on the inn to keep travellers away he would feel the pleasure of revenge and the magic would turn against him. But a spell of keeping travellers away would also be a service to others and would serve the landlord right. Then the magic would stay and do him no harm. It was so often this way with magic. How could he be sure it was not for his own pleasure and gain? But it was the only inn. There was nowhere else for them to sleep after a hard day's journey.

He left behind him a spell which cleared the inn of the bedbugs and made the cook clean the kitchen and buy fresh produce. It would not punish the landlord, but it would help other travellers. It would probably make the landlord rich as well, and Sandage regretted that. On the other hand, riches could be their own curse. Let the landlord take his chances.

Sandage hitched his cloak round his shoulders and trudged on, the castle just out of view, far, but coming closer now.

Day followed day and Caleb's hands healed swiftly under Flaxfold's care.

He slept ten hours a night, scarcely moving. In the mornings he walked down to the river and stood looking downstream.

Caleb slept a little most afternoons and sometimes sat with a book in his hands, turning the pages but not reading.

In the evenings they walked together sometimes. Not far. Caleb tired quickly. Or they sat together under the willow until the sun had quite gone. Then they sat in the kitchen and Flaxfold told stories until it was time to sleep.

She slept in the room she had used when Sam was little. Caleb had Sam's room. Flaxfield's room, though not locked, was never used.

Every morning, as soon as Caleb walked down to the stream, Flaxfold let herself into the study and closed the door behind her.

✳

Flaxfold found Caleb at the riverbank, he was wrapped in an old cloak, frayed at the hem, patched and worn.

"Why do you always look downstream?" she asked.

The water folded over itself and caught up the late autumn leaves that spun on its surface, dragging them under then releasing them downstream.

"Are you looking for Flaxfield?" she asked. "He's gone."

Their eyes followed the path of the stream that Flaxfield had sailed on his final journey in the willow basket.

"It should have been me," said Caleb. "I was his last apprentice. I should have done the last things."

"It was a good Finishing," she said.

"He never liked me."

A dragonfly, blue-green and bright in the sun, darted over the water, hovered, and swerved off.

"He liked all his apprentices." Flaxfold's voice was soft as the stream.

"He should be here still," said Caleb.

"The river takes things away," said Flaxfold, "and they never come back. That's the way of rivers. They always flow one way. Whatever you give to the river, you give it for ever."

Caleb nodded.

"Give me your hands," she said.

Caleb let the cloak fall away. His wounds looked different in the sunlight, less violent, like the bark of a tree, or the lichen on a wall. He held out his hands. The blisters had burst and dried, leaving scaly skin, flaking away, and sore, soft patches beneath.

"These aren't wizard's hands," she said.

Caleb looked down at them as though they were not his.

She lifted the cloak from his shoulders.

"Do you want to get better?" she asked.

He nodded.

Flaxfold took his hand and led him to the river. She pushed the reeds aside with her short legs, wading into the stream. Her feet made slow progress through the mud. She was sunk nearly to her neck by the time the water came up to his waist. They were still far from the centre, where the water was deep and the current strong. The mud had given way to pebbles and large stones. The water was clear, cold. She let go of Caleb's hand.

For the first time since she found him slumped at the study door, Caleb smiled. He spread his arms to feel the power of the current, letting the water rush past him. He leaned back and let his feet rise from the river floor. Turning over and over he gave himself to the river, allowing it to carry him downstream, then he struck out, swimming strongly back against the current. He laughed. Diving head first under the water he disappeared, then leaped out, clutching a silver trout in his hands. He brandished the fish at Flaxfold, who smiled and clapped her hands. Throwing the fish high into the air, plunging into the water again, ready to watch it as it fell back into the water and darted away. He put his hand to his shoulder to brush away something that was clinging to him, a leaf, perhaps, or pondweed. His fingers closed around a water-beetle. He looked at it for a moment, then lowered it gently to the river, watching it float away, blue-black in the sun.

Flaxfold waddled through the reeds back to the bank, found a solid patch of rocky ground, took off her shoes and washed them while she dangled her feet in the clear water to get rid of the mud.

Caleb was exhausted when he came out. She looked at him. The bruises had all gone. The scars remained, but their fierceness had faded. Taking his hands she dried them with her sleeve. She turned them over in her own. The palms were quite clean and clear of the last traces of the dead skin. The pus had dried up. Wherever the fire had touched his palms and raised the painful blisters there was line, a mark, sometimes curved like a snake, sometimes bunched like a burl on a tree trunk, sometimes raised like the veins on a leaf, sometimes sunk, the grain on a table. They were all there, healed, but not vanished. He would always carry them.

They stood together and looked downstream.

"Flaxfield's gone," she said again. "Look upstream instead."

"It should have been me," he repeated.

"Sam was a true apprentice," said Flaxfold. "You know that's true."

"He said I would be his last."

Flaxfold cut a small willow branch and stripped it of its

leaves, absently smoothing the soft bark.

"Things don't always turn out the way we think they will," she said. "He knew he would not live long enough to finish another apprenticeship. But then Sam came along."

"He shouldn't have started if he couldn't finish," said Caleb.

Flaxfold flicked the willow switch and it swished in the warm air. She laughed.

"You," she said, prodding him gently with the switch. "You? Rebuking Flaxfield for not finishing something? I remember when you were his apprentice. Have you forgotten?"

Caleb smiled.

"He left arrangements for Sam's apprenticeship. It will be finished," she said.

Caleb looked at his hands.

"Look upstream," she said. "What do you see?" ‖

The roffles stood at the four corners

of the planks that held Bearrock. They were waiting. All music stopped. Tremmort pointed to the woman and his mother looked in her direction. She beckoned her over. The woman shook her head, stared at them, moved her head a little and stared at Sam.

Sam had seen the effects of the world on faces that called at Flaxfield's door. He had seen what time and steel and sun and sorrow could do to a face, the wounds and the wear.

He had never seen a face like this one.

The skin was stretched tight, like the goatskin of the drum they had followed. Shiny, smooth, mostly, but puckered here and there, as though drawn tight by a tailor's thread. And she had no lips, like a snake.

Sam could not turn his eyes away. Her face fascinated him, as he had been captivated the first time he had seen a sheep's skull, half-decayed in a field, the flesh and bone equally presented, the gums, the teeth, the lips, the horror tongue.

She met his gaze, then, as though to make sure he did not miss anything, she lifted her arms, put back the scarf that covered her head, and he saw that her hair was half-gone in patches, and that her scalp showed through.

Tremmort called to her, "December. We're ready."

Without taking her eyes from Sam, she shook her head.

"He has not chosen this," she said. "It has chosen him."

The roffles had been watching this. Now, the one nearest to Sam stepped forward, took his hand and led him to the still figure of the corpse.

"It is you," he said.

A discontented sound rose from the crowd. Brakewood tried to pull Sam back and Tremmort said to his mother, "It shouldn't be him. Tell December to do it."

Greenrose asked December again, with silent eyes. The woman shook her head, drew her scarf up and wrapped it around her scrappy hair.

"Please," said Greenrose to Sam. "Please finish."

Sam remembered Eloise by the riverside at Flaxfield's Finishing. He thought of the dozens of Finishings he had listened to Flaxfield do. Holding his staff for support, he said the words. As he began the words a sigh breathed out from the crowd. The waiting was over. The Finishing was beginning. The words said, the roffles lifted the planks, carried Bearrock away. Sam and Tremmort, Greenrose and the girl followed, the crowd next. Sam wondered whether the woman, December, came too, but he did not turn to look. A fiddle found new notes, then the others joined in. The music moved their feet and their hearts.

Leaving the town, they passed a meadow, and here the others stayed. The roffles were much stronger than they looked, needing no help on the path. Sam's hunger had turned into a humming inside his head, a pain in his chest, a taste of wax in his mouth. Greater than the hunger was his fear of where they were going. He could see ahead of them the stunted turrets of the mine machinery, smell the fresh spoil, piled into heaps. The starlight shaped the sinister humps of earth that had been heaved out of the ground and now rose over them. They were taking Bearrock back to the mines and Sam would have to go into that depth and darkness where magic is twisted. He would open the door to the Finished World.

The woman they called December walked apart from the crowd, but never far off.

She had been looking for Sam. A week ago, more, she had left the town and taken the road to Flaxfield's. If he was leaving the wizard then the roads that led to the old man's house were the roads that Sam must take to get away.

Like the wizards who had gathered for Flaxfield's Finishing, December had tried magic to find Sam first. Like them, she found a broken thread, a misty window, a confused and shifting map. Sam was somewhere in their magic, but it was not clear where.

There was a magic that was muddling their minds, as powerful as the magic they were using to find Sam. Magic was hiding him from them, from her. Where magic fails then sense and experience and hard work and walking take over. December tried to see herself as Sam. What was he? A boy? Well, a young person. She remembered what that was like. What else? Alone. She remembered that, too. The memory made her stand up. She could not call to mind the child she had been without remembering the pain, the fear. Her room was so small she could almost reach out her arms and touch the walls on either side. Miners are not rich men and their houses know little luxury. Unable to pace the room she stood, closed her eyes and saw. What else? He was frightened. He may not know it, but he was. He hurt, too. She knew it. Flaxfield was all he had and Flaxfield had gone. What would he do? Where would he go?

She moved to her left. A looking-glass hung in the centre of the chimney breast. December faced it, looked long and steadily at her face. She knew every scar and every disfigurement. She lived daily with other faces, ordinary faces, and she knew the power of her face, the difference, the ugliness, the dreadful attraction it held for people. When she met someone for the first time she knew they could not keep their eyes away, did not like to stare. She knew they felt horror. She remembered getting her face.

What would Sam do?

He would walk, she decided. He would walk away, scattering what magic he dared behind him to hide his steps. But he was still young, still inexperienced. Would he think to scatter magic ahead of himself as well? The road a wizard walks can be drawn ahead of him. She thought Sam might not know that. It was her only plan. Following him would be impossible. Arriving before him might work.

And so she set off, looking for roads and trails. She kept far from Flaxfield's house, but looked always towards it. She had all but given up when the stars talked to her about Canterstock. It was the last place she would have expected. She was far from Canterstock and needed to pass back through her home town and the mines to get there.

The magic was restless now, hot and agitated. She felt it growing annoyed with her. It was like pushing her tongue against a tender tooth. Or eating something too hot. As long as she was careful it didn't hurt, but if she pushed, or troubled it too much the pain flared up, stabbing at her. It was more than she dared to do to use it to get to the college. She would have to walk.

She was road-racked, dirty and hungry. It would be better to take an extra hour and go home and eat and change. She would make faster progress.

The town was dark and busy. Nights were usually quiet in mining towns. The men worked hard and needed sleep. She joined the crowd, knowing there was a new death, blaming herself for making them wait for the Finishing. But puzzled, too. There should be no gathering tonight until she had finished the preparations.

She engineered her way through the press of bodies,

emerged into the cleared space. And there he was.

"Isn't that the way?" she said to herself. "You make a week's journey to look for something, and it was coming to you all the time."

Now that she had him, she would not let him go. He was nearly hers, but she would have to play him carefully. He would not come to her of his own free will. She walked apart from the crowd, but never far off. ‖

A second moon

rose up. It tugged against Axestone's hands, straining to escape and fly off into the night. Two moons. One, floating with patient face, ignoring the strands of cloud. The other, bobbing and dipping, soaring up and falling at the end of Axestone's twine. The real moon, blind and still. Axestone's moon, with hungry eyes, darting in the night, searching, hunting. And what the moon saw, Axestone saw.

He stood, eyes shut, arms raised, one hand on the bobbin that held the twine, the other hand against the twine itself, feeling every vibration, sensing the strength of the wind, directing the moon-shaped kite, seeing the country all around him from high above.

A castle. Roads, approaching. A woman, her head wrapped in a shawl. A man, riding. Another, older man, cautiously circling the castle then waiting, silent on the edge of the forest. The forest, knotted and tense, grey shapes leaping through clearings, spearing through undergrowth.

Axestone saw them with the eyes of the kite. He reeled it in. Opening his eyes, he looked around, half-blind, half-asleep, it seemed, until the magic swept away like smoke and he was himself again.

Now his ears heard the yelping from the forest, the beat of hooves, the breeze in the trees.

Khazib was the first to break cover. He rode up to the castle gate, dismounted and walked straight in, leading his horse.

Sandage, seeing Khazib from his own vantage point, walked slowly up, dragging one foot as though lame, head down as though frightened, shoulders hunched as though poor. A wizard's approach.

The yelps grew louder, nearer. Grey forms bounded clear of the trees, tongues wet, teeth bared. The wolves slowed, grouped, lifted their heads to the moon and howled.

They turned, saw Axestone, growled, leaped forward and ran straight for him.

Eloise, too, saw Khazib and Sandage enter the castle. She waited, the shawl over her head, her hands holding it tight at the neck.

The moon gave more than enough light to see them disappear through the gate, enough to see that they were met by figures, who greeted them. Then the darkness of the courtyard swallowed them and they were gone from sight.

She slipped the shawl from her head, spread it on the ground. The moonlight picked out the silver detail in the muted colour. The road ran clear as a stream towards the castle.

"This is it," she said. She looked up at the high walls, the round turrets. "This is not it," she said.

The baying of the wolves distracted her. She looked up and saw them circle in the moonlight. They looked around, then, as one, they ran to a lone figure on the edge of the forest.

Eloise knew it was Axestone. He was too far off for her to see his face, or even his characteristic stance. She knew him by the wizard-way he waited for the wolves.

Neither of them saw the shape of the dragon circling overhead. Neither of them noticed the glint of moonlight on his scales, the shadow of his wings against the sky.

Starback was a very old dragon. He had flown these skies before even Flaxfield was a boy, and that was many years ago. Starback remembered when Megantople, the fat roffle, toured around the fairs, charging people a penny a time to see him. But he had been away. He remembered when the college at Canterstock was a new place. He remembered the magic that had been learned there, when the students were more careful of the craft. He remembered this castle, the Palace of Boolat. Often he had played in the gardens, swum in the moat, scrambled up the walls and perched on the battlements to watch the feasts in the wide courtyard, the tournaments on the green just beyond the walls, the bright jackets of the men off to hunt wild boar in the forest, the rich coloured robes of the ladies.

But Starback had been away. Some of the time he had

slept. Some of the time he had lived in a distant country, where news of this place never reached. Some of the time he had fought, because dragons, even Green and Blues, need to fight sometimes. He had returned for Sam.

Now he was puzzled. He circled slowly over the castle. Where were the lights? The music? The clatter of horses' hooves on the cobbles? The trumpets, announcing visitors? The smells from the kitchens? The running feet of pages? Where was the life?

It had all been such a rush. If only Sam hadn't met that roffle. If only Starback had a little more time. If only Flaxfield had warned him that he was going. If only the wizards had listened to Sam. If only things were as he remembered them.

He dipped, tilted and flew down to the castle. He was tired and lonely. Since leaving Sam, Starback had felt an emptiness, like a pain. He had been looking forward to this visit. The castle was like home to him. He wanted company and friends. Now it looked deserted. Swooping low, he could see that there were figures in the courtyard, even though there were no lights, no torches burning. He shook his head. Dragon-sight doesn't need torches in the darkness, but he could barely make out what was beneath him. The castle was caught in a web of magic. Some-one in there had spun a veil of secrecy all around it and even Starback could not see through clearly.

He flicked his wings to fly higher. Still he slowly sank towards the castle. A moment of fear filled him and he flapped his wings more resolutely. The castle drew nearer. He could see more figures, running into the courtyard, pointing up at him. He was being tugged towards it, like a boat being hauled into harbour by a rope. He strained to fly up, struggling against whatever magic was pulling him down. Wings weren't enough. Struggle was only making it worse.

Old dragons know many tricks. Starback stopped struggling. He hovered for a moment, then allowed the magic to draw him down. The figures below him jumped with excitement. They cheered and yelled. Starback, wings outstretched, swooped towards them. All at once, they realized what it was to have a dragon flying towards them. He was an arrow, swift and deadly. They fell back, scattering. Starback roared. Fire flowed from his mouth. And with the fire, the thick, black shape of a broken dragon, that faltered, then flapped clumsily to the tower window. Starback's mind cleared. He saw what he had done wrong. He flicked his wings, taking him in a tight arc, down, round and back up, shooting high in the air, using the force of the magic that had pulled him down to send him soaring back up.

In the instant when he changed direction, he saw, clear as cruelty, the shape of one who was the centre and source of the magic. It was as though they recognized each other, and then he was gone, flying up and free.

The castle had changed. And Starback had led Khazib and Sandage right into the heart of a darkness that had eaten them.

He was lost. Since coming back he had been with Flaxfield and Sam. He had played like a young dragon again. He had watched over Sam and Flaxfield had trusted him with Sam. The old wizard had told him many times that he would not be able to finish Sam's apprenticeship and that Starback would be needed when the time came. And now Starback had let him down. He had led two wizards into danger, when he only meant to lead them astray. He had left Sam alone. For weeks he had flown over the countryside, tricking them into coming here. He had neglected Sam when Sam needed him most, only to fail in the task he had taken on instead.

Starback flew in a circle, high and distant, but never taking the castle from his sight. He could smell the magic down there, taste the malevolence. Something had been born here while he was away. Something that would reach out and hurt Sam. All other thoughts left his mind. He must find Sam and help him now. Forget the wizards. Forget everything except looking after Sam. He knew where Sam was. Starback always knew where Sam was. That was the way of things. Leaving the castle behind him, he flew towards the mines.

The wolves raced up the hill and surrounded Axestone, teeth bared, saliva dripping from their open mouths, hackles raised. They advanced slowly, eyes bright with anger.

The wizard looked over their heads and saw Eloise, alone in the night.

"All right," he said. "I know. It's all right."

The wolves lowered their tails and fell silent.

"I'm not going in there," said Axestone. "I know."

They waited.

Axestone raised his staff and signalled to Eloise. She tightened her shawl and walked towards him, stepping into the ring of wolves and shrugging her scarf back onto her shoulders.

"We have been tricked," said Axestone.

"I know."

"Did you see the dragon?"

"I thought it would be dragged down into the castle."

"Khazib and Sandage are in there," said Axestone. "We should try to rescue them."

"It is an old dragon," said Eloise. "It knows many tricks."

"Sam could be in there, too," said Axestone.

"I don't think so. I think the dragon has gone to find him."

"We made a mistake, losing Sam," said Axestone.

"Yes."

"He's in danger." The wizard reached out a hand and stroked a wolf. The animal turned his head and let him scratch behind his ears.

"So are we," said Eloise.

"I used my best magic to get here, and it was useless. All false."

"Mine, too, though the map was never clear, never fixed."

The wolves were restless, no longer in a circle round the two, but turned towards the castle, their hackles up, teeth bared, low growling in their throats.

"Not clear," said Axestone, "but there was no other place it could have been."

"We were brought to a trap," she said. "And we should get away, before it is sprung."

Axestone tossed the round kite into the air, fed out the twine until it hung over the castle. He closed his eyes. The wolves raised their heads and howled to the false moon, their cries breaking open the night.

Eloise spread her shawl over her shoulders, the silver threads alive in the moonlight. Axestone's hands were clenched on the bobbin, his knuckles white with strain, his fingers aching with effort.

The kite dipped, fell, spun high again then plunged down into the jaw of the castle.

Eloise shook him.

"Axestone!"

He was as though asleep. Eyes tight shut, lips straight and tight. Asleep, but in a nightmare. Desperate to wake, yet trapped in his dream.

The wolves bounded towards the grim walls.

Eloise shook him again. The twine was pulling at his hands. The kite was drawing him towards the castle.

The gates were opening. Dark shapes appeared, fanned out, then looked around. Half-upright, with the impression of more than four legs each, they had seen the two wizards and were coming towards them, guided by the twine from the kite.

Eloise shook Axestone harder, but he would not wake.

The wolves hesitated, then plunged forward towards whatever it was that had crept from the castle.

The twine thrummed in Axestone's hands. Eloise whipped her shawl from her shoulders and wrapped it round Axestone's face. He staggered, straightened and turned his eyes to her. He was released from the spell that had fuddled his mind, but his hands still gripped the twine from the kite and he could not let go.

For a moment the shapes from the castle had fallen back against the walls, clattering like cockroaches, ready to meet the attack of the wolves.

Eloise could see them clearly now.

"Takkabakks," she breathed.

The clacking creatures paused, as though they heard her.

The wolves were having the worst of the fight with the black shapes. They were falling back, getting ever closer to Eloise and Axestone.

Something was happening to the twine. It thickened and moved. Axestone stared at it. He tried to let go. His hands were clenched tight and he could not open them. The twine hummed, like the string of a fiddle. Before she could warn Axestone, Eloise saw an army of black beetles clinging to the twine, pouring over each other as they ran along it. They reached his hands and swarmed over them, up his arms, under the sleeves of his robe, dropping to the ground and scrambling over his feet and up his legs. He screamed in horror and jerked his hands back, but the twine held him tight.

The sound of wolves howling in pain carved itself into the night. The takkabakks were stabbing at them, killing the bravest, injuring those who darted up and retreated. The black shapes fell on the dead bodies and tore their flesh, scooping it into stinking jaws with jagged pincers. The rest moved steadily forward, jabbing at the wolves, advancing towards Axestone and Eloise.

Ash was watching the takkabakks through her window. She clenched her fists and hissed in pleasure whenever a wolf was stabbed. The takkabakks scrambled towards Eloise and Axestone, clattering and hissing. Ash looked up as a cloud folded itself over the moon.

"What's that?" she said.

She swung round to the black figure which squatted behind her.

"Look."

She pointed to the cloud and the moon.

Bakkmann shuffled forward. It clattered a question.

"He's trying to perform a Finishing," she said. "Quickly. It's a chance. Come."

Her grey robe flowed out behind her as she rushed down to the dungeons. Bakkmann banged against the walls of the staircase in its hurry to follow.

Ash threw open the door to Sandage's cell.

Bakkmann clattered with pleasure when he saw the old wizard.

"Can I kill him? Kill him? Kill?"

Ash nodded.

Bakkmann scuttled in and spat a jet of acid at Sandage, missing his face and sizzling on his shoulder.

"No," decided Ash. "Stop. No. Not this one."

Bakkmann hissed disappointment.

"Kill me," said Sandage.

Ash smiled.

"No," she said. "I need a quick kill today. You will be slow."

She darted to the next cell.

"Kill. Quickly," she ordered Bakkmann.

Bakkmann hurled itself at the dazed prisoner and stabbed into his heart, once, twice, then started to suck and bite noisily at the body.

Ash gabbled the words and the door to the Finished World opened. She leaned in. ‖

Part Four

WIZARD DOOR

Sam had never taken someone through

the opening to the Finished World before. All the things he had done so far for Bearrock he had done many times before, with Flaxfield to guide him. This last part, the final act of Finishing, was wizard's work. Sam knew what to do. He had just never done it. And he was doing it down the mine where magic was wild.

Everyone had fallen back at the entrance, save the roffles and Tremmort and Sam. They had walked deep into the earth, the path sloping steeply down. Burning torches lit the way. Sam saw the clean cuts in the wall where the miners had dug, the wooden beams holding up the roof. As they went he dipped his head to avoid bumping it. The roffles could still just about walk upright.

They reached the furthest point of the mine workings, where the wall in front of them was ready for the next day's shift. The roffles gently lowered their load to the floor and stood back, waiting.

Tremmort stared at Sam. Sam was trembling. He was

tired, hungry. His legs and back ached from the journey and from sleeping rough. His neck hurt where he was keeping his head low of the roof. He could taste the air down there, taste that it was different, not just from the dust of the digging and the tar that they painted the roof timbers with. It tasted like milk that is half a day too old and not yet curdled — not right, but not properly wrong. Sam could taste that magic was different down here.

"Can you do it?" asked Tremmort.

Sam nodded.

He took Bearrock's hand and started to say the words of Finishing. He could tell that Tremmort saw nothing. Sam didn't know enough about roffles to know whether they saw anything or not. But he saw the door open. He saw, for the first time, a crack in the ordinary world that opened up into a way to the Finished World. He saw Bearrock move through the opening. He thought he saw something of where the big man went.

Sam came to the end of the words and he drew his hand away from Bearrock's. The door to the Finished World was starting to close. As the big man stepped away, another hand took hold of Sam.

Sam flinched. He pulled back. Half-hidden in the Finished World a slender, grey-robed figure reached out and held Sam tight.

"No," Sam shouted. "Let me go."

He jerked as hard as he could, tugging the hand into the

mine for a moment. Then it was too strong and pulled back at him. Sam stared at the figure, trying to see the face. She was taller than Sam, strong for one so slim. Sam could sense that she was using the wild magic of the mines to keep hold of him.

He stumbled forward. He pulled again and he was nearly through the closing door.

Sam made one last effort. His weakened body was helpless against her determination.

"Come on through," she whispered.

He sagged, all strength spent. Her other hand found the seal round his neck. She tugged it. The leather thong grew tight. Sam's head dipped and he began to move towards her.

He was slipping through. And once you step into the Finished World there is no way to step back. The door closes.

Eloise stepped back and brushed beetles from her feet. She shuddered and felt sick as she felt them crawling over her skin. Axestone was alive with them. He was a living statue of black beetles, save for one area alone. The shawl that Eloise had thrown over him was clear of them. She reached out for it and tugged it from him. As soon as it had gone, the beetles swarmed over his face and head.

Eloise turned and retched, grabbing her stomach. She shuddered again, twirled the shawl into a rope and snapped it at the twine. It cut through and the connection between Axestone and the Castle was broken. Axestone fell to the ground. Eloise opened out the shawl and spread it over him. The beetles screamed and scurried out, some of them digging into the earth, others running away, others popping and dying. She swept it over him and he was clear of them. His face and hands and skin were cut and bitten. His eyes were filled with blood and he could not see the takkabakks scrambling towards them, the wolves running away and turning and yapping and snapping at them, trying to protect Axestone. ||

December stepped forward

and took Sam's arm. She looked through the gap to the Finished World.

"No," she said. "Not this time. Not Sam. Not now."

The grey figure shimmered with hatred and fury.

"Go," said December.

"I'll kill you."

The voice was not a voice. It was in December's head. Yet the threat was clear and real.

"No," said December. "You won't."

She felt her hand grow hot. She saw the half of Sam that was though the door burst into flames.

The grey figure laughed and pulled again.

"I know you," she said.

December looked hard. Shook her head.

"No," she said. "No you don't."

December raised her other arm, made a circle with it in the air. The flames died in an instant. She pointed. The grey figure froze. Froze and stopped. All strength gone. White crystals of frost formed on her lips, her eyes.

December pulled and Sam fell back into the mine and sprawled on the floor next to the body of Bearrock.

The door closed.

The roffles turned and walked away, taking Tremmort with them. Bearrock's son rubbed his eyes and shook his head as they made their way back to the surface. Whatever he had seen was already slipping from his memory.

December leaned over Sam. His eyes were closed. He trembled more than before. He lay curled up, his knees against his chest, his mouth half-open.

"Enough," said December. "You have done enough. More than you should."

Sam stopped shaking.

She put her hand to his head and rested it there.

"Wake up," she said.

Sam's eyes began to open. December stepped back into the shadows, waited till Sam stood up, looked around him, put his fingers to the point where the opening had been, dropped his hand to his side and shuffled towards the mine entrance. Then she darted away ahead of him.

Sam emerged into the starlight and found his direction in the sky. He followed the music, stumbling on the uneven ground in the darkness. December watched him, hidden. She made no move to help him, to show him the path, letting him stumble.

The music was slow, sad, with a strange, rhythmic thumping

underneath that Sam could not understand. As the road turned, the glow of torches revealed a scene that looked to Sam more like a picture from a book than real life. In the starlight there was no colour, save for the pools of light around the torches, and there the colours were deep, sombre. The black and white groups of people were dancing, and the thumping sound was the noise of clogs on boards. They moved slowly, their legs seeming to make no effort as one step blended into the next. The fiddles and the drum sang of loss and loneliness, and the dancers made no contact with each other, like blind beetles.

Children crowded round tables set with food. The men and women sat talking and eating on the ground, or stood in small knots of friendship, with mugs of beer and cider, beakers of wine.

Sam walked through them, ignored, yet not unseen. He knew they were choosing not to recognize him.

No one stopped him taking a chunk of bread and a slice of warm chicken. He folded the bread around the meat and raised it to his mouth.

He could not chew it, could not swallow. His mouth was still too dry, his tongue too big from the days without water, the lack of food. He spat it into his hand and didn't know what to do with it.

There was water in rough clay jugs. He didn't bother with a beaker. He sat in half-darkness, at the edge of torchlight, sipping slowly, watching.

Roffles were roffles, not men. But everyone spoke of the

miners as men. They did not seem like that to Sam. They had a likeness about them that meant that now he had seen them he would be able to pick one out in a crowd. Short, thick-set, with strong, wide shoulders, black, springy hair, they were fitted to life in low tunnels with picks in their big hands.

Watching them talk and eat and drink and dance, Sam felt his fear of them fade. They seemed kind to one another, gentle even. But they did not laugh much, seeming grim or serious. The children did not squabble or tease.

The water was making him light-headed. For a moment everything became blurred, then he was high above the crowd, looking down at them. He was a dragon again. Hunger gone, thirst forgotten, he soared above it all, rejoicing in the splendour of air. No longer black and white, in dragon's eyes the scene was rich in colour. The dance now was a pattern of precision and grace. No longer like beetles, the men were soldiers, princes, with movements of strong, elegant beauty. And the dancers were all men. The women watched and admired.

He saw a small procession returning from the mines, Greenrose, Tremmort, the girl, Goldengrove, the four roffles. He saw December and, seeing her, faltered in his flight, dipped down, unsteady, confused. Regaining his wings, he lifted and steadied. He could see himself, the jug on the ground beside him, the bread and meat in his hand, uneaten. He looked defeated.

Thinking of himself sent him back into himself and he looked around, the images becoming sharp and blurred, fading to black then reappearing with bright clarity, dream-like detail.

The music began to change, to speed up, the notes slid from sorrow to settled. Sam tried to stand, faltered, slid back down to the ground, tried and failed to raise the jug to his lips. And he was up in the air again, looking down.

The small procession had reached the crowd. The music soared; swift strings on the fiddle made a jig. The clogs clashed on the boards with new energy. Sam felt the music take him and he darted through the air in time to its beat. Women joined the men, took their hands and together they danced the night clear of sadness.

December moved towards Greenrose, leaned her head to the other's, whispered and drew back.

They were talking about him. He could hear them.

"I must have him," said December.

Greenrose shook her head again.

"He's worn out," she said. "And he was here for my husband while you were missing. He can stay with us."

"With me," said December.

Tremmort spoke to his mother, too quietly for Sam. But it was clear what he meant. He looked at December. "Take him," he said. "There's no room for him with us."

Sam smiled. It did not matter to him what they decided. He was not staying at the mines. Whatever happened, he would get away from there as soon as he had eaten and slept.

The dancing was changing again. The jigs were giving way

to other tunes, slow, solemn, joyful melodies, like sun on water in spring, like the upward ripple of leaves on a great tree before warm rain. The men and women wove intricate patterns of steps, always returning to the place where they began.

Sam flew higher, letting the music rise to him, watching the undulations of the figures below, like patterns in rich brocade.

If only he could be a dragon for ever.

Greenrose danced with Tremmort. The boy was surprisingly strong in his movements and graceful in his steps. Something of the sorrow of his father's death left him and Sam could see a new certainty wrap itself around the boy like a cloak.

The night was nearly spent. Parents picked up children and carried them, half-asleep, their heads resting on strong shoulders, through the dark town, home to a bed. Sam tried to remember if anyone had ever carried him like that. He was sure they had not. His had been a walking life.

Greenrose stooped to pick up Goldengrove, but the girl refused, taking her mother's hand and walking by her side.

Would they go back to work tomorrow, these sturdy miners, after a night of dancing? Or did a death bring a holiday? Sam knew nothing of the rhythms of life and work. Flaxfield never took time off.

December had not danced. Nor had she spoken to anyone save the family of Bearrock. Now she was making her way towards his sleeping figure. Greenrose saw her and crossed in that direction, too.

Another confrontation. Another argument about where

he would sleep that night. Well, he would settle it himself. Go back, wake up and go with Greenrose. Tremmort would have to accept it. One night should be enough. Two at most. He could repay them with a little magic to help them in these first days of loss.

They stood over him now. He must hurry to wake. He altered his wings to swoop, but they wouldn't obey his mind. Instead of lowering, he rose. Instead of finding himself he lost the sense of who he was, down there. Ears sharp with dragon sense, he listened.

Greenrose reached down and shook his shoulder. She turned to look up at December. Sam could see the panic in her face.

"Please," she said.

December stooped down, put her palm on his forehead.

The women looked at each other.

"He'll come to me," said December.

"He helped us," said Greenrose. "We should take him now."

"No," said December. "You know that wouldn't be right."

She beckoned to the roffles, who approached.

"What is it?" asked the little girl.

"He's dead," said Tremmort.

Sam screamed down at them. "No! I'm here. I'm coming back."

Their heads jerked up.

"What was that?" said Tremmort.

"Thunder," said December. "There'll be a storm before

morning. See the clouds." She draped Sam's cloak over him, laid his ash staff across his chest, folding his cold fingers round it to keep it steady.

Dense grey clouds rolled overhead, churning and changing.

"No!" shouted Sam. He tried to dive, but his wings flicked and held him up. "No!"

December whispered to the roffles. They laid Sam on their planks and lifted him to their shoulders.

Greenrose leaned over and kissed his cheek.

The rain started, slow, fat drops at first, then a sheet of water that drenched the small body as it was carried to December's house. ||

Leaving the castle

behind him, Starback flew towards the mines.

He just needed to be with Sam again. He was in danger. Starback knew he was.

Flaxfield had told him to take care of Sam, but it hadn't seemed to matter while the old wizard was around. Nothing bad ever happened to Sam, and there was nothing for Starback to do. In fact, it was more as though Sam looked after him.

The long days in the sun, when the two of them swam together in the stream. The short days of frost, when they broke the icicles off the eaves of the old house and Sam sucked them till his mouth was numb and he couldn't feel his tongue or his lips. The times when Flaxfield sent them away to gather herbs and roots, and Sam would use magic to make them laugh, even though he was strictly forbidden to. Trying to tell a boy not to use magic is like giving him a ball to carry all afternoon and never kick it or throw it in the air. Sam played with magic like other boys play with catapults and bits of string and sticks, making bows and arrows, throwing stones into water, climbing trees and stealing apples. Magic was his nature.

Even then, he was careful never to use it to make a job easier or to get himself something he wanted. It was all for joy.

By the time he was ten, Sam could make it rain on a single tree when all around there was a summer breeze in bright sun. He could walk through a storm and not get wet. He could swim among fish and not frighten them. He could catch a dragonfly in his hand and not hurt it. Magic spilled out of Sam like chestnuts spill from the branches in autumn, scattering all around, sweet and shining.

Sometimes, Starback thought he had never really known what it was to be happy until he had come to be with Sam.

And now Sam had gone.

Starback had seen something in those moments when he was being dragged down into the castle. He had seen through Sam's eyes. He had felt Sam's dry mouth, his desperate hunger, the tearing at his throat as he tried to eat. The fear of someone. Starback felt light-headed, dizzy. He saw a face. A woman. With a dark shawl covering her ugliness, hiding her lips, her cheeks. Only her bright eyes looking straight at him. Looking with recognition.

This woman wanted to get hold of Sam.

Starback's wings sliced through the night, hurling him forward, cutting through the miles. He would reach the mines soon. It had always been the mines for Sam. He knew that.

Sam could not escape them. They had been drawing him ever since the first day he had arrived at Flaxfield's house. Now he was there. Starback knew he was.

His flight had taken him very high. Now he plunged down, angled from the sky, rushing towards Sam.

His dragon eyes saw the dancing, the torches. The roffles with their heads bowed low. His eyes saw the people leaving the scene and making their tired way back to small houses, the narrow town.

He flew faster than he had even known he could, dropping like hail from the sky.

He saw the woman's face.

"No!" he shouted. "Not you!"

He was close now.

He saw another woman, a boy, a girl.

"No," roared Starback.

He saw the small body laid out.

He was close enough to hear clearly.

"He's dead," said the boy.

Starback screamed down at them. "No! I'm here. I'm coming back."

Their heads jerked up.

"What was that?" said the boy.

"Thunder," said the face. "There'll be a storm before morning. See the clouds." She draped Sam's cloak over him, laid his ash staff across his chest, folding his cold fingers round it to keep it steady.

Dense grey clouds rolled over their heads, churning and changing.

"No!" shouted Starback. He tried to dive, but his wings flicked and held him up. "No!"

The face whispered to the roffles. They laid Sam on their planks and lifted him to their shoulders.

The other woman leaned over and kissed his cheek.

The rain started, slow, fat drops at first, then a cloak of water that drenched the small body as it was carried to the face's house.

Starback wheeled round, lifted high and heavenwards. Flew straight into the castle of clouds and sped through, his face wet with rain, travelling far and fast. Away.

Axestone was badly wounded by the beetles. They had gouged him and left him weak. Eloise faced the advancing takkabakks alone. The wolves darted and snapped. Jaws seized black crooked legs and snapped them off. Crippled takkabakks flipped on their shell cases, legs waving in the air. The shells were shiny and hard, yet fragile. They cracked open under a fierce bite, but the insides were bitter and rank. Each time a wolf smashed its teeth through it tasted the slimy, soft inside and turned and vomited and slunk away.

Eloise wrapped her shawl around her left arm and prepared herself to drive off the takkabakks. She stepped over Axestone, putting herself between him and the grotesquely huge beetles that swarmed across the grass towards her.

She stepped aside to let a wolf pass and she stumbled back on Axestone. She tried to regain her balance. A takkabakk leaped at her and knocked her flat. The underside of its body was rough and furrowed, and it stank. It reared up, drew back a sharp leg and jabbed, straight at her heart. She raised her shawl-covered arm, the takkabakk stabbed, and tottered sideways as a wolf hurled itself onto it, tipping it over.

The sharp leg missed its target and jabbed into her arm, breaking off as the takkabakk rolled away. Eloise screamed in pain, turned, and her hand found Axestone's staff. She hauled herself half-upright leaning on it, then swung it round, slicing through more takkabakks. The staff glowed hot. She swung again. Standing, she brandished it. Dead wolves lay near to the castle. Three more dead lay near to her; two limped away, licking wounds; four more circled her, snarling at the remaining takkabakks.

Eloise panted with effort and pain as she swung the staff again. The takkabakks scratched their way back to the castle.

"Axestone?"

Eloise leaned over the wizard.

"Axestone? Can you hear me?"

He sat up, put his hand to his neck, leaned forward and vomited noisily on the grass. He spat, wiped his mouth with the back of his hand and sighed.

"Come on."

She helped him to his feet, giving him his staff to lean on.

"We need to get out of sight," she said. "Into the forest."

He let her lead him. Just before they plunged under the tree cover he whistled. The largest wolf bounded up to him.

"Go on," he said. "See if you can find Sam. Do what you can."

The wolf ran off and they pushed through the undergrowth and into the trees. ||

When Tremmort came in

he found December sitting in her chair in front of the window, looking out at the rain. She nodded a greeting, did not smile. Tremmort laid a basket on the table, put his hands in his pockets, took them out again and didn't know where to put them next.

"Are you going to sit down?" asked December.

"No."

"Then stand," she said. "Or go."

Tremmort stood, put his hands back into his pockets, took them out again and started to lift things from the basket.

"There's bread," he said, "and some damson jam. Mum says the jam needs another week or two before it's worth eating. Eggs, and some cold beef."

"Take the beef back," said December. "Thank you for the rest. Tell your mother it's welcome."

Tremmort put the beef back into the basket.

"Don't you eat meat?" he asked.

"Yes."

"Shall I leave it, then?"

"No."

Greenrose's family needed food as much as December did, and beef was expensive. Greenrose baked her own bread, kept hens for the eggs, picked the damsons herself from trees on common land. But beef always cost money.

Tremmort finally looked at the bed in the corner of the room. He looked away again, quickly.

"Is he dead or not?" he asked.

"Your mother always takes the stones out of the damsons," said December. "Not everyone bothers, or they miss some. It's good jam."

"What happened to him?" asked Tremmort.

"He came a hard way to the mines," she said. "Are you going to sit down."

"All right."

"Then take off your cloak first."

Tremmort hung the dripping cloak on a peg on the front door. The drops splashed onto the slate floor.

"When do you start in the mines?" she asked.

Her voice was soft, hard to hear against the driving rain outside, and the tapping of an ash tree against the eaves.

"Is he dead or not?" asked Tremmort. "He looks dead."

December smiled. "And how many dead have you seen?" she asked.

"My father." Tremmort said it just a little too loudly in his effort to sound unconcerned. "And others, carried from the mines."

"Does he look as your father did?"

"No."

"We shall need a fire, soon," said December. "The summer is gone."

The house was chilly. The drumming of the rain on the window made it seem cooler than it was.

December's house was just the same as Tremmort's in size and shape and age. They had been built at the same time. Rows of them, all alike. In other ways it was quite different. For some reason, Tremmort felt that an ugly person should live in an ugly house. December's house was beautiful. The miners' houses were plain, crowded with furniture to sleep and feed and sit a family. A picture on the wall, a colourful rug, a clay vase with some flowers, were all that most of them managed in the way of making the house look special.

December lived alone. All the space was hers, so the room seemed bigger, with more air. There were books and pictures she had painted herself, small, like jewels, bright as though the light shone from inside them. One wall was completely covered with a tapestry, so that it was as though there was no wall there and the room opened out to a meadow. It was landscape the like of which Tremmort had never seen. Not the flat, moor-bound country of the mines, but a sweeping green land, with gentle hills and a stream.

"Did you make that?" he asked.

"I don't have that skill," said December. "Only a really great weaver could do that."

"It's not like a real place," he said.

"Not everywhere is like the mines."

Tremmort stood up and went over to the tapestry. He wished he could step through the wall into the landscape.

"What are these trees?" he asked.

"Pomegranates."

The fruit hung ripe on the branches, pulling them down.

"Are they good to eat?"

"Sweet. Full of juice."

"And this?"

"A memmont."

"I've heard of them. Never seen a picture before."

"When are you going to the mines?" she asked again.

"I'm twelve in the spring. That's when I'm supposed to start."

"But?"

"But we need the money now, so I should start straight away."

"But?" asked December again.

"But." He put his hand towards the tapestry. Light and heat from it seemed to warm his hand and make it brighter in the darkling room. "But I don't want to go down there. I don't want to live underground."

"It is dangerous," December agreed.

He glared at her.

"I'm not frightened."

"No."

"I took my father down there. I know what it's like. I could work there. I just don't want to."

"What will you do?" she asked.

He pointed to the lower left corner of the tapestry.

"What is this?"

It was a house, a group of houses, and an inn with a sign, with trees framing the scene. By the inn a dragon, a Blue and Green.

"Is it a real place?" he asked.

"Yes."

"Have you been there?"

"Why do you ask?"

"How do you know it's a real place?"

"Why does it have to be?" she said.

"I'll go there," he said. "How do I get there?"

"You have to find the way yourself," said December.

Tremmort turned and looked her full in the face for the first time.

"You never help," he said. "I don't know what you live here for. You never really help people when they need it."

December waited for him to stop.

"Look at him," said Tremmort. "What have you done for him, eh? If he's dead, finish him and bury him. If he's alive, make him get up. Get rid of him. He should never have come here."

December met his eyes with her own, returning comfort in exchange for his challenge. "He didn't kill your father," she said.

Tremmort strode across the room, grabbed his wet cloak and flung open the door.

"What use are you?" he shouted, slamming it behind him.

December waited for the silence to gather, then she sat beside Sam and stroked his forehead.

"What use am I?" she asked. "Do you think it's time, Sam? Are you ready?" ||

It was six weeks

since the roffles had hoisted Sam's body onto their shoulders and carried him to December's house. He lay, motionless, white and cold on the bed in the corner of her room.

Every day December washed his face and hands in a potion she made fresh each morning. Every day she sat beside him and sang, songs of the mines, the dark tunnels and deep diggings. Songs of the sky, and the stories the stars told when no one was listening. Songs of the hearth, the fire glowing behind the iron bars, the embers cooling as the night shrugged off the dark and turned its face to morning. Songs of the woods, the shady corners where the rare herbs grew, the broad oaks and the silver birch, the rivers of bluebells and the green seas of ferns. Songs of books and baking bread. Songs of fishing for trout and swimming for joy. Songs of sorrow and loss. Songs of old men, long in years; songs of women, wide in wisdom.

She never left the house once. Food arrived at her door,

and gifts of flowers. People asked after Sam, and she said, "Time will tell."

Nothing happened.

Sam did not move. He made no sound. December lowered her face to Sam's. There was the gentlest suggestion of breath. She touched her hand against his chest. It was almost as though it rose and fell in breathing, but not quite.

Greenrose came often, and sat with December. She took Sam's hand in hers and held it, though it felt too cool, too still for her. Like Bearrock's hand when they carried him in from the mine.

"Why?" she asked.

"He should not have done the Finishing," said December.

"He did it well."

"I know. He would. He was taught well."

"Then why?"

"Finishing is not for apprentices. He has overstepped himself."

"You weren't here. Someone had to do it," said Greenrose.

"Hush. It isn't your fault."

Autumn bled away as Sam lay silent. The high, white, fat clouds that floated in the blue turned brown and stretched themselves thin against the grey sky. Nights grew bold and shouldered day away.

Sam saw none of this.

"Did he do wrong?" asked Greenrose.

"No."

"Then why did the magic turn against him?"

"Sometimes doing right hurts more than doing wrong."

"Can you make him better?"

"I don't know."

Greenrose let go of Sam's hand and took December's. The palm was hard and uneven, like her face. The skin was stretched and smooth in places, knotted in others. December could feel Greenrose's shock as she touched her. No one ever touched December. She knew that the woman had not expected the strange feel of her hand, knew she was wondering how her face felt. Knew she was wondering if the rest of her body was the same.

"What use am I?" December said. "Do you think it's time, Sam? Are you ready?"

December took Sam's hands, looked into the tapestry and searched for help.

The memmont was not right. There was a kestrel, high up, just to the left of the centre of the weave. December held her breath. Not the memmont. But the kestrel? It felt right. It felt as though it was right for Sam. But if it was wrong, then Sam would die.

This was the highest magic. This was more magic than even December had ever worked. It was this fear, the fear of getting it wrong, that had kept her from trying. That had kept Sam, lying between life and death in her little house. But he was slipping away. Tremmort's anger was right. She was hesitating too long. Perhaps she had already left it too late?

"Where are you?" she asked the tapestry. "Where are you?"

Her eyes caught a shape she had not seen before. Emerging from a forest, still half-hidden by trees, obscured by shade, was a wolf.

"Where have *you* been?" she asked. "Where have you come from?"

She thought she knew every detail of the picture, yet she had not noticed this grey figure bounding forward. The colours were soft, the wolf was in shadow, yet, even so, not to have seen it before.

"A wolf, then?" she said.

December put her hands on Sam's face and she breathed deeply, closing her eyes.

"Is that it? Is it a wolf?"

She began to sing of a wolf.

The rain spattered against the window. The wind whistled down the chimney. The ash tree tapped against the eaves.

December stopped.

The wind clenched and jabbed hard against the house. A rush of soot fell from the chimney, scattering wet and black on the tiles, rising up in grey dust.

"What is it?" asked December. "Tell me."

She moved to the hearth, dragged her finger through the soot and scooped some into her hand.

"Tell me."

The soot struggled in her hand. It curled round on itself

and lifted up, forming a shape, clumsy and crude, like a cloud picture, but clear enough.

December laughed.

"A dragon. It would be."

She cleaned her hands, checked the tapestry. There was a dragon, a Blue and Green, in front of a small group of houses, and an inn, with trees framing the picture.

December took Sam's hand again and began to sing. She sang of dragons.

As she sang her face grew tense. Her hand shook. She hesitated, breathed deeply and continued, her voice clear and strong, beautiful, as she was not. Another voice, and another joined hers. From outside the house, a howling. December heard, and ignored. Her eyes went to the tapestry. Not to the scene of houses and the inn, but to the dark fringe of forest. The shadowed wolf. Had she made a mistake? Was it wolves, after all?

Their voices joined with hers. The wolves ranged themselves in front of the house, barking, yelping and howling. ‖

The sudden, sharp stink

made the dragon turn his head and look. The fox slunk past, head drooping, sly and secret. The dragon lay still in the midnight forest, his long flight over. No stars broke through the canopy of thick branches.

He was quiet, as only a dragon can be quiet. The fox did not see or hear or scent him, a lame shadow by a stump.

The dragon needed the shelter of the forest, the company of animals and growing things. He could not be where there were people. Here, beneath the trees, he found something deeper than the darkness. Something in himself.

He slept. And he lay awake, unblinking. Beetles and woodlice, earwigs and mayflies scrambled over him, buzzed past his face, tunnelled beneath him, sheltered in the shade of his scales. He was a log, or an ancient stone, covered with moss. Part of the forest floor.

He enjoyed these ticklings and scratchings. To him, the creatures, with their crooked legs and jointy bodies, were as beautiful as a crinkled leaf or a folded petal.

He remembered other forests, other nights. Sometimes he dreamed, and sometimes he thought he dreamed but he was awake. Sometimes he dreamed he was not a dragon at all, but a boy. And sometimes, when he was awake and not dreaming, he thought he was a wizard.

But always, he was tired. Too tired to move. Too tired to eat or drink.

The fox stopped and sniffed the dragon's foot. Two fox eyes met two dragon eyes.

Then, he was gone, curling into the night forest.

A moth, with a fat, black body and grey powdery wings, flew in through the slit window, danced in the lamplight, diving and swooping near to the flame, then settled on the desk, spread its wings and came to rest.

Ash finished writing the sentence she had started, wiped the pen nib on a speckled rag, looked at the moth, pushed the blunt end of the pen against her cheek to calm an itch, then leaned back in her chair and waited.

The moth unfolded. Its wings flipped over and over till they opened out into a single sheet of notepaper. The black body trickled away into lines of writing.

Ash picked up the note, stood up and walked to the window. The castle was high and she was in the tallest turret. From the slit she could see for miles, across the meadow to the forest and over the tops of the trees into the distance.

She read the note. Read it again, though she did not need to. Placing the paper on her palm she turned it back into a moth. The lamp needed trimming and smoked a little. She lifted the glass chimney, the heat not seeming to affect her, then held the moth over the flame, watching its wings scorch, then flame for a moment before turning to ash. The fat, black body bubbled, dripped and dissolved. She wiped her fingers on the ink rag. Her lips curled in distaste.

"So late. Stupid," she whispered. "You've already let him slip away."

Sitting back down at the desk she began to write her reply.

Eloise and Axestone walked all day, all night, all day again, and slept a little when evening fell, then walked again, through the darkness.

He refused her arm. His face and hands oozed pus. Every step he took inflamed the wounds from the beetles more. His clothes rubbed against the sores. He shook off all her offers of help, offers to rest more.

"We must make progress," he insisted. "And you are wounded, too."

Eloise shook her head.

"It does not hinder me in walking," she said.

Axestone stared at her, challenging the lie. Eloise had covered her arm with her shawl, hoping to hide the wound. Axestone could see the bulge, the mark where the takkabakk's claw still stuck out from her flesh.

They stayed under the cover of the forest, though it made travelling slower. They spoke little. When they did it was always of the same thing.

"Did Flaxfield ever tell you anything of this?" asked Axestone.

"He said it would come," she answered.

The grass and ferns were night-wet and their shoes squelched as they walked.

"Did you ever know where you came from?" asked Eloise.

"No. Did you."

"No."

"It's as it should be," said Axestone. "Wizards should have no country."

"Did he tell you?" she asked.

"He said it would come."

"Did he say when, or how or who?"

Axestone paused, leaned against a birch trunk then drew back in pain.

"He told me there was a change in the magic," he said. "He told me that there were wizards who were growing greedy."

Eloise drew her shawl over her head. The night was cool. It left her arm exposed. The claw dangled from the flesh. The skin around it was raised and red, filled with poison.

"He said," Axestone continued, "that he had seen it beginning."

"He told me that," said Eloise. "He said he had seen what happened when a wizard learned to escape the magic when it turned against you."

"That was when the college went wrong," said Axestone.

"Do you remember." Eloise smiled.

They walked on, enjoying their stories. The memories soothed their wounds.

"Those village magicians who trained at the college did a lot of good," said Axestone. "They cured warts and they helped to make windows safe against the rain. I once saw one get a herd of cows out of a mire after a rain storm by giving the beasts wings and flying them out. You should have seen the looks on the animals' faces as they fluttered up from the mud."

They laughed, forgetting the castle and the creatures who had scuttled out of the gates.

"He took all the wings off straight away, but he missed one cow, which had flown away over the barn. That one flew about for a week."

"Hard to milk a flying cow," said Eloise.

"It wasn't just that. It was the cow pats, dropping down from the sky. No one was safe."

"They were good people, the college ones," said Eloise. "Not real wizards, but every village needed one.

"Not any more. Now they charge for every trick they work. They grow rich while the villagers pay."

"And they don't mind what they take the money for," said Eloise.

Axestone flicked his staff and withered a clump of ferns.

"Bloodsuckers," he said.

He turned back and looked at the waste he had made. He sighed. Bracing his shoulders to the task, he plunged his staff into the withered plants. Eloise watched him sadly. He mumbled, stirred the staff round and the ferns uncurled back into green fringed life.

Axestone nodded.

"That's the trouble," he said. "Let's sit down."

He slumped to the ground, lying flat. Eloise spread her shawl and sat next to him.

"Always more work to put a wrong right," she said. "Look at us now."

They stared at each other. Axestone's face was thin, drawn with pain. Eloise was grey. The poison was travelling through her.

A sudden, sharp stink caught their noses.

"It's only a fox," said Eloise.

The fox lifted his black nose from the dragon's foot, curled into the forest and was gone.

"Rest," said Eloise. "We can make up for lost time tomorrow."

"No." Axestone hauled himself up with the aid of his staff. "We must go on."

The forest swallowed them. The dragon scarcely bothered to watch them disappear. ||

Frastfil was in the middle of a question

when Smedge burst into flames and fell over.

"Where is he?" Frastfil demanded. Smedge thought the Professor was even more ridiculous when he was angry than when he tried to be pleasant. "If you don't find Cartouche, what will...?"

Quite what Frastfil would do stayed a mystery to Smedge. The boy was on fire. Flames flowed over him. His hair was a fiery torch, his finger ends, candles. He rolled over and over in his frenzy to put the flames out. Nothing made any difference. He blazed like a beacon. Frastfil screamed for help, the swift onslaught of fire taking him by surprise and driving all thoughts of magic from his mind.

Smedge shouted a dousing spell. The flames hesitated, shrank back, then flared up, more powerful than ever. The words jerked Frastfil into action. He dragged a curtain from the window, wrapped it round Smedge and shouted a spell of his own to stop the flames.

Duddle's face appeared in the doorway.

"What's...?" he started to say, then, seeing the flames, pulled back.

"Come and help," shouted Frastfil.

Duddle sidled in, keeping close to the wall, his hand against his face to shield it from the fire.

Smedge shrieked in pain, then, as though it had never been, the fire disappeared. He hugged his arms to himself, rocking back and forth, moaning.

Frastfil knelt beside him. The boy was completely unhurt. No burning to the skin. His hair was as neat and tidy as ever. His clothes unscorched. The room, too, was unmarked by the fire. Not even a smell of smoke.

He helped Smedge up from the carpet, moved him to an armchair.

"Does it hurt?"

He shook his head.

"Not now. Not any more."

His hand was clenched into a fist. He opened it. He was clutching a fat, white moth. The moth fluttered its wings, stopped, then unfolded into a note.

I know you've lost him already. Find him. Follow him. Or it will be worse next time.

"What's this about?" asked Frastfil.

✠

The wolves fell silent.

The swell of a soft song stood alone in the small room. December searched Sam's face for a response. The rain had eased. The heavy drops from the roof splattered in slow procession.

Sam's lips straightened. The curve of his mouth tensed. He grimaced.

December's song faltered. A solitary wolf yapped. She began again, stronger. Singing of a dragon's flight. She stroked Sam's forehead. Some warmth there, perhaps?

She lifted a potion to his lips. He made no response. Dipping her fingers in the cup, she put them to his lips, parting them gently. A few drops made their way to his mouth.

A wolf bumped against the door, nosing the wood. Claws scratched.

December rubbed Sam's hands between her own. He returned a feeble grip. She dabbed more moisture through his lips. A third time, his tongue reached out for it and she lifted the cup again. He swallowed a little, turned his head and the potion ran down his cheek. He coughed, gasped, then lay still.

"No!" said December. "No. Don't go now."

Her face was white. Her lips were pale as parchment. Her whole body shook. She tried to sing again, but had no voice for it. The notes would not hold true.

The wolves all set up a terrible howling. A heavy body hurled itself against the door, shaking it.

"Stay with me, Sam," she whispered. "Stay here."

Sam's breathing had stopped. His fingers were cold now, his lips blue.

December took the cup and filled her mouth with the potion. Leaning her face over Sam's she parted his lips and sprayed it between them, into his mouth. She shook him. He gulped. For a moment he stayed without motion, then coughed, gasped and panted deep breaths in and out.

December staggered back, sat in front of the empty grate and watched. ||

The ghost of the flames

still burned into Smedge's body. The pain had gone, but the memory remained. He walked the corridors of the college when everyone else was in bed. Almost everyone. He paced up and down, his shoes light on the polished wood, the smooth stone. Tamrin watched him. She had lived for years like a wild animal in the long passages of the grey building. She needed no magic to conceal her, no spells to hide her. She knew every dark corner, every long curtain, every obscure niche. And she was quiet. Mice did not hear her pass.

She watched him tumble ideas round and round in his head. He weighed them, sorted them, arranged them, tested them. His was a head full of plans. A head full of possibilities.

Again and again, though his feet took him all through the college, he returned to the same spot, to a high window that looked over the quadrangle. Again and again he seemed ready to do something, only to draw back and walk again through the dark passageways.

He came again to the window. Looked through the small panes between the lead lines. He pressed his hands against the glass. The stars looked back.

He said nothing. But Tamrin, who was skilled at watching people, saw the resolution made in the way he altered his posture. Something in him was decided.

She followed him down the stairs, through the wide door, into the night air of the quadrangle.

He kept to the colonnaded sides, not crossing the grass in the open, hugging the shadows. Tamrin was his shadow, though there was no light.

Smelling pipe smoke, she dropped back, just in time. Smedge had walked past the roffle, sitting in a niche in the cloister wall. Tamrin nearly walked past him, too, revealing herself as a spy.

"Young sir," said the roffle. "A cold night for a walk."

Smedge arranged a smile on his face.

"Megatorine, isn't it?"

"The very same."

The roffle pulled on his pipe and the tobacco glowed.

"Wasn't it you who brought that new boy here?"

"Mister Cartouche? It was. Why? Has he made a cake with frogs?"

"No."

"No. Then has he sent the cooks to the seaside for the day and cooked up a pot of porridge?"

"Why would he do that?"

"He's a boy, that one is."

"Well, he hasn't done either of those things."

"No, he hasn't. And shall I tell you why?"

Smedge was impatient to get away, but he waited.

"Why?"

"Because he's run away, that's why."

Tamrin hated this roffle. Smedge seemed to show a strange interest.

"How do you know that?" he asked.

"My brother told me."

Smedge leaned against the wall and watched the roffle do those things that people do with pipes — fiddle with the stem, examine the tobacco, puff two or three times sharply, then draw in slowly. Megatorine was in no hurry to add anything, so Smedge did.

"I've been worried about him," said the boy.

"Oh, yes."

Tamrin screwed up her eyes in hatred.

"He seemed to need some help, and we would have given it to him."

"Yes," said the roffle. "Help and a thick ear. That's what all boys need. Still, he's gone now."

"I thought," said Smedge, as though it was just a casual thing, "that I ought to go and find him. See if I can help him. Bring him back here, if he'd like that."

"There'll be no need for that," said the roffle.

Tamrin knew Smedge's moods and she could see that it

was taking him all his time not to cast a painful spell on the roffle. And there was something about Megatorine's attitude that told her he knew that as well and he didn't care. He seemed to be teasing the boy.

"No need?" asked Smedge.

"No help. You can't help a cat with a bottle of stones, can you? Or you can't help a cow with a bag full of burst balloons."

Tamrin had never had a conversation with a roffle before and she was puzzled at first, then she realized it was Megatorine's way of frustrating Smedge, to get him to speak more directly.

"He's not a cat or a cow," said the boy.

"No," said the roffle. And then he produced a bit of news, with smile and flourish, like a conjurer finding a coin behind your ear. "No, he's not anything. He's dead."

The air was soft. The water in the fountain in the centre of the quadrangle twitched and tumbled with the noise of a stream over pebbles. Tamrin blinked. She saw Smedge control the smile that had threatened to move his lips. She saw the roffle's keen eyes examine the boy. She felt the understanding that they reached at that moment. They were both pleased that Sam was dead, but neither of them would say it.

"That's terrible," said Smedge. He kept the excitement from his voice by speaking slowly and in a low tone. "How did it happen?"

"Do you mean am I sure?"

Smedge nodded.

"My brother was there. He saw the other roffles carry him away on the mine trusses. He heard them say it. He saw the boy, cold, dead."

"Why?"

The roffle tapped his pipe against the wall, pushed his stubby fingers into the bowl, put it into his mouth without trying to light it.

"He was starved to death, almost, then he did a Finishing for a miner."

"He can't do that. Not a Finishing."

"He did."

Tamrin pressed her cheek against the stone, felt it grow wet, closed her eyes.

Megatorine continued, "Finished himself at the same time. Just what you'd expect."

"I'm so sorry," said Smedge.

Tamrin's eyes flicked open. She wanted to hurt him. A lot. She wanted to slam him against the wall until his head cracked.

"So you won't need to be leaving the college tonight, after all," said the roffle.

"Ah, no. Well, perhaps. I may just go out anyway."

"Do you want to find a fly with a paper tail, then?"

"No."

"Or is there a heap of ribbons with a badger's baby underneath that you need to stroke?"

Smedge moved away from Megatorine.

"I think I'd like to be by myself," he said. "Such sad news."

Tamrin watched him slip unobserved through the gate. She saw the roffle hitch his barrel-shaped bag onto his back and slip after him.

Stepping out of the shadows and into the quadrangle, she lifted her eyes up and interrogated the stars. She asked them for an answer and they replied, clearly. Usually they gave an answer which was not an answer, a riddle more than a reply. This time Tamrin read them like a name on a book. *Look inside yourself,* they said. ‖

The garden was ragged

under the grey sky.

"Be yourself," said Flaxfold. "It's the easiest way."

Caleb smiled.

"If I could get the hang of that it would be all right," he said.

"You're impatient," she said. "That's the trouble."

"I want to be the best. Is that so wrong?"

"No, that's a good thing. But the trouble is, you never will be."

Caleb's smile disappeared. He bent to pick up his bag and sling it over his shoulder.

"Don't go like that," said Flaxfold. "Let us say goodbye as friends."

Above their heads, the ash tree tapped against the window of Flaxfield's study. Its branches were almost bare now, stripped by the wind.

"Where will you go?" she asked.

"Small roads," he said. "Paths that look old and not much used. I'll see what places they lead me to."

Flaxfold put her hands into the deep pocket at the front of her apron.

"And what are you looking for?"

"Sam."

"I was afraid of that."

"I don't want to hurt him."

"Then why look?"

Caleb walked away, slowly, more because he needed to move than because he was going anywhere yet.

"I can feel that there's something," he said. "When I'm not thinking about anything, or when I'm half-asleep, it's as though there's another person there with me, watching me. Do you understand?"

Flaxfold walked alongside him. They had left the garden now. Flaxfield's house stood behind them, the road, ahead.

"I know exactly," she said. "But what has that to do with Sam?"

"It started the first time I saw him," said Caleb. "I thought he had been making a fire. I could smell smoke."

"Do you think he caused it?"

"No. Perhaps. But I think he can help me to understand it."

"What sort of person is it?" she asked.

Her grey hair had come undone and a strand of it fell over her face, blowing in the light wind. She brushed it back behind her ear.

"Are you going to stay here?" he asked. "In Flaxfield's house?"

"Why not?"

"It isn't yours."

"Who else should be here?"

"It's easy to say, 'be yourself'," said Caleb. "But Flaxfield stopped all that for me."

"Flaxfield helped people to be wizards," she said. "Is that what you are?"

"It's not exactly a person," said Caleb. "Sometimes it's more like an animal, watching me, sniffing me. Then, other times, I almost hear its voice, talking to me."

"Perhaps Sam went to the mines," said Flaxfold. "You might find him there."

"That's the last place he'll be."

Flaxfold nodded.

"Goodbye, then," said Caleb.

"No need to *be* the best," said Flaxfold. "Just do the best."

Caleb walked off.

Flaxfold went back into the house and to Flaxfield's study. She watched him through the window till the two roads diverged in a yellow wood and he dissolved into the undergrowth. ‖

Greenrose could hardly

see Sam and December. There was no light on in the house. The wolves had howled all night. No one in the town had slept. Doors were bolted. Mothers hugged their children to soothe their dreams. Just before dawn, the howling stopped and the wolves bounded away.

Something grey and swift dodged away from December's door. Greenrose feared a wolf and hesitated. Then, seeing nothing, stepped to the house. She knocked, and when there was no answer, opened the door.

She didn't know which of the two to go to first. Sam was sprawled on the bed.

December was grey. Her face, so damaged already, was twisted and thin, as though sucked in. She half-sat, half-lay in the chair, her body at a painful angle.

December stared back at her. Or through her, as though she was not there.

"Flaxfield."

Greenrose turned to Sam.

He was calling out a name. His hands were searching the air.

"Flaxfield!"

"No you don't," said Greenrose, looking at each in turn. "I'm done with death for this year. Don't you dare die."

Sam was crying now and calling out Flaxfield's name more urgently. Panic was creeping into his voice and he was flicking his head from side to side.

Ugly December sprawled in front of her. Greenrose drew back from her, as she would from a spider, or a toad.

"Flaxfield."

Greenrose turned to Sam.

"You'll have to wait," she said.

She gently straightened December's arms, moved her to the side and made her comfortable.

The woman felt cold and clammy. Sweat stood out on her forehead. Her hands were damp. Her hair clung to her head, showing the bald patches more clearly than ever.

The mines are a hard world. Death walks the underground tunnels. The slow death of disease from breathing the dust. The quick death of a roof fall. The dark, lonely, drawn-out death of suffocation. December had walked into that hard world one day. She asked for food and was given a meal by an old widow, with no children, who scarcely had enough to feed herself.

"That's the way of it," said December as she settled into

her bed, for the woman had given her the spare room for the night. "That's always the way of it. The ones who have least give most." The sheets were frayed and not too clean. The floor was sticky under her feet. The pots the dinner had been cooked in did not look as though they had seen scouring for more than a year. The widow was old. Scrubbing hurt her hands and her eyes had dimmed beyond seeing grime.

People avoided her. Neighbours whispered to the old woman, whose name was Fleur, and told her to send December away. They hated to look at her in the street. The few who used to call at the old woman's house stopped, in case December opened the door.

Fleur didn't care. She couldn't see December's face too well, and she loved having the company, the help, the extra food that December's work in the garden brought.

Near to death when December arrived, Fleur improved with the better food and with the herb drinks that December made, the oils she rubbed into the woman's aching joints. So it was, that when a child fell ill, someone suggested that December could make a potion that could help. The child recovered and a joint of gammon appeared on Fleur's doorstep. A miner, crushed under one of the same roof timbers that the roffles had used to carry Bearrock to his rest, knew he would never walk again, never go back to the mine and earn money to feed his family.

When December appeared at the man's door, his wife swept her away with her hands.

"Don't bring bad luck and your ugly face round here!"

December returned home and waited. Four days later, the woman knocked on the door.

"He says you're to come," she said.

"No."

December closed the door.

The woman rapped hard.

"He thinks you can make him better," she said.

"I can't."

December tried to close the door again. The woman held it open.

"Why not?"

"Because I am not welcome in your house."

She closed the door again.

The woman sat down where she was and wept. December could hear the sobs through the door. She sat, picked up her embroidery and began to stitch. For over an hour the two women sat, almost within arm's reach of each other. The one, silent, sewing, the other, sobbing slowly.

The miner's wife knocked again on the door.

December's face showed no emotion, no question as she held the door open.

"Please."

"No."

"Please. He'll never walk again. You can change that."

"No."

"We can't pay you. You know that. But please come."

"No."

"Why?"

"He wants you to."

"No."

"Why don't you come?"

"Why do you ask?"

"Because there is nothing I can do for him."

The woman sank down to the floor again. She coughed with tears, drawing in her breath with pain.

December closed the door.

That evening, just as the birds were singing their last before roosting, December knocked on the miner's door. The half-light did not help her face. The miner's wife drew back as she saw her. December did not smile, though she noticed. She always noticed.

"How is he?" she asked.

"Please, come in."

"Why?"

The woman did not hesitate, but answered from her heart.

"I want you to."

December stepped inside.

It was a year before the man walked again. He always dragged one foot a little. He always felt some little pain after walking a while, but he walked. He worked again. His family were fed and cared for.

December was not liked, but people came to her first now, for help.

Then, when a bad fall killed seven on one day, December took over the arrangements. She washed and prepared the bodies, made them ready and, when the miners lined up to carry the bodies to rest, she sent them away and told them to come back the next day.

When the next day arrived, Fleur peered through the window and said, "Is it roffles?"

"Yes," said December.

"We haven't seen roffles since I was a girl," said Fleur.

"About time they came back, then."

"Are you going to do the Finishing?"

"Yes," said December.

"I knew it," said Fleur. "I knew you were a wizard. A proper one, not just a village wizard."

That was the day a sort of pride came back to the town. The bodies were carried away by the roffles, in the mining tradition. The band and the dancing came back, and the funeral feast.

"When all this is over," said Fleur, "it will be my turn next."

"No need to think of that," said December.

"I don't mind. Now you're here."

"I'll take care of you," she promised.

Spring came and December took care of Fleur as she had promised. She performed the Finishing, and the roffles carried her, shoulder-high, to the place.

As the band played and the men lifted their feet in the

slow, thumping dance, December said, "There's nothing to keep me here now. I'll be gone by the end of the week." She drank her wine and went home to the empty house she had shared with Fleur.

The next morning, early, when December opened the door to shake out her duster, the street was lined with miners and their families. No one had gone to work. No one had stayed in bed to recover from the dancing and the drink. They had arrived, silently, early, the whole town.

The man whose legs had been crushed stood at the front, his wife holding his hand. It hurt him to stand long, but he had been the first there. The pain showed on his face.

"Please stay," said his wife.

"Why?"

"You belong here now."

A rumble from the crowd approved her words.

"No," said December.

Voices barked back at her.

"Yes!"

"Stay here!"

She raised her hand for silence.

"I'll stay," she said. "For now."

They applauded and the miner's wife stepped forward and put her arms around December's neck, hugging her.

December gasped and drew back, raising her hand as if to strike the woman.

"I'm sorry," said the woman. "I'm so sorry."

December lowered her arm, took the woman's hand in hers.

"No. It's good. Thank you."

She lifted her face and her voice to the crowd.

"Thank you," she said. "Now, it's time for us to go to work."

She closed the door, leaned against it, feeling the knots in the wood on her back.

"I'll stay till it's time," she said. "But I don't belong here."

Greenrose remembered that morning. Remembered the strange embrace and the way December had recoiled from it. Now she recoiled from touching December and she rebuked herself for it.

December's body was limp in her arms. Sam called out, "Flaxfield."

"Come on," she said. "You know how to make people better. I don't. What am I supposed to do now?" ||

Pages from an apprentice's notebook

MEGATOLLY'S QUESTION

PART 1. ARE THE LEAVES THE TREE?

There are many ways to answer this part of the Question.

A) The leaves are not the tree, they are part of the tree.

So, ARE THEY AN ESSENTIAL PART OF THE TREE?

B) Yes, it would not be an oak unless it had oak leaves.

So, DOES IT STOP BEING AN OAK IN THE WINTER WHEN THERE ARE NO LEAVES?

C) No. It is still an oak.

So, THE OAK DOES NOT NEED LEAVES TO BE A TREE? THEY ARE NOT ESSENTIAL.

D) Yes, it would not be an oak if it did not have leaves.

SO, THE LEAVES ARE THE TREE?

Here the clever person will say that the oak is all of the parts of the tree, the trunk, the branches, the twigs, the bark, the leaves, the acorns, all at once.

And here the very clever person will say that they do not need to be there all at once, as long as some of them are there.

Which ones?

Clever people sometimes get a headache at this point. Less clever people go away and try to climb an oak tree or to get inside a hollow one, or to look for roffle holes.

Megatolly's Question also asks about each part of the tree.

Which part of the oak is the true, essential part?

The trunk.

But a trunk alone is not an oak.

Trunk and branches are an oak. But there has to be the possibility of leaves, the possibility of acorns.

Megatolly added a second question to his first, great question.

HOW OLD IS AN OAK?

A) An oak is as old as its trunk.

WHAT ABOUT ITS BRANCHES?

B) There are new branches and old branches.

ARE THEY ALL PART OF THE THING CALLED OAK?

C) Yes.

SO A BRANCH WHICH IS A HUNDRED YEARS OLD IS A TRUE PART OF A SEVEN-HUNDRED-YEAR-OLD OAK?

D) Yes.

SO, IT IS, IN SOME WAY, SEVEN HUNDRED YEARS OLD?

E) Yes.

AND A HUNDRED YEARS OLD?

F) Yes.

BOTH AT THE SAME TIME?

G) Yes.

AND A WEEK-OLD LEAF ON THE SAME HUNDRED-YEAR-OLD BRANCH, ON A SEVEN-HUNDRED-YEAR-OLD OAK IS A TRUE PART OF A SEVEN-HUNDRED-YEAR-OLD OAK?

By now, the clever person will have stopped trying to answer and will just listen.

A week-old leaf, a day-old leaf, is a full part of a seven-hundred-year old tree. It is, in some ways, one day old and seven hundred years old. It knows all that the tree knows. It is the tree. Without the tree it will die. Without new leaves the tree will die. They are not different things. They are the same thing. Old is new. New is old. Leaf and acorn, branch and twig, trunk and bark. And we have not even begun to think about the roots yet, they are all the tree, all oak.

That's how it is with dragons.

And boys.

*

The night is never as quiet

as you think it is going to be. Alone on the turret, Tamrin could hear the sounds of darkness. Only the stars were silent. Everything else creaked in its own way. The walls crumbled infinitesimally. The lichen spread with slow sighs. The air carried memories of song and sobbing, talk and trees.

Tamrin sat, eyes closed, legs straight on the cold stone, arms by her sides, face upturned to the cool night air.

So, when Vengeabil finally appeared in the small doorway, it was after a symphony of approaching sound. Feet on the steps, coat brushing against the wall of the narrow spiral, breathing getting deeper, mumbles of complaint, a tapping of wood.

He sat opposite her and waited.

"He said that Sam's dead."

"Yes."

"How do you know?"

"Not much is said in the college that I don't hear."

Tamrin opened her eyes and saw him, sitting, propped against a staff. She closed them again.

"Is it true?"

"Some roffles are liars. Good liars."

"Is it true?"

Vengeabil tapped

"Smedge has gone."

"I saw him go," she said.

"Did the roffle follow him?"

"Yes."

"Where do you think he's gone?"

"He can't be dead, can he?"

"The nights you've lain awake, looking into the corners of the room, did you know Sam would turn up one day?"

"Yes. Always."

Vengeabil tapped the staff against the roof.

"And now?"

"The stars told me to look inside myself."

"And what do you see?"

"He is not dead."

"Where do you think Smedge has gone?"

Tamrin opened her eyes and glared at him.

"Is that all you can say?"

"What are you going to do?"

"I need to know."

"You already know."

"I need to know."

Vengeabil stood up. He leaned against the staff.

"What shall I do?"

Tamrin seemed smaller, younger. She looked up at the man then dipped her head and tears fell straight from her eyes to her coat, not bothering to run down her cheeks first.

"Where do you think Smedge has gone?" he repeated.

Tamrin could hardly speak.

"That's nothing to do with this," she said.

Vengeabil strained to hear what she was saying.

"It's not about Smedge."

Vengeabil stooped down, put a strong hand on her shoulder.

"Everything is about Smedge," he said. "Where do you think he's gone?"

"I think he's gone to find Sam."

"What are you going to do?"

"I'm going to follow him."

Vengeabil smiled.

"It will be quite a procession," he said. "Smedge, the roffle, then you."

"Tell me he isn't dead," said Tamrin, looking up.

"I can't say that."

Her head drooped again.

He helped her to her feet.

"You'll need this."

Tamrin took the staff. Then tried to hand it back.

"I am not ready for this."

"No. But it isn't yours. Yours hasn't been made yet. Or if it has, I know nothing of it. This is mine. Look after it. It hasn't been used for a long time."

"I can't take it."

"I won't let you go without it."

They made their way silently to the gate. Vengeabil kept them hidden from the porter as he stepped into the town square with Tamrin.

"You understand you have to return as soon as you've finished? Perhaps you should stay here and wait."

"Yes."

"It won't be easy to come back. Not once you've breathed the air away from here."

"Please," she said. "Tell me I'm right. Tell me he isn't dead."

"I'll be watching for you coming back," said Vengeabil. ||

Greenrose had no magic, here,

in December's house. She was helpless, a cat thrown into a river. Confronted with the choice of whether to help Sam or December, she didn't think she was able to help either.

The boy writhed and called out. The woman lay broken and near to death.

Holding December in her arms she said, "Come on. You know how to make people better. I don't. What am I supposed to do now?"

The wolf nosed the door open. Its grey head wet from the rain. Its eyes bright against the dark. It swerved inside, half-crouched, ready to spring.

Greenrose moved to put herself between the wolf and December. Her quick movement alerted the wolf and it snarled, baring its teeth at her. She waited for the others to appear.

"Get out!" she shouted. "Go on. Out."

The wolf lifted its legs carefully, like a dancer, and

advanced. Greenrose searched for something, a knife, a heavy candlestick, a doorstop, anything to use as a weapon.

"Flaxfield."

Sam's voice was growing fainter. The recovery that December had given so much to achieve was pouring away, like the rain running from the eaves. His life was emptying.

The wolf turned its head from Greenrose and moved with deadly grace towards the boy.

Greenrose tried to stand up and grab the wolf. She was a miner's wife. She knew what danger was. She had seen men carried up from the pit, broken and dead. She had seen what a dead miner looked like who had been five days underground, trapped by a fall and drowned in water that sprang up from a released spring. Bloated and wrecked. She had once seen what was left of a woman who had been attacked by wolves on her way home in the dark. She knew what teeth could do to flesh. And still, when the wolf made towards Sam, she was ready to take it on, to fight it away. Though she knew that it was impossible. So, she tried to stand.

December's hand gripped her arm. Greenrose pulled. The grip was firm, strong. Greenrose screamed and slapped December's hand, pulled her arm to free it. The grip tightened.

The wolf bounded onto the bed and crouched over Sam, lowering its mouth over his face.

Greenrose slapped December's face, over and over, not minding the feel of her hand on that slick skin, that ruined flesh.

The wolf lifted its head, turned and grinned at her. His long tongue licked and lolled. Then he lifted his head and howled.

Greenrose used all her strength. She dragged December from the chair. Tugging all the time at her arm, she hauled her to the ground. Her feet slid against the cold floor, failing to grip and move towards the wolf. It was too late, the wolf forgot Greenrose, turned again to Sam, opened its jaws wide, showing long, yellow teeth, and closed its mouth around Sam's face.

December's eyes opened. She looked at Greenrose, but there was no light of recognition or intelligence.

"Leave him," she said. Her voice was cracked.

Greenrose slapped her again, part anger, part frustration at trying to rouse her from this trance.

"He needs help," she shouted. "You should help him."

December slumped back again, her head knocking on the floor. Greenrose winced, pulled her up into her arms.

"I'm sorry," she said. "I'm sorry."

Afraid to see what had happened, unable to stop herself, she half-turned. She looked again at the wolf.

It was licking Sam's face, snorting, nose to nose, growling, low.

Greenrose hugged December to her.

The wolf lay down beside Sam, licking still, pressing their bodies close to each other.

Sam's left hand moved to find the wolf's back. He stroked the fur. His breathing grew more steady. He had stopped calling out. Smoke trailed from his nostrils as his breath returned.

The wolf stared at Greenrose. She felt uncomfortable, but

no longer afraid. He stared until she remembered December, remembered the woman in her arms.

Carefully, she let her lie on the floor. She put a cushion beneath her head. The door was rattling against the wind. Greenrose closed it, looking over her shoulder at the wolf.

In the absence of magic, common sense and experience work wonders. Greenrose boiled a kettle, searched December's shelves and cupboards, found jars of herbs, bread, preserved fruit and jars of jellied meat, fresh milk and butter.

She infused the herbs she knew, helped December to drink a little, covered her with a rug, made a clear broth and fed her with a spoon. She had lost all her feelings of revulsion at the woman's face. She lifted the spoon to December, for her to take the broth. She had no lips. The flesh of her face met in a slit beneath her nose. And the nose was half-gone. Greenrose stroked her cheeks and fed her.

Sam was asleep now. Not as he had been, but a proper sleep, with deep, clear breathing and his face relaxed. His hand still stroked the wolf's fur.

The wolf lay still, protective, giving warmth and life to the boy.

Greenrose relaxed and nursed December.

December opened her eyes again. This time she saw Greenrose, Sam, the wolf. She smiled.

"Thank you," she said.

"Hush."

Greenrose leaned forward and kissed her cheek.

"Hush." ‖

Smedge had been walking

all day. He had to keep moving. He could not use magic to make better progress. Every step had to be taken, every mile walked, every bridge crossed. Over the years, Smedge had become expert at making it seem as though he was making spells as carelessly as all the other pupils in the college, but he held back, allowing all the other explosions and flourishing of spells around him to mask his own careful use of magic. There were times when he was forced to do it, to pass a test or play a game. Most of the time the others were so delighted with their own skills they didn't bother about him. In the marketplace of magic that was the college, Smedge chose not to set up his stall.

He could have been at the castle in a day. As it was, he had walked for ten days already and was not halfway there.

He could have sent a message, as a moth or a beetle by night, or a wasp or a bluebottle by day. But his orders were very strict. He was not to use magic to contact the castle in any way, except as he had been instructed.

Magic is like a fire. It can burn the one who builds it as easily as the one who stumbles into it. And the smoke rises.

He did not hide, but nor did he attract attention on his journey. The second day a farm cart pulled out of a field as he approached.

"Take a ride," the farmer invited him.

"I enjoy the walk," said Smedge.

The farmer's smile slid away. He pushed his hat down a little over his eyes, to shade them from the sun and get a better look at Smedge. He was not so friendly now.

"It's a long walk to the next place."

"But not too hot for the journey."

Summer had handed over the year to autumn. The cart was laden with sweet hay, the second cut, cut and dried and stooked, ready for storing for the winter. The leaves were beginning to blush at the approaching nakedness of the trees. Horse chestnuts gleamed on the path.

The man nodded, clicked to the horse and began to drive away, mumbling under his breath.

"Wait," called Smedge.

He did not want to ride next to the man, did not want to talk, to be drawn in to giving a reason for his journey, an explanation of where he was going. A lie can always leave a trail, and he could not tell the truth. But the refused offer would be the talk of the next village that night. The farmer would grumble to his wife about the surly boy who would not ride with him. He would share the story with his friends over a mug of beer. Before he knew it, Smedge would find that the story was ahead of him as well as behind him.

"Please," he said. "I'd like a ride with you. If I may."

Magic would silence the man. But magic would send up smoke.

"Are you going far?"

The wagon rocked pleasantly on the rough road.

"To see a friend."

The farmer nodded.

"I'm sorry if I was rude back there."

The farmer did not seem to think that much was required of him for the conversation.

"He hasn't been well," said Smedge, making sure that he told nothing but the truth, but not enough truth for it to be true. "And I wanted to be alone on the journey. To think about things."

The farmer leaned back against the wooden board and breathed deeply. The wagon was a world of perfume. The reassuring smell of the horse, the sweet scent of the hay, the soft, secret aroma of the old wooden wagon, the almost-living fragrance of the farmer's leather waistcoat. The dying year exhaled its essences.

"You're welcome to a meal with us and a bed for tonight," said the man.

There was a limit to Smedge's willingness to be polite and not attract attention, and the man had just reached it.

"I have family, a few miles further on," he said, trapped at last into a lie. "They're expecting me."

"Then perhaps you'll be so kind as to work a little spell before you go."

"I'm sorry?"

"In exchange for the ride. Perhaps you'll cast a spell to make the horse last another year before he goes to the slaughterhouse, or you might make it so the wheels on this wagon never break or turn into a ditch."

"What makes you think I can do that?" asked Smedge.

The farmer looked under the brim of his hat and smiled, knowingly.

"If you want to find a fool in the country, then you'd better take him with you," he said.

Smedge jumped down from the wagon.

"On your way," he said.

"As you like."

He watched the wagon draw away, then, without moving, he muttered a few words. The front wheel snapped. The wagon toppled over, hurling the man into the ditch and spilling the load of hay.

Smedge walked up and stood over him. The man was dazed, but not dead. He stared up at Smedge, who said, "You're lucky you are going home tonight. You could have died in that fall."

The man groaned.

Smedge held the man's gaze for a moment, then, stepping

back, he disappeared. In that instant, all memory of him was wiped from the man's mind. When Smedge appeared again he was half a mile away.

After that, he avoided roads, walking when he could behind the cover of hedgerows and through woods. He sometimes travelled by night. He spoke to no one. But the magic had been worked and its smoke rose up. ||

Tamrin followed Smedge

as autumn pushed summer aside.

At first she followed closely, not keeping him in sight, but making sure that he was never too far ahead. The real problem was the roffle. He was always between them. And her legs hurt. She stooped a little, sometimes, trying to make it easier. The pain in her face was worse, too.

Tamrin had not left the college since the day she arrived. She was a creature of corridors and corners, of attics and cellars. The world outside, when she had seen it, had been seen from the turret, from high up.

She found pleasant conversation and gentle hospitality from the houses and the workers along her way. While Smedge avoided contact, she sought it out. She feasted on the facts she learned from them all. A whole village toiled all day in the field, bringing the last harvest in before the rains ruined it, and she helped to gather stooks and load them onto carts, and afterwards ate cheese and bread, fruit and ham, drank cider and snoozed until it was evening, then leaned on Vengeabil's staff and tracked on after the boy and the roffle, ignoring the pain. A family gave her a bed for the night, up in the eaves of their cottage, and shared a pot of stewed chicken with toasted almonds sprinkled on the top and a spoon of thick cream stirred into each bowl. They told her tales of ghosts and made her listen to the creaks as the house adapted to the wind, then laughed at her and she laughed, too, and the joke turned into memories of family members, long gone, not forgotten.

She often left a small, secret spell behind, to thank the ones who had been kind to her. Some turned her away, and she slept under the sky, but even to these she gave a small reward, in case it should make them happier, more generous to the next caller.

She thought the trail might be hard to follow. She watched a hawk circle round the fields, then swoop on a small creature whose safety had been reaped with the wheat. Smedge had been careful not to leave magic behind him, but there was something else. Just as a snail leaves a wet trail on a path, just as a wounded fox leaves a trail of blood, just as a civet leaves a stinking smear of itself, so Smedge left something behind him that Tamrin could sense and follow. She only once saw it made real, other times it was like a half-remembered dream. Just once it was there in the road, for all to see.

The broken cart was half in the ditch. The farmer groaned. His leg had snapped like the spokes of the wheel. He had been sick and the vomit pooled alongside his face, sour-smelling, slimy.

Tamrin bent over him and touched his forehead. He was hot, sweating.

"I'll get help," she said.

His farmhouse was not far along the road, and his two sons were quick to come and lift him onto a hurdle and carry him back. Tamrin helped the pain with a drowsy spell, but he still cried out when they lifted him onto his bed.

"You'll eat with us and stay the night, won't you," his wife insisted.

"And you'll mend the leg?" he asked.

"Thank you," said Tamrin. "I'd like to stay. But I can't mend legs."

"We won't ask more than what's right," said the woman. While she prepared for dinner the elder son fetched someone from the village.

Tamrin saw that this woman was only a local healer, not a wizard. She watched as the woman straightened the broken leg, strapped a splint to it and made it tight. Then Tamrin silently added a spell that would keep the wound clean, knit the bone well, and heal it in half the time it would usually take.

Dinner was simple but good.

He explained how the accident had happened.

"The wheel just broke," he said, when he had finished telling the story. But Tamrin had seen the traces of the spiteful magic.

The sons were big men, with faces browned by work in the fields and hands like hammers.

"What brings you here?" asked the older one.

Tamrin ate quietly.

"Leave her be," said his wife.

"What does she know, then?" The elder son stared at her.

"She's going to the castle," said the father. "Aren't you?"

"I don't know," she answered.

"You have friends there?"

"No."

"So why are you going to the castle?" asked the other son. He had not spoken till now, but had watched everything carefully.

"I don't know that I am," she said.

"Leave her alone," said the wife, "she helped us out, didn't she?"

"We don't know that," said the elder son.

"What castle?" asked Tamrin.

"We'll finish our dinner first," said the woman. "There'll be time for this later."

It was clear that when she spoke like this no one argued.

Though pressed to stay with them for longer, Tamrin left after one night. The year was bleeding away and she needed to keep up with Smedge. There was no more smoke from careless magic. Tamrin tracked him right to the edge of the forest, the very gate of the castle. Her legs hurting more and more. She watched while autumn surrendered to early snow.

Flaxfield would have said that the seasons were out of joint these days. Tamrin knew nothing of that. She only knew that she had run out of ideas. She could not go into the castle. She could not leave. It made her face hurt, her head heavy.

She sat for five days in snow, watching, listening. Crouched like a crow against the wind, she waited. She saw the takkabakks swarm in and out. Watched them circle the forest, trying to penetrate its denseness. They were hunting, and she felt a sick fear that Sam was in there, hiding from them. The forest shrugged them off and they rattled back into the castle. As soon as the gate closed, wolves ran up and scratched at it, their heads to one side, listening.

She neither moved nor ate. Her legs were fixed in a twisted crouch, her back bent. The pain in her face had dug deeper, closing one eye, making her deaf on one side.

She knew Smedge was in there. She feared Sam was, too. All she could do was watch.

More days were swallowed by longer nights. When she finally tried to stand she found she could not. She leaned to her left, slowly lay down and felt the darkness cover her, like a cloak. ‖

Ash lifted her head and turned

to the slit window. She sniffed. Laying aside her pen, she crossed the room and looked down over the dark fields and hunched forest.

He was nearly here.

Too far away to be seen, Smedge was approaching the castle and she could sense him.

Her hands were white against the stone. With her back to the lantern, her face was shadowed against the night sky. A single flake of snow passed the window. Then, as though summoned by the first, more. She could count them, singly, then in groups, then too many, and the black fields began to turn white.

She left the turret room. The winding staircase, the narrow passageways, the locked doors, the high, arched ceilings. As she passed, a moment of yellow light lit them then died.

It was a place of noises. She ignored the moans and the screams that came from behind the locked doors. Ignored the laughter, which was worse than the screams. Ignored the hammering and the click of tightening ratchets that came before the screams. She ignored the scuttling of sharp feet on the stone floors as her creatures hurried to get out of her way.

Khazib was chained to the wall. He did not look up when she walked in.

"I don't need the chains," she said. "I could hold you here without them. You know that."

Khazib was as though asleep.

"Do you want to know why I use them?"

She walked up and down in the small cell, the yellow light that glowed from her moving on the ceiling. Her bare feet made wet, slapping noises on the slimy floor. Cockroaches that did not scurry away fast enough crunched as she stepped on them.

She stopped pacing and waited for him to answer. He kept his head low, his face turned to the wall.

She moved her hand in an impatient order. Instantly, one of her clacking creatures leaped forward, pounced on Khazib and jabbed a long sharp tongue into his shoulder, drawing blood. Khazib screamed in pain and surprise, his head jerking up so he faced her.

The takkabakk dropped off and scrambled away to a corner.

"Where is he?" she asked.

"I thought he was here," said Khazib.

"Then you will have a very unhappy stay with us," she said.

Khazib looked at the blood flowing from his wound.

"It's poison," said Ash. "And if I don't treat it, it will kill you, slowly, spreading through your body."

"Good."

Ash moved the toe of her shoe over the floor.

"But I won't let it. I will make you better and then it will stab you again. And over and over and over. Poison and pain, poison and pain. For ever."

Khazib panted with pain.

"The chains," she said. "Do you know why I use them?"

"To humiliate me," said Khazib, as though answering an easy arithmetic question. "They don't. They humiliate you."

She didn't lock the door as she left. There was no need. ||

Miners left early for work

and Sam's first thought every morning was shaped by the sound of their boots on the cobbles.

At first it had troubled him, crept into his sleep and curled up in his dreams. The clump of the boots was sometimes thunder, sometimes the crashing of an old tree, felled, sometimes a hammering on the door. Many times he called out in fear before he woke. December stroked his face, whispered that it was just a dream, told him about the morning walk to the mines, the boots, the hard street. She helped him from bed and took his arm as he limped to the window. Drawing back the curtain, she showed him the men, unspeaking, intent, preparing themselves for a day of darkness underground.

Sometimes he thought the work in the mines was more to be feared than the thunder, or the knock on the door.

She helped him back to bed and he would sleep again, for hours sometimes, until she brought him food and a cool drink.

Sometimes she lay on the floor next to his bed and slept as well. She moved more slowly than she had. And, if Sam noticed, always with pain.

Greenrose came to the house every day. She lit the fire now that the days were colder. She lifted the heavy kettle that December had once found so easy to put over the hot coals. She cleaned and cooked, sweeping December away when the woman tried to help her. Without her visits, December and Sam would have starved or died in the cold of the night. They were both so weak that they needed her nursing.

Greenrose never got used to the wolf. She pretended it wasn't there. For its part, as though it sensed her dislike, it kept out of her way. When she needed to tidy Sam's bed, it slipped off and curled up by the fire till she was done. Its eyes never left her. As soon as she was finished it bounded back beside the boy and settled down.

In the evenings, just after the men had come back from the pit and were safely inside their little houses, eating their supper, the wolf would swerve through the door and run out for an hour. They heard him howling into the night air.

"What is he saying?" asked Sam, when he was well enough to take notice. Wisps of grey smoke curled out of his mouth when he spoke.

"Nothing to our danger," said December. "I think."

Greenrose never fed him. There was no spare money for meat for a wolf. If he ate, it was on these evening runs.

They sat, not close, but on his bed. December looked at

the tapestry, trying to remember if the wolf breaking cover from the forest had really been there or if it was part of the delirium that had seized her in the days after Sam began to recover. There was no wolf there now.

The snow was deep now, and Ash stood in the castle doorway, watched Smedge hesitate at the great gate, then draw in a deep breath and walk through.

He was startled to see her waiting for him and she saw that he was frightened and hungry too.

Ash led him to the turret, making sure they passed near to the kitchen. The scent of roasting meat greeted them and bade them farewell within the space of several seconds. She hardly ate at all, never felt hungry, but she remembered what it was to be hungry and knew that Smedge would be wounded by the closeness of food he dared not ask for.

"You've had a long journey," she said.

The stair was narrow and wound round and round so he could not see her ahead of him, just the dying yellow glow on the ceiling. He felt along the wall for guidance.

The desk stood in the centre of the turret in a pool of light. She sat. He stood.

"You lost him," she said.

"He had help," said Smedge.

He had bad memories of this room.

"But you lost him."

"Yes."

"Well, I found him," she said. "I had him in my hand. Understand?"

"Where is he?"

Ash flicked her fingers.

"There are doors I can go through," she said. "He opened one of those doors and I met him. I held him. I nearly led him through. I nearly brought him here. Here."

She paced the room and glowed with heat and hate.

"He got away. He was helped."

Smedge tried to keep away from her. The heat was uncomfortable.

"I couldn't see the other side of the door."

"Wasn't there any way to ask?"

Ash stopped still and stared at him.

"I have to be careful when I go there," she said. "I am not exactly ... welcome. Though there are some who would like to keep me there for ever. You understand?"

Smedge remembered things, half-remembered them. From when he had first met Ash. He nodded.

"All that matters," she said, staring hard at him, "all that matters is finding him and bringing him here. Do you understand?"

Smedge's hair began to singe.

"Yes. I understand."

"What about Frastfil?"

"I have him under control."

She nodded. The hair stopped smoking.

"You've done well there."

"Thank you."

"Come to the window."

The fields were deep in snow. The forest tops were white clouds.

"I have two of them secure here," she said. "Two others ran into the forest. My creatures have hunted them for weeks. The forest barred their way. Every path is blocked. Every attempt to hack down new trails has been met with strong magic."

"Who is helping them?" he asked.

"There is no *who* any more. It is everything."

"I was hindered on the way here," he said.

"Come with me. I'll explain as we walk."

They walked the same route she had taken earlier. She watched him as he heard the screams.

"There are moments," she said. "Moments when everything changes. There was one of those moments when the roffles went to live underground. There was another moment, when I came here."

He took his glasses off and polished them, attentive.

"I thought no one knew how the roffles came to live underground."

"Everything is known by someone," she said. "At the beginning, magic was different. Magic spilled out and what wasn't used just trickled away harmlessly. The college is a memory of those days. It's just a box of tricks today, with no real magic."

They were going deeper into the heart of the castle. The noises were more unpleasant. Smedge struggled to block them out.

Khazib looked up as they entered, his face drawn with pain.

"This one was looking for him, too," she said to Smedge. "And I think he knows more than he is saying."

Smedge looked away from Khazib.

"No," she said. "Take a good look. That is what happens to people who stand in our way."

Smedge looked. The creature with the crooked legs looked at him and looked hungrily at Khazib at the same time. It had enough eyes to look many places at once.

"Or people who fail," she added.

They closed the door as they left.

"You said two of them," said Smedge.

"You would not enjoy seeing the old man," she replied.

She watched him eat sitting at the long table in the kitchen. They ignored the misshapen, squat figures who lurched between range and spit, turning meat, scalding pans, stirring pots, chopping hunks of meat, sawing through bones. The steam and the hissing of fat from roasts filled the air.

Smedge did not like to think what it might be that he was eating, so he chewed resolutely, needing to be fed more than he cared what fed him.

Smedge found that something in the piece of meat he was eating would not chew away. He hoped it was gristle as he took it from his mouth and put it on the side of the plate.

"Old magic can only travel one way," she said. "Do you understand?"

Smedge knew better than to pretend to her.

"No."

"No. It can go in one direction," she said. "It can go where we want it to go. Or it can go against us, but not both."

The food was all gone, and he was still hungry.

"You have a question?" She missed nothing.

"I am afraid to ask."

"Ask."

"Who is in control?"

"What do you mean?"

"Do we control the magic, or does the magic control us?"

He felt his skin grow hot as she struggled to keep her anger in check.

"I'm sorry," he said.

The heat subsided.

"No," she said. "It is a good question. It is the only question."

She walked with him, to his old room.

"There is a second question," she said.

Smedge looked at the room. It had not changed. A bed, some books, a small desk, a chair.

"Which way do you want the magic to go?" she asked.

"Your way," he said, without hesitation.

"Of course. Then you will stay here for the winter. Learn. Play with the two wizards we have captured. Tease them."

Smedge shuddered at the thought of what teasing might mean, but it excited him, too. "See if you can find anything from them. More than anything else, we need to find the boy."

"Why is he so important?"

She looked through the window, slender and tall like the one in her own room.

"Flaxfield was a great wizard," she said. "He was our greatest enemy. When he died, I should have been free of here. Because of the boy, I'm still a prisoner."

"They still talk about Flaxfield at the college," said Smedge. "But he's dead now."

"Come to the window," she said. "All that he had, all his strength and power is with the boy now."

Smedge remembered the clumsy apprentice who had caused such trouble in the college.

"Him?"

"He doesn't even know it himself," she said.

"What about the girl, Tamrin?"

"Watch her," she said. "When the weather breaks, you will go back. She is connected to him. I don't know how. But she is important. Keep watching her. If he is still lost, she will lead us to him."

"She hates me," said Smedge. "She won't tell me anything."

"Then you must find another way with her. Understand?"

She left him then. The breath of the night-wind brushed his face.

Out of sight, covered by the rim of the forest, Megatorine looked at the castle and saw the outline of the boy framed in the window.

The drear and naked branches arched above him, the melancholy, long roar of the wind in the trees. The snow stretched on for ever.

"Time to go under," he said. "He'll keep till spring."

As the days passed, Sam and December grew stronger. They left the house sometimes, walking to the end of the road. Then, with the wolf following them, as far as the edge of town, and then to the fields beyond. Sam recognized the area where the dancing had happened. He smiled as he recalled the sound of the band. Sam hobbled, his legs bent, back crooked, his shoulders hunched. The illness had damaged him badly. Progress anywhere was slow, but he could walk a long way now.

December could lift the kettle now and did more of the work, but Greenrose still came every day and sat with them and talked.

Then the night came when the wolf returned with snow in its fur. Sam and December went to the window and saw the soft flakes settling on the dark streets.

"It will soon be time for us to go," said December.

"This is the worst weather for a journey," said Sam.

"Which is why we must go soon," she said. "Do you think they are not still looking for you?"

The wolf moved closer to Sam. The boy stroked him, absently.

"Where are we going?"

December stirred the fire and settled the pot on the stove.

"That is your decision to make," she said.

"I used to dream that I was flying," he said.

December ladled a rich soup into bowls and cut slices of bread.

"We will travel by night," she told him.

"Why are they looking for me?"

"It will be cold, but safer in the dark."

"I miss Flaxfield," said Sam. "It was all right till he died. I was safe then. No one was looking for me."

"They have been looking for you all your life," said December. "You just didn't know."

Sam ate his soup, dipping the bread into it, spooning it to his mouth silently.

"Flaxfield hid you well," she said.

"Why are they looking for me?"

December smiled. Sam was used to her smiles now, the thin lips, and he saw nothing strange in them.

"I thought you were looking for me," he said, looking away.

"I was."

"Why?"

"Not to hurt you."

"Did you know Flaxfield?"

"In a way," she said.

The wolf walked to the door and sat with his back to it.

"Where are we going?" asked Sam.

"You must decide."

Sam looked over his shoulder at the tapestry.

"Is that a real place?"

He pointed to the inn.

"It is."

"Then we'll go there."

December took his dish. She washed the bowls, put them away in the cupboard, covered the fire and blew out the lamp.

"Get your cloak," she said.

Sam was drowsy after the meal; he stared at her.

"We're going now."

"Why?"

"I have been waiting for you to tell me where we are going. Now I know." ‖

Just the worst

time of year for a journey. In the end, Eloise and Axestone preferred to travel all night, sleeping in snatches.

"We can't escape," said Eloise.

The forest held them clenched in its fist. Forests are old in magic.

"It's full of voices," said Axestone.

Some were the voices of the trees themselves. Some were the voices of those who have become lost in the forest and never escaped. There are the voices of the animals, the beasts that live there, that hunt, and are hunted. And the voice of the wind. And the voice of the forest itself. Because a forest is not just the trees that are in it. A forest is a thing in itself. It is one tree and many trees.

"Listen to them," said Eloise.

Eloise curled her body round the trunk of a slender ash, pressed the side of her head to the smooth bark, the wounded arm dangled by her side, dead now, black and stinking. Her shawl covered her shoulders and spread beyond them to the tree, making her seem to melt into it, to be part of it.

Axestone stood in a clearing. The trunks of the trees around him like the stone pillars of a great hall, their branches the vaulting. He kept his arms relaxed by his sides, his head still, his breathing slow and regular.

"We can't go on," he said. "This is where it ends."

Summer had gone and autumn had nearly run its course. The wind was stripping the leaves from the trees, opening up the canopy of the forest. Now the fist that held them was a skeleton, but its grip was as tight as ever.

"Winter will kill us here."

"As good a place to die as any," said Eloise.

The berries and roots they had eaten were gone. Hungry, cold, wounded and exhausted, they had each done what they could to learn from the forest itself how to get out. Eloise was white with hunger, black with poison, her lips pale, her fingers so slender they looked as though they would snap. Axestone's clothes hung on him, tied tight at the waist, made for a bigger man. His cheekbones pressed against the skin. His eyes sunk deep. His flesh scoured by the beetles, raw and wet with festering blisters.

They settled back into the forest to die.

Anyone walking into the space would not have seen them. Eloise's shawl had become the green-silver of the bark. Axestone, brown-cloaked and motionless, seemed no more than a tree himself, in autumn hues.

They stayed like this for four days. Each lost to the other. Each absorbed in listening.

On the morning of the fifth day, Eloise uncurled herself from the ash. Her shawl shimmered as she stepped back, blazed blue and bright green, sky and new leaves. She staggered a little, then seemed to wake and look around her.

The air was crisp and her breath smoked in front of her face as she breathed out. Overhead, the trees laced themselves together, black against grey.

Eloise found Axestone, more by sense than sight. She laid her hand on his shoulder and spoke, softly.

"It's done," she said.

The voices were singing in their ears. Axestone's face was the colour of his cloak.

"We can go now," she said, taking his hand and raising it from where it hung by his side.

She stroked his cheek. The colour faded, the brown and green draining away, leaving his skin as before, healed, fresh. He opened his eyes.

"I thought the singing was in my head," he said.

They looked around them. The singing was everywhere. It came, not from the trees, nor from the movement of the wind in the branches, but from the forest itself. Solemn and joyful, it made their hearts glad.

"The year is ending," said Eloise.

Axestone rolled his shoulders, lifted his arms above his head and stretched. He moved one foot, carefully, then walked forward, enjoying the sense of movement.

"Is it ending well?" he asked.

The singing changed. Still solemn, it took on a graver tone, a note of warning.

"Well enough," she said. "For now."

He nodded. His face was restored. The cheekbones no longer pressing against the flesh. His clothes no longer hung half-empty from him. Eloise had colour in her cheeks, and her eyes were bright again. The broken leg of the takkabakk had fallen from her and lay on the ground. She had a scar, but no more poison, no wound. Axestone smiled.

"The forest fed you," he said.

"We were never prisoners," Eloise said. "We were guests."

The singing grew softer.

"Do you know where we go now?" asked Eloise.

"Yes. You?"

"Yes."

The old lost road through the woods stood clear and open before them. As they walked it the singing grew ever softer, ever sadder until they broke through the cover into the open fields and the singing stopped.

The sky was grey and low. A single fat flake of snow fell, hesitated on the grass, then melted away, followed by another, and then another. By the time they were half across the first field the snow was beginning to settle.

"It's a long way from here," said Eloise.

"Yes," said Axestone.

"And just the worst time of year for a journey."

"And such a journey," he said.

They lowered their faces against the snow and walked.

Ash pursed her lips and swept her hand across the embers of a fire she had lit on the stale floor of her room. She swore. The folds of her grey dress were spread around her as she sat on the cold floor. A beetle scratched its way over her foot. She leaned forward, picked it up and put it to her lips without thinking. She crunched it, sucked the soft pulp from inside, licked it clean then dropped the empty husk into the remains of the fire.

Smedge pressed his elbows to his sides and looked away.

"I don't understand it," she said.

She wiped her forehead, leaving an ash-grey stripe over her eyes.

"Look."

Smedge couldn't interpret the magic the fire had produced for her.

"There are three of them," said Ash. "The girl has disappeared. The dragon has disappeared, and the boy is in three places."

"That can't be right," said Smedge.

Ash wheeled round.

"Of course it isn't right," she screamed.

Smedge's face exploded into a fountain of fire. Ash clicked her tongue in irritation. She let the fire burn for a few moments, watching Smedge flail his hands helplessly at the flames, and hearing his screams, then she blew softly in his direction. The fire snuffed out in a second. Smedge was unharmed, but shaking from the pain and shock.

"I know it can't be right," she said slowly. "But it is. No girl. No dragon. Three apprentice boys. What can we do now? How can I find him in three places?"

She paced the room.

"Not there. Not there. There and there and there," she mumbled. She wrapped the grey robe round her face and pulled it tight.

"There. Not there. Not there. There. How?"

Smedge slipped out of the room, leaving her half-sobbing the questions to herself. ‖

Saliva ran from the corners

of Sam's lips. He had trouble keeping his mouth tight shut when he was making an effort.

The strain of walking slowly was telling on December. She was a swift walker. Pushing the road behind her gave her a feeling of intense joy. For all the years she had spent at the mines, she still regretted the loss of freedom, the sense of movement. She liked places best when they were disappearing behind her. And she liked them to disappear swiftly.

Sam's crooked legs, his bent back, his pained steps, slowed them down more than she had realized they would.

Hunched forward, he was too short for his cloak. It dragged behind him, slowing him more. The snow melted into it and weighed it down. His bag, which he had hauled on his shoulders all the way from Flaxfield's to the college, and then on again to the mines, rolled off his rounded back, so he clutched it instead in his arms. December had tried to take it from him, to help. He snarled at her and the smoke, which dribbled most of the time from his nostrils or the sides of his mouth, billowed out hot, the grey gilt-edged.

December had planned the journey with her own pace in mind. They would have reached the inn before the snows locked down the roads and made travelling impossible. Now, at Sam's pace, they would not be halfway there before they were trapped.

They spoke little. Sam crept relentlessly on, ignoring the pain in his legs and back. He looked sideways often at December. She pretended not to notice.

At night December used just a little magic to make two spaces for them where they could sleep, dry and warm, usually under trees, but sometimes in a ditch, diverting the sluggish green water away from them, covering them instead with fragrant air and soft, summer breezes. It wasn't for herself. She needed to do it to keep Sam alive.

She slept a little away from Sam, who always slept with his arms around the wolf, his head lying on the grey fur.

It was at night, when he thought December was asleep, that Sam tried to cast a small spell.

He had done this twice in the house before they left. Once, to make the fire burn brighter when he was cold. Nothing happened. Then he tried to give Tremmort a headache, out of spite, but the boy was bright as brass and Sam sulked.

He thought that once they were away from the mines it would be all right. He cast a Searching Spell, to see the road ahead of them for the next day. Nothing happened. He closed his eyes, expecting to see the road, the turns and hills, any dangerous banks or icy slopes. Nothing.

The next night, snug in the safety of December's spell, he attempted to clear a space in the cloud so that he could ask the stars what to do. The cloud spread in all directions, unmoved by his spell.

He clutched the bag to him harder than ever, fumbled inside it, and fell asleep.

A day came when they woke and the road was not there. The snow had fallen so heavily that all was covered.

December could have walked on, treading lightly over the fine snow, hardly disturbing it. But Sam's steps were laborious, heavy. He sank with each step.

"I'll stay here," he said.

And die, she thought.

He was not many steps from death. His face was grey. His body shrunken. Except for when he darted them at her, his eyes seemed never to focus, but to stare at something out of range.

And all the time now, like claws, his fingers scrabbled inside the bag. She could not know that he was clutching at his notebook.

The wolf had been running in circles, its paws just breaking the snow. Now it leaped, landed and ran without even denting the surface.

It stopped, turned its head, and, its long tongue lolling out, seemed to laugh at them.

"The hedgerow," said December.

The snow was only a thin crust on the top of the thick hedgerow. It made a path they could walk on.

"We don't have much time," said December. "Look at the sky."

Low, grey clouds, full of more snow, spread over their heads like a tent.

Had Sam been able to cast a Searching Spell, he would have seen Eloise and Axestone, staring up at the same grey sky many miles away.

"Five more miles," said Eloise.

"Or ten," he answered. "Who knows for sure?"

"Or ten," she agreed.

"There's only one way to find out."

They trudged through the snow, wishing that magic could ease their way.

"Do you know what's happening to him?" asked Eloise.

"He's very sick."

"Will he make it?"

Axestone shrugged.

"The winters are getting colder," said Eloise. "I've never seen snow like this before."

"The world is shifting," he said. "Magic is different. Everything changes."

"We need him to live," she said.

"I'm doing what I can. There's one hope left. But it means he will not get to us until the spring."

They walked a long way in silence. Eloise covered her face with her shawl to protect her from the driving wind, the sharp cold. Axestone let the wind cut his face. He was as though not there. Eloise left him to his work.

They turned a corner. Trees that had blocked the view of the road ahead were on their left now and they could see, a mile or more away, a small group of houses, an inn, and smoke rising from the chimney pots.

"We're there," said Eloise.

The sky began to release the snow that had weighed the clouds all day. Axestone lifted the hood of his cloak.

"And here we stay," he said. "Longer than we would like."

Eloise agreed that the wait would be hard, but as she pushed open the door of the inn and saw inside, she was glad to be there.

A fire blazed in the hearth, its glow lighting the glaze on the blue and white plates on the shelves. The copper pans glowed. Armchairs opened their hands to receive them. Five oak tables with oak chairs around them stood ready to support tureens of soup, platters of roast meats, dishes of turnips and cabbage, mugs of beer and wine, pastries and puddings. The stone floor was as clean as quartz.

"Welcome," said a soft voice.

They greeted with hugs, as old friends do.

"It will be a long winter," said Eloise.

"He is nearly there," said Axestone. "Nearly safe."

He looked around the cosy room.

"But not as well-provided as us. There is still hardship ahead for him."

Hardship that December feared would kill Sam.

The wolf had disappeared far ahead of them, leaving its tracks in the snow to mark the line of the hedgerow.

Sam's knees were drenched where he dragged them, bent-legged and painful. His hands were never still, stroking the cover of his notebook. His finger ends picked at the metal clasp, making a criss-cross of tiny cuts. His lips moved constantly. He no longer tried to hide from December his attempts to make a spell, any spell. She wondered if it was worth keeping him alive any longer. Whether he would ever recover enough to be any use. But, magic or not, she would not let another person suffer, would never leave him to die alone in the snow.

She put her hand under his arm, leading him. He had shaken her off before. This time he allowed it. Stumbling, half-blind from the glare of the snow, he muttered and fumbled in his bag. When the wolf returned, Sam did not see him. Did not see the pitched roof of the cottage, the thin smoke from the chimney, the drifts of snow against the walls that half-hid it from view. Did not know that the little food the crofter and his wife had stored for the winter was scarcely enough for two of them, certainly not for four. Did not know that they did not hesitate to offer their hospitality, though they knew it would put their own lives at risk, that they would rather starve together than send this frightening woman and the mad boy out into the snow to die.

He slept for most of the time they spent there. December cooked and cleaned to earn their keep. At first the woman begged her to be sparing with their small supply of food, to make it last as long as possible. After ten days, perhaps twelve, the woman noticed that the cheese in the larder never grew less. The bacon joint never grew smaller. The pile of logs in the wood store by the fireplace never seemed to need replenishing. The crock of flour was as full as ever, the milk in the churn as fresh, the butter as wholesome and not rancid.

She whispered this to her husband, just before they fell asleep.

"Leave it be," he advised.

"I'm frightened of her," she said.

"That face would frighten anyone," he agreed. "But we are eating well and we are warm. If she stays, then we will see the winter through safely, and that's more than I would have thought a week or two ago. Go to sleep."

"But what about that boy?"

"He'll die here, and we'll bury him in the spring," he said. "When the ground's soft enough to dig."

They slept well.

December heard every word. The cottage was small. Sam heard, too. Outside, the wolf heard everything, watched, and waited.

✠

At the inn, Eloise slept little. Many nights she left her bed hours before dawn and sat in the parlour, in front of the dying embers of the fire. She fed it a little, to keep it in till the morning, listened to the creak of the sign as it swung in the wind. Axestone kept to his room, though he slept little, too. He watched through the window, and sometimes he caught the sound of a wolf howling to the moon.

Their host slept well, and waited. ||

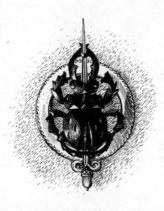

Part five

DRAGONBORN

Sam arrived at the inn on a Friday,

which was a good thing, because they always ate trout on a Friday and the fish were fresh from the stream.

Sam and December had left the crofter's cottage just as the first warm breezes of spring had unlocked the scents from the garden and the fields.

They waved Sam and December into the distance.

"I thought he would die," said the crofter.

"It's not over yet."

Eloise was the first to see Sam. She was standing at the window of the inn parlour, looking for Axestone. The tall wizard walked up from the stream, holding the trout at his side. Ten fish, brilliant in the spring sunlight. He strode effortlessly up the slope from the stream, his brown robe brushing the grass. As he saw Eloise he raised his arm in triumph, brandishing the fish. She smiled. Next to her, Flaxfold sighed.

"It was always trout on Friday in the old days," she said.

"Always," Eloise agreed.

"It won't be long now," said Flaxfold.

"If he's right."

Axestone threw the door open.

"In the kitchen," said Flaxfold.

He grinned at her, like a rebuked schoolboy.

"They're too fresh to stink," he said.

"Did you clean them?" she asked.

"Of course."

Leaving the fish on a marble slab in the cool larder, he joined them in the parlour, a glass of small ale in his hand. He plunged into a leather armchair and drank, his left arm dangling to one side and stroking the soft, grey fur of the wolf.

"How much longer?" asked Flaxfold.

"They should be here before nightfall," he said, looking down at the wolf. The animal stared back, bright eyes unblinking.

"They're here now," said Eloise.

Flaxfold's eyes filled with tears when she saw Sam.

"That poor boy," she said.

"I'll help him," said Eloise.

"Leave him. He won't thank you."

December raised an arm in greeting when she saw their faces at the window.

"I'll get them a drink and something to eat," said Flaxfold, going to the kitchen.

Eloise hugged herself, partly in sorrow at the bedraggled and crooked shape of Sam, partly in excitement and anxiety at what was to happen next.

"We're there," said December. Sam looked up. A small group of houses and an inn, with trees to one side framing the view. On the inn, a sign swung gently. Sam felt as though he had been there before. As though he knew the place already. As though there was something missing, but he couldn't remember what.

He kept his hand inside his bag, stroking the cover of his notebook. Unfastening it, he opened it, wondered what page his hands had felt in the darkness, drew in a deep breath and made a playful, teasing spell, to make the inn sign swing faster, further. Nothing happened. Smoke dribbled from his nose.

They stepped into the inn and Sam saw Eloise first, then Axestone, still in the armchair.

"So," he said to December. "It's a trap. I should never have come with you."

Eloise came to him and took his hand.

"No, Sam," she said. "No. We're your friends."

"Him?" said Sam, looking at Axestone. "He's not my friend."

The wolf, hidden by the chair, stood and slid round. He brushed against Sam's legs and looked up at him, his tongue lolling out as though laughing.

Sam stroked him delightedly.

"If the wolf is your friend, then so am I," said Axestone.

He stood and looked down at Sam. The wolf moved away to stand next to the huge wizard. Sam saw, at last, that Axestone was more wolf than fox, more true than trick.

"And you are all my friends," said Flaxfold, pushing through the kitchen door and putting her arms around Sam. "Welcome, Sam."

Then she folded her arms around December and kissed her face. "How are you, my dear? It's been a long time."

"Too long," said December.

"You must be hungry."

"A little."

"Trout tonight," said Flaxfold, "but that's a long way off. "Come into the kitchen and we'll talk there and eat."

Sam sat down on the floor. The wolf nuzzled against him.

"You can eat in bed," said Flaxfold.

Axestone picked him up, as though he weighed no more than a trout, and carried him up to a wide room with a window that looked over the stream, a polished floor, a soft bed and a bowl of fresh flowers.

Flaxfold helped him to eat a little soup, then sat with him till he fell asleep, his hands still in the bag, holding his notebook.

It was a sombre meeting at the kitchen table. December told them how she had found Sam at the mines. She looked away from them when she came to the part about Bearrock's finishing.

"We nearly lost him," said Eloise. "Thank you."

She took December's hand.

"I thought I knew what it was, that was pulling him through," said December. She had left her hand in Eloise's, just for a moment, not to seem impolite, then drew it away.

"Evil is always familiar," said Axestone.

December nodded.

"It was more than that, though," she said.

They listened to the rest of the story, Axestone nodding at the parts about the wolf.

"The people in the cottage were so kind," said December. "Even when the snow had cleared I still had to stay until it was warm enough for him to travel."

"Will he live?" asked Eloise.

"I don't know."

"Will he live to be any use to us?" asked Axestone.

"Living will be enough," said Flaxfold.

"It won't," he said. "You know it won't. Isn't that right?" he demanded of December.

She nodded. "That's right. He is the one we've been looking for. No doubt about it."

"I never did doubt it," said Flaxfold.

Axestone threw up his arms in defeat.

"All right," he said. "We were clumsy and unsure. If we had trusted him straight away he would never have gone on the run, never have been hurt, never have turned up, twisted and broken and limping along like this. If you had been there," he pointed an accusing finger at Flaxfold, "we would have known he was Flaxfield's apprentice."

"He died suddenly," she said. "I was here. It's where I live when I'm not helping the small apprentices."

"All the same," said Axestone. "It would have been better if you had been there."

"And we would not have lost Khazib and Sandage," said Eloise. "And Caleb." Her face was solemn, her voice low.

"We have made mistakes," admitted Axestone. "The question is, is it too late to mend things?"

"You missed Flaxfield's Finishing," said Eloise, taking the older woman's hand in hers.

"I would have missed it anyway," said Flaxfold.

Flaxfold, her small, plump body and her pleasant face, grey hair and homely manner, seemed an odd person to lead this discussion, but when she spoke they all deferred to her. She had welcomed them to the inn many weeks ago, fed them and entertained them, kept them hopeful through the long winter, and it had been her presence which had soothed Sam when he looked about to fight them. Now she spoke.

"I have known Sam since he was a tiny boy," she said. "You know how I helped Flaxfield. You know what I did for the two of you, when you were his apprentices."

Axestone and Eloise nodded. December kept her eyes slightly averted from the woman.

"Flaxfield knew," she said. "I knew, that Sam was the one who would take over from him. Flaxfield put everything in place. And now it's all at risk. If Sam dies, or if the journey he has taken has broken him, then I think we have lost. The

Castle of Boolat will rise up, Magic will be dark. People will suffer and the land will be covered with pain and distress."

"And us?" asked Axestone.

"I think you know what will happen to us and to the other wizards of the old way," said Flaxfold. "And it will not be pretty."

"It isn't about us," said December.

Flaxfold smiled at her.

"Indeed it is not," she said. "You know best of all of us what he is like now. Will he live and will he ever be strong again?"

December placed her hands on the table, the palms against the wood.

"Sam has no magic," she said.

"Nothing?" Axestone spoke quickly.

"Nothing," she said. "I've watched him. I've seen him try. There is nothing inside him to work magic any more. Even his notebook is empty."

"Then we're lost," he said.

"Empty can be filled," said Flaxfold. "Broken can be mended."

"Can it?" asked Eloise.

"Sometimes," said Flaxfold. "How?"

December paused.

"Well," she said. "We know that he's being hunted. That hurt him. The college was bad for him, and that has hurt him, too. The journey itself was difficult, and an ordinary person would have died. Then he used up everything that was left inside him to perform a Finishing."

Flaxfold put her hand on December's arm.

"If it were not for you, he would have been dead long ago."

"And you," said December to Axestone. "And the wolf."

He nodded.

"Go on," he said. "How can we mend him?"

"He dreams," she said. "And he calls out 'Flaxfield' all the time."

"He never really knew anyone else," said Flaxfold. "People came to the door, but they never stayed. He went with Flaxfield to Finishings, but never really met people there, never talked to them. Flaxfield was all he knew."

"After you left," said Eloise.

"Yes."

Eloise continued. "I went to fairs with Flaxfield, and to markets. We travelled all over, staying for weeks at a time sometimes. I played with street traders' children, learned how to fight and how to make up. And he had people to stay, often. We were never lonely."

"I was never lonely," said Sam, "but I was alone a lot."

They had not heard him come in.

"How long have you been there?" asked Axestone.

Sam hobbled in, looked around.

"We'll go to the parlour," said Flaxfold. "It's more comfortable."

The day was drawing to a close. The sun low. The air cool and fresh. The spring evening gave a strange clarity to everything, a more vivid colour, a deeper, cleaner atmosphere.

The fire in the parlour had smouldered to grey ash. The low sun caught the copper pans and blue-and-white plates, painting them with an intense glow.

"Tell me more about the markets and fairs," said Flaxfold, when they were settled.

"Tell me about the wolf," said Sam.

The creature moved across, sat with his head on Sam's lap.

"What do you want to know?" asked Axestone.

"Is he yours?"

"No. He belongs to himself."

"That's not a straight answer," said Sam.

Flaxfold smiled and folded her hands on her lap.

"There's a connection," said Axestone. "Sometimes. With a lot of effort. I can see what he sees, hear what he hears."

"How?"

"Scratch your head," said Axestone.

"Don't make me look a fool," said Sam.

"I don't know another way to explain."

Sam scratched his head.

"How did you do that?" asked Axestone.

Sam shrugged.

"Close your eyes. What do you see?"

"Trees," said Sam. "Above my head. And moss. And a fox. Earwigs and beetles."

He opened his eyes and saw the others looking at him intently.

"Was it a memory?" asked Eloise.

"What else?" said Sam.

"How did you do it," asked Axestone, "scratch your head, see pictures with your eyes closed?"

"It just happens," said Sam.

"Like breathing. Or swallowing," said the man.

"Yes."

"That's how it is with the wolf."

"All the time?" said Sam.

"No, not all the time. Only when I make it so. It costs a lot."

"Did you send him to look for me?"

"We did it together," said Axestone.

Sam stroked the wolf.

"Thank you."

There was a long silence.

"The fairs," said Flaxfold.

Eloise smiled.

"It seems so long ago," she said. "Flaxfield had work to do there. Not that it seemed like work. He walked about among the stall-holders, talking to them, buying what he needed, string, shoes, selling a few things that he took with him."

"I never understood the things he bought," said Axestone.

"Or what he sold," said Eloise. "Little parcels that he had made himself. Bottles of tincture. Sometimes just a piece of paper with writing in a strange language."

Axestone laughed.

"Now we buy and sell the same things ourselves," he said.

"What are they?" asked Sam.

"Not apprentice things," said Axestone, not unkindly.

"Anyway," said Eloise. "All I wanted to do was buy some sweets and maybe a scarf, and look at the entertainers."

"Jugglers," said Axestone.

"Fire eaters," she said. "Tumblers and puppet shows."

Sam wished that Flaxfield had taken him to the fairs.

"One day," said Eloise, "there was a juggler, and I loved watching him. He juggled balls at first, then knives, then burning torches. I watched the whole show. When it was over, he came round the crowd with a hat for money. I didn't have any and said I was sorry, but thank you for a lovely show. He started to shout at me, and I didn't know what to do. He said I was robbing him by sitting at the front and then not paying. I was so embarrassed that I put my hand in my pocket, took out a toffee and put it in his hat. It was all I had. Then he was really angry, and started to call me names. He made fun of my clothes, which were old-fashioned and not very colourful. You remember what Flaxfield was like."

"I always left you nice clothes," said Flaxfold.

"Yes, but after you left, we didn't look after them very well," said Eloise. "I was a bit of a scarecrow. Anyway. People were laughing at me and he was enjoying hurting me, making me feel silly. That was when Flaxfield arrived.

"He asked the man to apologize to me. The man laughed at him and started to make fun of him as well. All the crowd were having fun. He was a clever man, good with words and quick on his feet, as you'd expect a juggler to be.

"Flaxfield let him have his say. Then he told the juggler that I was only there to teach him how to juggle properly. The man laughed; then, when Flaxfield told him what a poor juggler he was and needed lessons, he got angry. The crowd were laughing at him now. Flaxfield had begun to turn them around. Flaxfield pulled me to the front of the crowd, threw the juggling balls at me and told me to juggle."

Eloise looked at them, her eyes bright with the memory. Sam was holding his breath. Even the wolf was attentive.

"I was thirteen," she said. "Do you know how awful it is for a thirteen-year-old girl to stand in front of a crowd? And to be asked to juggle? I wanted to fall through the ground and go and live with the roffles. They started to jeer at me. 'Juggle,' said Flaxfield. So I did. I was wonderful. It felt wonderful. The jeers turned to cheers. The juggler was furious. He picked up his knives and started to juggle them. But he dropped one and it clanged on the cobbles. He stumbled and another one came down the wrong way. He grabbed it by the blade instead of the handle and it cut deep into his hand. This made him so angry that he threw it at me. I caught it, added it to my act and juggled it up with the balls. He threw another, and another. I caught them all."

Sam screwed up his shoulders with pleasure.

"In the end," said Eloise, "the juggler was covered in blood from his hand. The crowd jeered at him. I was applauded and congratulated and the crowd made him give me the money in his hat because I was a better juggler than he was. I gave him the toffee though."

Flaxfold nodded.

"He didn't like his apprentices to be made to feel small," she said.

"He bought me a set of juggling balls," said Eloise. "That night, when we got home, I tried to show him how good I was. I dropped them all."

"Why?" asked Sam.

"He said if I wanted to be a juggler the only honest way was practice."

Sam remembered the day he had used magic to get the trout.

"What about you?" asked Flaxfold, looking at Axestone. "Have you got a Flaxfield story?"

Axestone looked through the window. The light caught his eyes and made them seem like polished stones.

"Not as much fun as that one," he said. "I made a kite." He stroked his cheek and paused, remembering. "Such a kite. I've never made a better one. Well, perhaps. But never one I loved so much. It was shaped like a tortoise and its head went in and out of its shell as the wind took it. I flew it all afternoon and I was getting tired, so I lost control of it and it got stuck high in an old elm. I was tired and hungry, but I wasn't going to lose that kite. By the time I had climbed the tree I was covered in scratches, sweating like a roffle's dog and so thirsty I could have drunk the water from a stagnant pond.

Well, you can guess what I did. I freed the kite, took hold of it and let it glide down to the ground, carrying me with it."

Sam held his breath, thinking how Flaxfield would have felt about that.

"Flaxfield knew, of course," said Axestone. "He made me climb back up the tree, carrying the kite, and lodge it back in the branches. Then I had to climb down again. He was waiting for me on the ground. We looked up at the kite together. 'Now,' he said. 'Supper, or the kite?'"

"What did you do?" asked Sam.

"By this time, I was so tired and hungry that I left the kite where it was. I stamped off, in a temper. Flaxfield climbed the tree himself. He rescued the kite and climbed back down again, making sure he didn't tear it. It took him three hours, and it was night by the time he got down. He was cut and bleeding from the branches, tired to death. He was old even then."

"That sounds like Flaxfield," said Eloise.

"After supper," said Axestone, "we sat together and worked on the kite. He never said I was lazy or stupid to use the magic like that. He just helped to make it a better kite. He showed me how to put a special magic into kites, one I have always used since."

Sam found that he was crying. No noise. Just slow tears bathing his cheeks.

"I miss him so much," he said.

"We all do," said Axestone.

Sam turned to Flaxfold.

"What do you remember about him?" he asked.

"Too much to tell here," she said.

"I have a memory," said December.

Eloise looked surprised.

"You were never his apprentice," she said.

"I met him once. When I was little."

"What happened?" asked Sam.

"I had hurt myself," she said. "Well, I was hurt anyway. And nothing would take away the pain."

Sam looked hard at her, at the too-smooth skin of her face, the no-lips, the patchy hair.

"How did it happen?"

"That's a different story," she said. "I'll tell you that another day."

"Who was looking after you?" he asked.

December looked around at the faces in the room. "It's not that story I'm telling you now. This is a Flaxfield story."

"Sorry," said Sam.

"I was being looked after. Very well. But I was in pain all the time. I had potions and salves that helped. They made it bearable. Without them I would not look as good as I do."

She smiled at them.

"But there was never a time when I was without pain. I never went to the fairs or markets. I kept away from people as much as I could. It hurt me more to be looked at. Most people just turned their faces away. Some looked frightened. Some laughed. Other children were the worst. So I tried to stay away from everyone.

"It was evening. Cool, the sun nearly gone. I was sitting on the river bank, watching the fishermen. They paddled to shore, picked up their little boats and put them over their heads, walking back home like mushrooms. I was watching them so closely that I didn't hear Flaxfield approach until it was too late.

"I didn't know who he was. He sat down next to me and we watched the boats disappear. I had been crying. The pain was bad that day. He picked up a stone and threw it into the river.

"'I can throw further than you,' he said.

"I found a good stone, smooth, flat, just the right size for my hand. I skimmed it over the water, watching it bounce far beyond where his had fallen. He took another stone, flicked it, without effort, and it skimmed along over the water, easily outdistancing mine.

"'See?' he said.

"He looked straight at me, into my face. I didn't know what to think. He didn't seem uncomfortable like most people. He wasn't laughing. And, the thing I hated most, he didn't seem to be sorry for me. I was angry with him for being so much better than I was. I hadn't had any magic for a long time. Since I got hurt. I was frightened of the magic I had once had, so I left it to die inside me. But I wanted so much to beat him that I roused it. I took another stone. It was heavy, rough, no good at all for skimming. Underneath, the soil clung to it, and where it had been lying tiny creatures scuttled for safety, exposed to the light. I threw it, without really trying, but used magic to keep it above the water. It went far beyond his, splashed clumsily into the river, almost halfway across.

"'Very good,' he said.

"'I win,' I said.

"'Ah, no,' he said. 'I win. I challenged you to a throwing match. I won that.'

"I didn't know what to say. I had hidden the magic, a little. But he knew I had used it. I knew I had done wrong, so my pain came back all the stronger, fed by the shame.

"'Do you want to do tricks?' he asked me.

"I didn't understand, so I said nothing.

"'You're making your magic starve inside you. It will never quite die, but it will be thin and weak, useless, except for tricks. You can do tricks if you like,' he said. 'But if you want to do real magic, you must be an apprentice. You must learn properly. Which do you want?'

"I told him I had been an apprentice once before and it had gone wrong.

"'I know,' he said.

"'Being an apprentice made me look like this,' I told him. 'Being an apprentice made me hurt all the time.'

"'I know that, too,' he said.

"'No,' I said, 'I don't want to be an apprentice. Not unless it can make me better. Can it?'

"'Will it make you look different? Will it take away the pain?' he asked. 'No. Can it make you different?' He took another stone. A smooth, grey stone, slender stripes of deeper grey running through it, not quite oval, but almost. 'How badly does it hurt now?' he asked.

"'Very much.'

"He gave me the stone. 'Show me,' he said, 'if you can just do tricks, or if you can be a wizard.'

"I didn't understand.

"'Hold it. Stop thinking about anything. Just let the stone be itself.'

"I thought he was mad, but he was interesting. So I did it. I looked down into the stone. I stopped thinking about myself, the way I looked, the pain, the terrible things that had made me like this. And as I held the stone, it seemed to melt into my hands, and my hands seemed to melt into the stone. Then, I stopped being myself at all and I was the stone."

December looked down at her hands, remembering that evening.

"What happened?" asked Sam. "Did the pain go away?"

"The pain never goes away," she said. "But I learned that it didn't matter. That the way I looked didn't matter. So I said yes, I wanted to be an apprentice again. I wanted to be his apprentice."

"But you said you weren't," said Sam.

"He wouldn't accept me," she said. "Someone else was ready. So I went there instead."

"Who?" asked Sam.

The wolf stood up, turned around, licked Sam's hand and sat down again.

"I never saw him again," said December. "I wish I had. I wish I could have said thank you."

Sam's eyes filled with tears again. He blew his nose and smoke billowed out of the sides of the handkerchief.

"Tell us about Flaxfield, Sam," said Eloise.

"I don't know what to say."

"Just say anything."

"I remember one day," he said. "In his study."

Axestone couldn't stop himself from interrupting.

"You were in his study?"

"Yes."

"How often?"

"All the time," said Sam. "Why?"

"I have never been in there," he said.

"Nor I," said Eloise.

They looked at each other and then at Sam.

"Are you sure?" said Axestone.

"Yes."

"Go on, Sam," said Flaxfold.

"I was in his study," said Sam, "and he let me take a book from the shelves."

He told the story of the strange language and his own anger at feeling cheated.

"He said, 'Trust what you have chosen. There is a reason. Sometimes it has chosen you,'" said Sam.

"That's Flaxfield," said Axestone.

Sam remembered the old wizard's face over the book, the

bright eyes, the lips that smiled more than they rested, the quick hands. More than anything he remembered Flaxfield's voice, always helping him, making him feel good about himself. He remembered the way they started to work and then turned it into a game. The way the wizard's mind darted about like a dragonfly, bright and beautiful.

"How did you make the dragon?" asked Flaxfold.

Sam took a plate from the mantelpiece. He dipped his finger into the soot in the fireplace.

"There should be salt," he said, "and a leaf, and other things."

"Just pretend," said Flaxfold. "Just to show us."

Sam traced the letters on the side of the plate. Green and blue smoke dribbled from his nose and fell into the plate. Sam drew back, startled, then leaned forward and looked down. The smoke hovered for a second and then, contracted, gathered together over the plate and, in a moment, formed itself into a tiny green and blue dragon. Sam sat back in fright. Then he fell back, unconscious. ‖

The dragon woke

from a blue true dream of sky. He dragged his claws on the forest floor. Beech mast and acorns, the dropped twigs of autumn and the sweet brown earth under the greenly fallen leaves. He had been roused from something deeper than sleep.

The dragon drank in the scented woodland air, the ears of his ears awake, the eyes of his eyes opened.

Lifting himself from the sleep that had swallowed him, he scrambled up the trunk of a wide oak, scampered along the topmost branch, looked down at the forest top that spread in all directions away from him and, with an effortless push of his legs, launched himself into the high air.

This was his birthday. He was new made in limitless sky, over the endless earth. ‖

The clatter of branches

overhead woke Tamrin.

She turned over, wincing at the stiffness in her legs, her neck. Her hair was tangled and twined with small twigs. She was thirsty, tired. Sleep was slipping from her like a slow shadow.

The branches closed in again and she saw the flash of blue and green against the paler blue of the sky.

"Steady," said a voice. A hand rested on her shoulder. She lifted herself onto one elbow, pushed her hand back through her hair to keep it out of her eyes.

"I've been asleep," she said.

"Six weeks," said Vengeabil.

"How did you get here?"

She struggled to sit up. A cloak which had been covering her slid to the ground.

"I lost Smedge. I lost Sam," she said.

"You did well," said Vengeabil. "But you shouldn't have done it at all. You should have stayed at the college."

"You could have stopped me."

He looked down at her.

"And what good would that have done?"

"Where is Sam?" she asked.

She stood up. Straight. The pain in her face and legs had gone.

"How did you get here?" she asked again.

"Underground," said Vengeabil.

He leaned against his ash staff.

"I need to know what Sam's doing," she said. "That's why I followed them."

"Do you know now?"

"No."

"You should have stayed. He will be back. You'll see him again."

"I don't want to wait."

Vengeabil sighed.

"Sometimes, waiting is all there is. The important thing is what you do while you're waiting."

"What shall I do?"

"What you have been doing all along. Learning."

"I can only learn the real things from Sam."

"That's right," he said. "And you shall. But he's not ready to teach you yet. Or for you to teach him."

"I'm ready."

"Not quite. And you both have to be ready."

Tamrin scratched her head and tousled her hair.

"Do you want to see the Deep World?" he asked. "We can

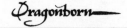

go back that way."

"What about Sam?"

Tamrin was walking up and down in the clearing.

"Sam is safe for now. We need to go back. I came through the Deep World. The snow was too thick for me to come any other way. The roffles led me to you."

"I want to go to Sam."

"You will." Vengeabil took her arm. "You will, but not yet. We have to go back to the college, and wait, and work."

"I hate the college."

"I know. But it's time to go back."

"I'm thirsty."

"The roffles will look after that. Once we go into the Deep World."

"Time for what?"

"Time you learned how to be a proper wizard. Time to get you ready."

Tamrin followed him through a parting between two bushes, round a huge rock and into a small opening that had been hidden in the ground.

"Are we really going all the way back to the college this way?" she asked.

"Just follow me."

Tamrin took a last look round at the world up top and then plunged down after Vengeabil.

"What do you mean," she said, "be a real wizard?" ||

Pages from an apprentice's notebook

COINS. You can never tell the value of a coin by its appearance. A heavy coin may be worth very little. A small coin may be the most valuable. A coin does not lose its value no matter how many times it is spent, but a coin is only worth as much as people are willing to give you for it. You can buy a chicken if the farmer will sell it to you, but if he won't sell you will go hungry, even if your purse is heavy with coins.

Learn what your coin is worth before you spend it. Find out what is for sale before you try to buy. Don't be deceived by the appearance of the coin. Find out what it is really worth.

And half-a-crown is a single coin, but it's a shilling and a shilling and sixpence as well. And it's five sixpences. And it's ten thruppeny bits. And it's half-a-crown. All at the same time.

> Look closely at a person, but
> look deep, and look
> around.

*

Sam set the places

at the kitchen table.

Flaxfold, Eloise, Axestone, himself, December, Starback, and an empty place.

The trout were frying in butter, the almonds toasting to sprinkle on top at the last moment. Thick slices of bread. Axestone had insisted on a salad as well, fresh leaves from the garden, tossed with herbs and sweet oil, sharp vinegar.

"Where shall we sit?" asked Eloise.

"Wherever you like," said Sam.

Flaxfold poured cider into clay bowls, apple juice for Sam.

Starback scrambled onto his chair and squatted on his haunches, then slid down and lay in front of the oven.

December looked at Sam with quiet pride. He was alive, more than alive. He was well. The moment that the small dragon had appeared on the blue and white plate he had fallen backwards, unconscious. They all sprang forward to help him, but he rolled, gasped, stood up and laughed. His legs were straight, his back lost its crooked twist, his eyes were bright and clear.

He laughed again and smoke and flames burst from his mouth.

"Sorry," he said. "I'll get rid of that."

He ran out of the door and looked high into the sky.

They followed and stared with him.

"How far away?" asked Axestone.

"I don't know," said Sam. "Minutes. Not much. I can see us."

"Dragons have good eyes," said Flaxfold.

A shape was already forming high and far from them.

Sam clenched his fists and hugged himself tight.

Eloise took Axestone's arm and whispered, "He's both at once. He's Dragonborn."

Axestone nodded.

"I've heard of it. I've never seen it before. I didn't believe it was true. When I need to see with the wolf's eyes, I disappear into the wolf. I stop being Axestone. Until it's over."

"I know," she said.

"But this." Axestone pointed at Sam.

Flaxfold stood with her arms crossed, her white hair flocked by the breeze, smiling at Sam.

Starback was close enough for them to see his wings, pick out the blue and green against the sky.

Sam sighed and relaxed. His fists unclenched, and he raised his arms.

Starback circled round and round, dipping and soaring.

December felt ashamed of her face in the presence of such beauty and made to walk away, back into the inn. Sam put his hand on her shoulder. She looked at him and he smiled.

"Thank you," he said.

December's face broke into a smile of her own. She regretted her shame. It was her face. As good as any she needed. Better than some more regular.

"I'm a dragon," said Sam.

"I know. Dragonborn."

"You did it," he said. "With the tapestry."

"No. I just saw it there. No one did it. It's what you are."

"Part of what you are," said Flaxfold.

They all looked up.

Starback looked down. He saw a group of houses and an inn with a sign, with trees framing the scene. Circling low, he came to rest beside the door of the inn, completing the picture.

Sam looked at Starback. Starback looked at Sam.

"It was always a dragon," said Flaxfold.

"Always," said Sam.

They left him and Starback and went inside.

Being a dragon and a boy at the same time was like learning to swim. Sam splashed around at first, gulped some water down and half-choked. But soon enough he knew the difference between one and the other. Now, he blew a little smoke for a few hours, but that stopped and he didn't mix up Sam and Starback. He was sitting at the table and curled up on the floor by the oven both at the same time, with no sense of strangeness.

"There's an empty place," said Eloise.

Sam sipped his apple juice.

"Who is it for?" she asked.

"Who is missing?" asked Sam.

"Khazib," said Axestone.

Sam remembered the day they stood side by side at the riverbank and he looked up at them, dark and light versions of the same thing.

"Sandage," said Eloise.

The old man had brought Sam water. He deserved to be here now.

"Caleb," said Flaxfold.

"Oh," said Sam. "Him."

"Waterburn is missing, said Eloise. "He did not join us for Flaxfield's Finishing.

"There is a reason he was not there," said Axestone.

Flaxfold raised her eyebrows.

"Waterburn is Flaxfield's only apprentice who did not come," he said. "There's a reason. Who took Sandage and Khazib? That was strong magic."

"Dangerous magic," said Eloise. "Whoever is in the castle is at war with us."

Starback rolled on his back and scratched behind his ear.

"Why don't people all use the magic properly?" he asked.

Axestone put down his knife and fork. He took a deep drink

of the cider and refilled his bowl from the jug.

"You have a notebook?" he said, at last.

Sam looked down.

"We all have a notebook," said Axestone. "Do you want to see mine?"

"No," said Sam.

"No?"

"Notebooks aren't for sharing," said Sam, who thought he would die before he showed someone the inside of his notebook.

"Everything is for sharing," said Axestone. "Just be very careful who you share it with."

He left the room and came back with a book very like Sam's. As the huge wizard sat down again, Sam noticed that Eloise and December had also produced books. December's book was the least like Sam's. Eloise's book, again, was very like his.

Axestone opened the book and found a page.

"Most of the time," he said. "An apprentice makes his own entries in the notebook, from what his master teaches him. Right?"

Sam nodded.

"But sometimes, Flaxfield would give me something to copy, word for word. Did he do that with you?"

"Yes. Sometimes. Not often."

He turned the book to Sam, who read what it said. ||

Pages from an apprentice's notebook

MAGIC IS LIKE MUSIC, LIKE READING. There are dots on the page, there are words in the book. Anyone can pick out a clumsy tune and there are people who can become good at playing, but who don't care for what they do.

To make real music, music that people sing to, dance to, music that people carry with them in their heads all day, music that sets the teeth on edge and drives the heart to race with fear, music that alarms and consoles, that inspires anger and love and tenderness, music that will drive men from their homes to fight and to die, music that changes worlds — to do this there has to be something more. There has to be the dedication to learn, to practise, to go hour after hour, until the fingers ache and the joints of the body scream out for rest. There has to be a hunger in the heart to make the music, not just for an audience, but for the performer first. And there has to be, inside, at birth, unexplained and unexplainable, a quality, a talent, a natural gift that singles out a boy or girl from all the rest.

So it is with magic. You will meet many who have no gift, but who have learned a few spells. There will be more, who, without knowing they have a gift, and, who have never been taught to use it, will work magic every day, unnoticed, sometimes good, often bad. And there are those, gifted and trained, who become what we are, skilled artists in magic, using our talents with training and knowledge. We are never quite at home with the rest of the world. We have privileges, but we also carry burdens they know nothing of.

Now, whenever magic is worked, it does more than was meant and it lives a life of its own. So never, never make magic just to make

life easier, or to do something quicker.

Always keep your magic

for something that

matters.

*

The other books were open

at the same page. Eloise and December and Axestone had exactly the same words in their notebooks.

"This is what we live by," said Axestone.

"But not all of us," said Eloise.

"What happened?" asked Sam.

"We don't know," said Axestone.

"Not exactly," said December.

"Not all of it," said Flaxfold.

"We have lost Khazib and Sandage," said Axestone. "They may be dead. We may be able to rescue them."

Starback stirred, Sam felt a tumbling movement in his stomach and his head was dizzy.

"I took them there," he said. "Starback took them."

"There's a time," said Eloise, "when you and the other part of you are coming together. It's a time of confusion. Starback led them to a place where they couldn't hurt you. But he led them to a place he remembered from many years ago. Long before you were born."

"I don't understand. How can Starback be older than I am?"

Flaxfold patted his hand.

"This isn't the time for that question."

"We didn't know about Starback, then," said Axestone. "It's only now that we know what he did and why he did it. You should know better than we do."

"If Starback is old, why don't I remember all the things he remembers?"

Axestone stroked the wolf's ears.

"Perhaps you will, one day."

"Things fold over each other, like sheets in a linen press, like pages in a book, like a map that has been creased by age. Sometimes the edges fray," said Flaxfold. "Just give it time and see what comes."

"It's enough to know that he didn't want to go to the college, didn't want you to go and that he tried to protect you from the others."

Sam closed his eyes.

"He waited for me outside the college," he said. "To stop me from going in. Then he left, before I arrived."

They sat in silence, then closed their notebooks.

"What happens next?" asked Sam.

"That's for you to decide."

"I left the college to find a new master," said Sam. "To be an apprentice again. Now, I don't know."

"What else can you do?" asked Axestone. "You won't go

back to the college."

"No. I won't."

"There is a battle ahead," said Eloise. "We need all the fighters we can get. All the magic we can find."

"If you go off," said December, "you will not be able to help in that fight."

"Why should I fight? I've seen the harm that magic can do. I've felt how it hurts."

"Not yet," said December. Her quiet voice interrupted Sam.

"Enough," he said. "I've felt as much hurt as I want to."

"You haven't really tested your magic since you came here," said Flaxfold.

"I don't need to. I know it's there again."

Sam stood up and went to the door, Starback scuttled after him.

"I've decided," said Sam. "I won't serve another master, not after Flaxfield."

Axestone raised his voice.

"A spoiled apprentice is dangerous," he said. "If you don't stand with us, you may find one day you'll stand against us. You can never be a real wizard without a master. Not until your apprenticeship is finished."

"And will you be my new master?" asked Sam.

"If you ask," said Axestone, "I have to say yes."

Sam smiled.

"I don't think you'll need to worry about that," he said. "I have given up magic. I have given up the search to be a wizard. I don't want it any more."

"It isn't that easy to walk away," said December. "I tried it once."

"Perhaps," said Sam. "But it nearly killed me. And because of it other wizards are now captured. Perhaps dead. I won't do it. I won't go on. You'll have to fight your fight without me."

"What will you do?" asked Eloise.

Sam shrugged.

"I'll just be me," he said. "I'm going for a walk now."

Sam fastened his cloak and left.

Starback dodged round his legs and ran out, leaped into the air and soared overhead. ‖

Ash didn't like the spring. She liked

cold days, dark nights, the smell of smoke in the autumn air, the grey of charred wood in the forest, the black of beaten iron from the forge.

"There are three of them again," she said.

"You've found them?"

"The boy and the dragon are together. The girl is on her way back to the college."

"What shall I do?" asked Smedge.

"Go back to the college," she said.

Smedge nodded.

"But you can't go looking like that," she told him.

Smedge stood a head taller than when he had arrived. He was wearing a black leather jerkin and black boots. He was a little taller than Ash now. His spectacles had gone.

"I'll say goodbye to Sandage and Khazib," he said. "I can leave in a couple of days."

The air in the tower room thickened. Smedge struggled

for breath. Ash yawned, drawing in deep lungs full of the grey smoke. She smiled.

"You've enjoyed yourself too much with those two," she said. "You're forgetting your place."

Smedge was red-faced with the effort to breathe. The smoke was hot and scorched his nose and throat as he gasped.

"What have you learned from them? Nothing," said Ash.

"They don't know anything," said Smedge. His words were choked, almost impossible to hear.

"Then leave them," said Ash. "Go back."

She opened the door. The smoke poured through, clearing the room. Smedge leaned forward, his elbows on his knees. He coughed, gasped, retched and wiped his arm across his mouth.

"Don't waste any time," said Ash. "Tidy yourself up and go back."

"What am I to do?"

"Keep on doing what you've been doing. You're to make sure Duddle gets his way, as long as he does what you tell him to. And you're to make that fool Frastfil carry on ruining the college. I want the library destroyed. Everything that could hurt us is to be thrown out."

Smedge pulled off the leather jerkin and kicked the boots from his feet. He held his breath. His hair straightened it-self into a neat parting. He shrank down, till he was about an inch taller than when he had arrived, not quite as tall as Ash now.

"Get your uniform," she said. "Don't waste time here. Send

me news when you arrive. Close the door behind you."

Smedge made to leave.

"Most of all," said Ash.

"Yes?"

"The girl, Tamrin. Never mind that she hates you. Make her your friend. Spend time with her. Get her trust. I want to know what happened when she disappeared. That is the most important thing. What happened when she disappeared? I want to know everything about her. Understand? Whatever else you do, never let her leave the college unless you know where she is going. Understand?" Ash interrupted him as he tried to answer. "Just go. Don't get it wrong."

"What will you do?"

"Never open a door unless you know what's through it," she said. "Never open a door unless you close it again."

Ash smiled. A black beetle spilled out of her mouth and fell to the floor.

"I want to leave this place," she said. "I want that boy here. I have things to do. I need him to let me out. Don't let me down. Now go."

Smedge was glad to leave the room. ‖

When Flaxfold went to wake Sam

he had gone. His bed had not been slept in. She summoned the others to the kitchen.

"It's a bad look out," said Axestone.

"I'm not chasing after him again," said Eloise. "He's made a choice."

December tapped her fingers on the table top. Her eyes were constantly on the window. Flaxfold laid her hand on December's. She felt it tremble.

"You brought him here," said Flaxfold. "You did all you could."

"I didn't think we'd lose him," said December. "I thought he'd choose to stand with us."

"He's very young," said Eloise.

Axestone stood up and paced the room.

"It's because he's young that he's dangerous," he said. "He's an open door. Anything can walk in, take him over." He glared at them. "You know what I'm talking about. He would be a very powerful enemy."

"We already have many powerful enemies," said Eloise.

"Well, he'll be the worst of the lot of them, if he falls under their influence," Axestone shouted.

"Please," said Flaxfold. "Sit down."

He slammed into a chair and banged his arms on the table.

"Where do you think he's gone?" he demanded.

Flaxfold smiled at him.

"It doesn't matter," she said. "What matters is where are we going now? What are we going to do?"

"Back to the mines for me," said December. "I've got work to do there."

Flaxfold squeezed her hand, let it go and leaned forward and kissed her.

"It's always work with you," she said. She stroked the ruined cheek. "Why don't you stay here a while? We can talk about old times, walk in the orchard and enjoy the blossom. I've got cider in the cellar from last year's apples that I haven't brought out yet. It's too good for bad-tempered men. We could enjoy it together."

December allowed Flaxfold's hand on her cheek for a moment, then drew away.

"I have to go," she said. "There'll be time for rest another day."

"What about you?" she asked Axestone.

"I'm going to camp out by the castle," he said. "See what I can discover."

"Don't try to rescue Sandage and Khazib," Eloise warned him. "Not on your own."

"No," he agreed. "Not that. But we need to prepare ourselves."

"Why did the dragon lead us there?" asked Eloise.

"He was confused," said Axestone. "Sam was getting ready to share a life with him. He muddled up the past and the present. He remembered when the castle was a good place. He must have thought he could keep them there, away from Sam. You remember what it's like when you first find your other way." His wolf-grey eyes looked directly at hers.

"Yes," said Eloise. "Yes, it's unsettling for you and for the other one."

"There was more than that, I think," said Flaxfold. "I think he was attacked. I think he was misdirected."

"We all were," said Eloise. "In ways we'll probably never understand."

"What about you?" asked Flaxfold.

"I'll go with Axestone, see the castle, keep him company on the journey. But I won't stay. I'm going home. I need to see the river and the green shade."

"That's all settled, then," said Flaxfold. "We part. We'll meet again."

"What will you do?" asked December.

They looked at Flaxfold. ‖

Tamrin stepped out into the sunlight

of the town square, Vengeabil following her. She had never noticed the small area of shadow by the side of the horse trough, next to the shoemaker's. They moved away from it before anyone could see that they had appeared from nowhere. Tamrin did not even look over her shoulder to see if she could still make out the entrance to the Deep World. There were more of them than anyone ever suspected.

They moved, side-by-side, towards the college. The high, grey walls filled almost the whole of one side of the square. After the soft light and gentle shapes of the roffle world, it was a strange sight. Tamrin hardly recognized it. She hesitated.

"Come on," said Vengeabil. "No time to waste."

"I don't want to go back," said Tamrin.

"But you're going to, so the longer you think about it, the harder it will be. Best to just do it."

"What shall we say?"

"Nothing."

Tamrin stopped and took Vengeabil's arm. He allowed her to stop him.

"We've been gone for months," she said. "It was summer when we left. It's spring now. We can't just go back in."

Vengeabil took his arm back and put his hand on Tamrin's shoulder. She was twelve, taller than most girls of her age, slender as string, her face not yet set into the patterns of what she would become. But her journey through the Deep World had changed her. She was not quite the little girl who had set off after Sam and Smedge. Then, she had been like a wild animal cub. Now, she had the poise and presence of a creature that was beginning to know its own strength.

"They won't ask," said Vengeabil. "They won't really have noticed. Come on."

Tamrin threw her questions at him as he led through the shoppers and loblollies in the square.

"You can't just leave for months and no one notice, can you?"

Vengeabil shrugged.

"You're just the strange girl who couldn't fit in. I'm just the odd-job man who lives in the stores and potters about the place. We're both sort of charity cases, tolerated, but not liked or wanted. No one cares if we're not there for a while. No one notices."

Tamrin paused at the gate, but Vengeabil took her arm and swept her through before she had time to object or turn around. He nodded to the porter and ducked into the first door they came to.

Once inside, Tamrin felt easier, and much more unsettled. It was all as she had known it. It was all different. The bobbing spheres of light, the crashes and smells from the classrooms, the tingle of magic in the air all around her. She had not noticed before how much magic there was there, how it spread like smoke, touching everything, filling the air, leaving smudges and stains on the walls, the floor, the cups and plates in the dining hall.

"Was it always like this?" she asked.

Vengeabil looked grim.

"As long as you've known it," he said. "Not before."

"I don't remember it as bad as this."

"You've seen what magic can do," said Vengeabil. "You've tasted it, now. Not watered down, but the full strength. You've felt how dangerous it is."

"Yes."

They made their way down to the stores, through the curtain and into Vengeabil's private rooms. He walked around, opening cupboard doors, looking into the pantry, touching whatever came to hand, getting familiar with it again.

Tamrin sat at the table and waited.

When he sat next to her it was with a sheet of thick paper, a pen, an inkwell and a jar of powder with a sprinkler top to dry the ink.

"Do you want to be a pupil at the college?" he asked.

"No."

"Do you want to be a real wizard?"

"Yes."

"How do you want to learn to do that?"

Tamrin looked him in the eye.

"I want to be your apprentice," she said. "Please."

"Very well."

Vengeabil dipped the pen into the ink and wrote his name. Tamrin looked at it and smiled. Then he told her what name she was to write. She frowned.

"Are you sure that's right?"

"Write it," he said.

He sprinkled the drying powder onto the wet ink.

"Now," he said. "Your first lesson as an apprentice. You are to work no magic at all until I tell you to. Do you understand?"

"How long will that be?"

"It will be until I tell you."

"Is this what it will be like, being an apprentice?"

Vengeabil smiled.

"It's one of the things it will be like."

Flaxfold didn't wave them off. December left first. No one saw her go. Axestone and Eloise left later the same day. Flaxfold heard the door shut. She finished cleaning the range in the kitchen, washed her hands, had a small mug of the weak cider for everyday drinking, locked the front door, slid the two bolts, top and bottom, put the key into the small drawer of the hall table, and went upstairs. The first-floor corridor ended in a small door. Flaxfold unlocked this. It led to another corridor. She took the third door on the left, opened it and went in. Closing it behind her, she took a book from the shelf, sat at the table and began to read. Sometimes she stood and looked out of the window, as if she was expecting someone. ‖

Starback sprang up to the height

of a haystack, spread his wings, levelled, then plunged into the stream. Sam felt the shock of the cold water from where he stood on the riverbank. Then, with a yelp of laughter, he threw himself in after the dragon. His arms and legs flailed. He hit the surface with a slap and a surge of water.

Starback grabbed him and dragged him down. They struggled against each other, playing against the current and diving down till Sam scraped his legs on the pebbles on the riverbed.

Starback held Sam's leg in his mouth, dragging him along. The water streamed over their heads. Sam forgot for a moment which he was, boy or dragon, dragon or boy, and breathed in a lungful of water. A water beetle slipped into his mouth. Sam tried to spit it out. He thrashed about, turning and grabbing, till Starback swept up, broke the surface and flung Sam on the grassy bank. Sam coughed, the spasm jerking his ribs in pain, spewed up water, coughed again, grabbed his chest. He moaned, more water trickling from his mouth and down his nose.

"Kitchen boy."

Sam looked up.

Caleb pushed Sam with his foot. Not a kick, but not gentle enough to be friendly.

"What are you doing here, kitchen boy? Washing the stink off?"

Through all the months since Flaxfield had died, through all the pain and danger, nothing had hurt him so deeply as the news that he was dirty and that he stank. He tried to get up and face Caleb. Caleb pushed him again with his foot. Sam slipped. Caleb put his foot on Sam's chest, pinning him to the ground.

Sam pushed his fingers into his mouth, trying to dislodge the beetle. It was swirling round in there, jabbing his tongue and the inside of his cheeks. He felt himself feeling sick and wanting to throw up.

Caleb laughed.

"Cat got your tongue? Or is it something else?"

Caleb unfastened the silver and jet clip at his neck. He threw it into the air and it hung, then fell, then opened up into a black beetle, bigger than Sam's fist. It circled, swooped, rose and circled again. A swarm of beetles from all directions gathered around it.

"Come on, kitchen boy. Say something," Caleb taunted him.

The huge beetle dived and flew straight into Sam's face.

The others followed, swarming all over him. Into his ears, his nose. He closed his eyes tight shut but he could feel them probing with sharp legs. Caleb took his foot away. Sam scrambled to his feet and lunged in his direction. Caleb stepped aside and Sam fell again.

He was drowning in beetles, being eaten alive by them.

He summoned up all his strength to throw a spell at Caleb, to shake off the beetles with magic.

Nothing.

There was nothing there.

No magic.

Sam had travelled a long way since the day he had said goodbye to Flaxfield on this riverbank. Many miles. Many months. Many wounds. Many changes. And this was to be the last change. The last journey. To follow Flaxfield.

Sam closed his eyes and gave himself over to the beetles. He stopped struggling, felt their claws, their jaws, the rip of flesh, the probing legs.

His mind took him away from the attack, away from the pain and he slid down the bank, into the water, ready to follow Flaxfield and find an Unfinished death.

Starback watched Sam splutter and lunge towards the bank, out of the water. He laughed at the boy's discomfort and flicked his tail and plunged deeper and further into the water. Choke it out or swallow it whole, a water beetle will do no harm. Sam would be back soon enough.

He felt a dragon's delight in the cool green water, the brush of the weeds, the swift dart of the fishes, the ooze and squelch of mud. Swimming was like flying. Green and Blues are born for it. He twisted round, flicked free of the mud and let his wings push him through the water. He was heading back to the riverbank when a sudden current pushed him back.

Starback felt something of Sam slide into the water. A sharp pain jabbed into his head, between his eyes. He felt sick.

The dragon turned his face upwards and flew out of the river, up, high above the trees. Looking down, he saw the boy, a black shape on the ground, shimmering alive with the movement of the beetles which covered him.

The boy's mind returned him, back from the water, back into his torn body. Through the pain, he could smell smoke. The beetle in his mouth exploded, burnt up and turned to ash.

Caleb laughed.

The dragon swooped and dived, straight at Caleb. Caleb felt the movement of the air, heard the swish of the wings, caught a glimpse of blue and gold in the corner of his eye.

The boy was beginning to pass out with the pain and terror when he heard Caleb scream.

The dragon opened his mouth and let fly a burning scream of rage.

The beetles ran off the boy, popping and fizzing, bursting open and dying. The fist-big beetle flew up high and hovered.

The boy sat up and saw the dragon rocket towards Caleb, mouth open, flames pouring out. Caleb shouted and pointed.

Tried to conjure a protection spell. The dragon struck. His jaws seized Caleb's head and jerked it to one side.

The boy heard bones snap.

The dragon shook Caleb as a terrier shakes a rat. Caleb's head lolled to the left, one side of his face burned away. He sagged and fell.

The boy shouted, "Stop."

The dragon looked at the boy, took Caleb in its jaws and tossed him into the river.

The boy stood and watched what was left of Caleb drift downstream.

The dragon moved to the boy's side.

They watched. Together.

Sam spat the foul ash from his mouth, scooped water into his hand, washed round and spat again.

"We killed him," said Sam. Starback breathed out smoke.

Ash fell to the floor and screamed and kicked and tore her grey robe. She threw herself at Bakkmann. It clacked its jaws and fought back, losing a black leg before escaping and scuttling down the stairs. Ash sobbed with fury.

When her rage had died down she looked through the slit window.

"It is not over, boy," she said. "Not over."

She wrapped herself in her robe and went to the dungeons, to comfort herself with the prisoners.

✠

Sam stepped into the water again, letting the cool flow soothe his torn flesh.

Starback swam slowly round, waiting for him to recover. Many times Sam filled his mouth with water and spat it out, to get rid of the taste. At last he left the river, walked away and lay down on his back on the fresh grass in the shade of a tree.

He looked up into the green arms of the willow. The wounds from the axes had healed. All up and down the riverbank, the willows bore the scars of their contribution to Flaxfield's Finishing. Sam leaned on his elbow and looked at them. New bark was growing over them. He stood and went to the water's edge, his eyes following the stream that Flaxfield had taken. Starback nuzzled against his leg. Sam scratched the dragon's head, felt the comforting motion in his fingers and the soothing touch behind his ears at the same time.

"We're home," said Sam. "Safe and home again."

"Dragonborn," he whispered.

Starback licked Sam's hand. ||

THE END

envoy

Sam trudged up to the house, keeping his eyes away from it. He wanted nothing more than to be in Flaxfield's house again. The glimpse of it, in the corner of his eye, empty of the old man, silent and hollow, was more than he could turn and gaze on yet.

He pushed open the door. The kitchen was fresh and clean, scented wth herbs. A loaf of bread, a bowl of figs and a bottle of cordial stood on the kitchen table. Sam picked up the bread and smelled it. He squeezed the sides of the loaf. It was fresh. Almost warm.

Sam climbed the stairs and stood in front of the study door. Laying his hand on the polished oak, he felt that the sealing spell he had lain on it had been removed. He pushed the door and stepped in.

Flaxfold laid down her book and smiled at him.

"Hello, Sam."

Starback darted across and wound himself round her legs,

then lay at her feet. Sam drew back, half-turned to go.

"Won't you sit down?"

"I thought the house was empty."

"No."

Sam closed the door behind him.

Flaxfold's arms rested on a sheet of paper. A pen, an inkwell, a glass of cordial stood to one side.

"You've been hurt," she said.

Sam touched his fingers gently to his bitten face.

"Yes."

"We can deal with that," said Flaxfold.

"Where are the others?" he asked.

"Gone home."

Sam sat opposite her. The ash tree outside the window was in bud. Green against brown.

"I didn't want to be with them. I didn't want to fight their fight."

"What do you want to do now?"

"I had no magic just then," he said.

"You walked away from it," said Flaxfold. "Magic does not like to be rejected."

For a moment, Sam remembered Vengeabil, the library, the same question, day after day.

"Is it too late?" he asked.

"Never too late," she replied.

"I want to be apprenticed," he said. "I want to be a wizard for myself. Not to join in a fight. Just for myself."

"Sometimes," said Flaxfold, "a day comes when the fight comes to you. And then you have to decide to fight back or walk away. Wizard or no wizard."

"When that day comes, I'll see what happens," said Sam. "But I won't be a wizard just to look for that fight."

Flaxfold nodded.

"I've never seen you do magic," he said.

"No. That's right."

"Do some magic for me," said Sam.

"No," said Flaxfold.

Sam fidgeted with the clasp on his cloak.

"Can you?" he asked.

Flaxfold picked up her book and started to read. Sam waited for something to happen. He watched her carefully. She looked up, smiled, turned the page and read on.

"I want to ask you something," said Sam. "I think."

Flaxfold looked up.

"Trust what you have chosen," she said. "There is a reason. Sometimes it has chosen you."

"Please will you take me as your apprentice?" he asked.

Flaxfold put aside the book, turned the paper over, signed her name at the bottom. She handed Sam the paper, the pen.

"Of course," she said.

They signed.

Flaxfold found a lump of hard wax and a candle. She dripped the hot wax onto the indenture.

"You seal it," she said.

Sam undid the leather thong and pressed the seal into the wax.

"You know about this?" he said.

Flaxfold nodded. ||

Acknowledgements: To Denise, Ellen and Ben at Walker Books, for encouraging me and for the care and attention they have taken. To Felicity at Curtis Brown, for keeping me at it. To Jim Kay, for drawing the book exactly as I had seen it. To Gerard Manley Hopkins, Ted Hughes, T. S. Eliot and others who didn't know they were writing some of the best parts of this book. To St Alban's Hull, who gave me more than they'll ever know and who I miss more than I can ever say. To Cath Fuller, who believed me. To the Athenaeum, Liverpool, for providing a quite place where no one can find me. To the Travellers Club, Pall Mall, for their hospitality. To Ursula le Guin, Alan Garner, Susan Cooper and others, who demonstrate that fantasy is not the same as whimsy, or spy stories with added spells. To everyone who reads this book with pleasure.

To my family, as always.